ELEMENTAL

In the next instant Sabrina was pulled against him. An arm curved around her and a gentle hand cupped the back of her head. Without knowing exactly why, she stood on tiptoes and—

Bay kissed her. Her low sound of protest was muffled by his sensual mouth. He hardly allowed her to breathe but she secretly didn't mind. If he was that into it, so would she be. She kissed him right back.

An elemental tension crackled in the air when he raised his head. His hands moved, closing over her slender shoulders, keeping Sabrina in front of him.

"I—you—we shouldn't have done that," she managed to say.

"Oh no? You didn't seem to mind."

from "The Ivory Cane"

BOOK YOUR PLACE ON OUR WEBSITE AND MAKE THE READING CONNECTION!

We've created a customized website just for our very special readers, where you can get the inside scoop on everything that's going on with Zebra, Pinnacle and Kensington books.

When you come online, you'll have the exciting opportunity to:

- View covers of upcoming books
- Read sample chapters
- Learn about our future publishing schedule (listed by publication month *and author*)
- Find out when your favorite authors will be visiting a city near you
- Search for and order backlist books from our online catalog
- Check out author bios and background information
- Send e-mail to your favorite authors
- Meet the Kensington staff online
- Join us in weekly chats with authors, readers and other guests
- Get writing guidelines
- AND MUCH MORE!

**Visit our website at
http://www.kensingtonbooks.com**

When You Kiss Me

JANET DAILEY

ZEBRA BOOKS
Kensington Publishing Corp.
http://www.kensingtonbooks.com

ZEBRA BOOKS are published by

Kensington Publishing Corp.
119 West 40th Street
New York, NY 10018

All Kensington titles, imprints, and distributed lines are
available at special quantity discounts for bulk purchases
for sales promotion, premiums, fund-raising, educational, or
institutional use.

Special book excerpts or customized printings can also be
created to fit specific needs. For details, write or phone the
office of the Kensington Special Sales Manager: Attn.: Special
Sales Department, Kensington Publishing Corp., 119 West
40th Street, New York, NY 10018. Phone: 1-800-221-2647.

Zebra and the Z logo Reg. U.S. Pat. & TM Off.

ISBN-13: 978-1-4201-0667-1
ISBN-10: 1-4201-0667-8

First Printing: July 2009
10 9 8 7 6 5 4 3 2 1

Printed in the United States of America

Contents

When
You Kiss Me

SOMETHING
EXTRA

Chapter 1

The pinto, a mixture of chestnut and white, reluctantly submitted to the pressure of the reins and turned away from the rich grasses of his pasture. His head bobbed rhythmically from side to side as he plodded down the rutted lane. Fifteen summers had passed before his soft brown eyes. He no longer pranced and tossed his brown and white mane, or tugged at the bit between his teeth. Through the years he had grown fat and lazy, saving his energy to swish away flies and tear at the long green grass so that he would have the strength to see another long South Dakota winter sweep by.

The horse didn't need to look at a calendar to see the month of September preparing to make way for October. All he had to do was look at the trees and their green leaves that were dotted with red and orange, or to raise his brown eyes to the blue skies and see the birds gathering to begin the migration south at the first sign of cold. The waving fields of wheat next to his pasture had ripened and grains of gold hung heavily on their slender stalks. The days were still warm but the nights held a chill. The pinto had already begun growing his shaggy coat to ward off the cold northwest winds.

A heel dug firmly into his side and he snorted his disapproval before amiably breaking into a rocking canter. The rider on his back was light and the hands holding the reins were gentle. The pinto's dark ears pricked forward as a brightly plumed pheasant took wing ahead of them. But there was not the slightest break in his stride. A hand touched the side of his neck in praise, followed by a checking of reins. The aging pinto gladly settled back into a shuffling trot and finally to his plodding walk again.

The young woman astride his bare back sighed deeply, letting the circled reins drop in front of her while placing her hands on her hips. Her bare legs dangled from his fat sides as she balanced herself easily on his broad back. She squinted her own soft brown eyes at the sun's glare, feeling its warmth on the skin not covered by her white halter top and blue shorts. If she had looked for them, she would have seen all the signs of autumn that the horse did. But her gaze flitted over the landscape, looking but not seeing.

Anyone looking at her would have seen a figure that was not overly curvy or too skinny, but somewhere in the middle. It couldn't be said that she was tall in the saddle, since she was five feet four, an average height for an average female. Her hair was the same warm brown shade as her eyes, and was thick and cropped in a feathery boy-cut that allowed its fullness and natural wave to frame her oval face. Even her features were average, not possessing any startling beauty, only a pleasing wholesomeness.

When she'd been younger, Antoinette Smith, her mother, used to moan about her lack of glamour. Her father always used to gather her in his arms in one of his giant bear hugs and in his laughing voice teased her.

"You have a pair of very nice eyes to see with, a nose to breathe and smell with, pretty lips, and a gorgeous set of white teeth, thanks to the dedication of your dentist, considering how you always argued with your mom and me about brushing them." Then he would lift her downcast chin with his hand and study her face closely. His voice would become very serious. "And by my latest count, you have two thousand, four hundred and thirty-seven freckles, which you ought to thank the good Lord for, because He's the one who sprinkled gold dust all over your face."

She would be scowling by that time at the faint freckles that were there and not there, so light were they. Her father would then tickle the corner of her mouth to get her to smile.

"And He also gave you a matching set of dimples!" he ended triumphantly. Even though Jolie knew her dad was on her side no matter what, she always felt better after one of his pep talks. It was only when she grew up that she realized he'd been trying to make her content with the way she was, with the things she couldn't change. Yes, she had long ceased to curse the fact that she'd been endowed with both freckles and dimples, and learned to put up with the good-natured teasing that they always earned her.

Even though Jolie seldom got a second glance when she was walking down a street in town and couldn't have won a beauty pageant to save her life, there was a consolation prize: she was known as an excellent listener, had a ready smile, and could carry on a conversation without giggling. She'd been the kind of girl that got invited home to chat with moms while her girlfriends were invited to parties. After hearing tales of what went on at some of these, Jolie wasn't sure she would have liked it, but she never had the chance to find out for herself.

She was home now after a little more than three years into which she had crammed a four-year college education. Okay, she had her degree but now what? What came next? Inside Jolie felt a surge of restlessness that heightened her sense of dissatisfaction.

Home. Everything was different and yet essentially the same. Home. A three-hundred and sixty acre tract of land sixty miles from Yankton, South Dakota, where for the entire twenty-one years of her existence, Jolie's parents had farmed. It had been a good life and a hard life at times, the difference dictated by the weather and its effect on the crops. But it was her parents' life and not hers.

The pinto paused to munch on a tempting clump of grass until Jolie raised herself out of her indifference to lift his head away.

"If you eat any more, Scout, your sides will burst," she admonished him. Dutifully the horse plodded on. "Poor old Scout," Jolie sighed. "You've changed too, just like me. Whoever said you can't go home again was right."

Her parents had lived by themselves for the last three years and had grown accustomed to it. They no longer knew how to treat Jolie. She wasn't a child anymore but to them she wasn't grown up—not quite. Madelaine, her older sister by one year, was married and already had two children as well as a life completely separate from Jolie's. Change was the only constancy. And that included John Talbot.

Jolie saw his pickup parked on the turnout from the country road. Tall and sunburned, he stood on the edge of a wheat field, the muscles of his arms evident in the late morning sunlight. A stalk of wheat twitched between his teeth as he lifted a hand in greeting. Without any effort his long stride carried him to the edge of the field as Jolie drew level atop her pinto. His large hands encircled her waist and lifted her to the ground. There John lowered his head and with the ease of habit claimed her mouth in a kiss. Jolie responded just as naturally, liking the warmth and the closeness of his body next to hers.

"Hi." The gleam of quiet affection in his tawny gold eyes was comfortable and pleasing, as was his slow smile. "It's been a long time since you've come out to visit me in the fields."

Snuggling against his shoulder, Jodie nodded agreement as his strong arm held her there. She slipped her arm behind his back and around his waist. The pinto began contentedly grazing on the grasses near the lane, ignoring the couple walking slowly toward the lone cottonwood by the fence.

"Dad says your wheat is ready for harvest." Jolie chose the main topic of local conversation. It was a safe subject that steered clear of her restlessness. John plucked another stalk of wheat before sinking down on the ground beneath the cottonwood. He stripped the golden grains from its head, tossing two into his mouth.

"Still a little too much moisture," he decreed. "Another day of sun like this and it'll be ready." He pushed the straw hat back on his head and gazed out over the sea of wheat. "It's going to be a good harvest."

"Dad's shoulder is bothering him, which means rain before tomorrow night." The blade of grass in her hand split down the middle at the nervous pressure of her fingers and she tossed it away.

"You can tell him from me that he can hold it off for another couple of days." John smiled and drew Jolie into his arms.

She turned her head just as he was about to kiss her and his lips instead found her cheek. But he wasn't deterred, letting his mouth wander over her neck and the lobe of her ear, which was half-covered by her hair. For Jolie, there was nothing soothing in his caress and her lack of response made her feel uncomfortable. She wriggled free, plucking another blade of grass and studying it intently.

His measuring eyes were on her. Jolie could feel him studying her face and she tried to seem nonchalant.

"What's wrong, Jo?" he asked quietly. If he was annoyed or hurt, nothing in his voice revealed it.

"I don't know," she sighed. She glanced back at him hesitantly, letting him glimpse the melancholy expression in her eyes. It would have to do for a silent apology.

"You've been home a week now. No callbacks on any of your job applications?"

"I haven't applied anywhere."

His eyebrows raised briefly at her flat statement, but his expression remained impassive otherwise. Jolie drew in a deep breath as she averted her eyes from his face. He always seemed to know so much about what she was thinking and she couldn't even begin to guess what was going on in his mind.

"I've got my diploma," she said at last, "and I don't even know what I want to do with it."

"Home economics graduates always make good wives," he said lightly.

"Too bad I majored in history then," she shot back. She knew perfectly well that he knew that and that he'd been teasing her, but his remark had a slight—very slight—edge. As if he was testing her. But how could she possibly tell John that she didn't love him, or at least not the way she wanted to love the man she would marry? What was worse, she felt so guilty for not loving him.

John Talbot was a dream come true, but he was someone else's dream and not hers. Still . . . he was good-looking, extremely so, and solid and dependable. Just looking at his face, so clean-cut and handsome, made Jolie wonder if she wasn't out of her mind for not snatching up a man who'd waited faithfully for the last five years for her to make up her mind. She didn't deny that John had a magnetism that attracted her, but nothing happened—no bells rang, her heart didn't beat any faster—when he held her in his arms. It wouldn't be fair to marry him when she knew this.

"Do you ever wonder why I didn't call you while you were at college?" his quiet baritone voice asked.

Jolie nodded, too full of her own feelings of guilt to reply vocally. "I was pretty sure you liked me, maybe even loved me a little, but I knew you weren't in love with me." John lifted her chin as it moved inadvertently down toward her chest. "You were eighteen and I was twenty-four. I decided it was only fair to you to wait until you'd graduated and grown up some. But I guess absence hasn't made the heart grow fonder, has it?"

"I feel awful about it, John," Jolie whispered, "but you're right. I'm not in love with you. I do care about you, more than anyone I've ever met."

"Yeah." For just a moment, his fingers dug into her shoulders, revealing the pain that his face didn't show. Then he released her and lay back against the tree trunk. "The way you feel wouldn't satisfy either one of us for long." His smile was slow and regretful with a trace of bitterness to it. "So what are you going to do now? Are you going to stay around here?"

"I don't think so." There was an almost imperceptible shake of her head as Jolie replied. "I thought if I came back here to the farm it would give me a chance to get my thoughts straight. After three years of nonstop classes, endless assignments and part-time work, I feel as if I'm still rushing around. I thought coming home would calm me down, but it's only made me more confused. I don't want to take just any job, but I can't keep living with my parents. I have the feeling they were more than happy to become empty nesters."

"It will all work out."

"I hope it does . . . for both of us. John?" His gaze moved from the landscape to her again. "Is it too much to ask that we still be friends?"

He reached out a hand and ruffled her hair the way he'd done when she'd been a teenager. "Of course." He smiled, getting quickly to his feet. She rose to stand silently beside him. "Don't be so solemn, honey." He traced the curve of her cheek with his finger. "It's not as if I'd suddenly discovered you weren't in love with me. I think I would have been more shocked if you were, and a little bit afraid that you were lying."

Jolie stood on tiptoe and planted a soft kiss on his mouth, her eyes brimming with tears she didn't feel she had any right to shed. "Aunt Brigitte will have my scalp for letting you go."

"Don't tell me your romance-obsessed aunt is here," John laughed.

"Aunt Brigitte is permanently single. How can you possibly consider her romantic? Mom swears she would be surprised if Aunt Brigitte had ever been kissed."

"Don't you believe it. That's one woman who knows exactly what love is all about." That was a puzzling statement to Jolie and one that John was going to let her think about by herself, evidently. "Well, Jo, your uncle will be wondering where I am, so I'd better shove off."

She didn't realize at first that he was leaving until he was already several steps away from her. "John— I'm . . . I'm sorry," she called after him.

Jolie didn't miss the slight stiffening of his shoulders before he turned and waved. Yet his stride quickly carried him toward his pickup. Jolie watched him drive off before she walked over to her plump horse still contentedly stuffing himself with grass.

The screen door slammed behind her as Jolie entered the two-story frame house. She didn't feel any better or worse than before she'd left that morning. Only one thing was definite: she would not be looking for a job anywhere near home. It wouldn't be fair to John, not that he was the type to jump off a cliff. Actually, he was the opposite, the kind of guy who met problems head on and never had second thoughts.

"Hello! Who's there?" The imperious question came from the sun porch.

"It's me, Aunt Brigitte," Jolie replied, sticking her head around the door with a wave of her hand. "Where's mom?"

"In town getting groceries." When Jolie would have gone on to her own room, her aunt motioned her into the room. "Come sit with me."

Brigitte's iron-gray hair was drawn into a severe bun at the back of her head. Jolie had always regarded her aunt, who was twelve years her mother's senior, as being stern and practical, but in the light of John's statement, Jolie wondered how accurate her assessment was. Brigitte's features had the uncompromising lines of maturity, but it suddenly seemed possible that she'd been pretty back in the day, especially when her aunt smiled as she was doing now.

"What have you been doing since you got back from college?" Her aunt's questions generally sounded like commands, but then she'd been a teacher for the last thirty years, Jolie mused.

It wasn't often that her aunt made the weekend trip to see her only sister and spend two uneventful days on the farm. This was one of those rare times.

"Relaxing from the grind of all the finals, mostly. And trying to figure out what I want to do next."

"That sounds as if it's a tremendous problem." Jolie saw her aunt's lips quiver and almost break into a smile. Brigitte Carson glanced up, noting the troubled expression on her niece's face. "Hmm. It is, isn't it?"

"Yes." Jolie sighed heavily and turned away from her aunt's searching gaze.

"Where have you been this morning?"

"Out with John."

"I bet he had an answer to your dilemma."

"Yes, he had a suggestion." Jolie's voice was soft and simultaneously firm. "But I'm not in love with him, Aunt Brigitte."

It was her aunt's turn to sigh and she did. "I'm sorry to hear that. Sorry for you as well as John. He'd make a perfect husband and father. Are you sure about what you feel?"

"What is love?" Jolie asked quietly, turning away from the window to her aunt. "I'm twenty-one years old and I don't have a clue."

"That, my dear, is an eternal question that will be asked as long as there are people on earth." Her aunt's eyebrows raised significantly. "At least, I do know you really aren't in love with John or you wouldn't ask."

"Which is a tricky way of getting out of answering it." A flash of depression turned down the corners of Jolie's mouth. "And please don't quote mom's old line about love being many things to many people."

"Well, all right. But the kind of love I believe you're talking about—bells ringing, sun coming up, everything but the cartoon bluebirds—is rare."

Jolie suppressed a snort.

Her aunt shot her a considering look. "There are different kinds of love, you know. For starters, selfless love, but very few people can love freely and completely and expect nothing in return. No, give-and-take is generally how it works—"

"Does it have to be work?" Jolie interrupted her.

"Sometimes," her aunt laughed. "If you want love to last, then yes, you do have to put your heart into making it happen. You'll learn."

"Who's going to teach me?"

Brigitte looked at her a little sadly. "I couldn't say. Anyway, you're very young. Although some people search for love so hard that they never find it."

"Did you, Aunt Brigitte?" The withdrawn expression on the older woman's face didn't stop Jolie from asking.

"Yes, once. A car accident took him away from me." A melancholy smile touched her usually stern mouth. "And that love completely spoiled me for second best, which has made my life very lonely."

"I'm sorry," Jolie began, wishing she hadn't been so thoughtless.

"You didn't know," he aunt said simply. "But I think the kind of love you want can cost very dearly. Perhaps that's why it's so precious."

Jolie heaved a sigh. "Do you think I'll ever find it?"

Her aunt's reply was brisk. "Not with that mopey expression on your face. Nobody would be interested." From experience, Brigitte Carson put just enough sharpness in her teasing words to snap Jolie out of her blue mood.

"Thanks very much. But I still need something to do in the meantime. I'm not looking forward to leaving here and still, I don't want to stay."

"Sometimes, Jolie, it's difficult to make a decision when you're surrounded by the people you know. You want their suggestions even knowing they're not helpful. The best thing for you to do would be to take off for a week or two. Go somewhere by yourself, relax, and have a good time. It's surprising how clear everything becomes afterwards."

Jolie shrugged. "There isn't anywhere I particularly want to go."

"Really? There has to be some place that you've always wanted to see."

A light shone for a moment in Jolie's eyes as she thought of her long-held childhood wish before she blinked it away.

"There is, yes," she admitted, "but it's basically out of the question. I haven't saved much and I have to use that to start out on my own. It wouldn't last long."

"It doesn't hurt to talk about it. Where would you like to go—if you could afford it?" Brigitte persisted.

"Ah, maybe this is going to sound strange to you, but I've always wanted to go to Louisiana where my great-grandmother came from. I remember Grandma telling Madelaine and me the stories her mother had told her about the plantation home where she lived." Jolie glanced over at her aunt, shyness creeping into her voice. "I can't help wondering if Cameron Hall is still standing."

"It's interesting how that one lone ancestor of ours has managed to still be so much a part of our lives." Brigitte's thoughtful gaze scrutinized Jolie. "You were named after her, of course. Jolie Antoinette. Somehow all the girls got French names down the years."

"I don't mind. Jolie is much more romantic than Jane Smith could ever be," she laughed.

"Indeed it is. Let me think. Perhaps there's a way

you can get there." The wheels were turning almost visibly in her aunt's mind as Jolie watched her set down her book and stand.

"I don't see how."

"I have a fair amount of money saved apart from my retirement fund and I never did decide what I was saving it for. I didn't get you a graduation gift because I wanted you to pick it out. It seems you have." Her aunt smiled. "An everything-included trip to Louisiana and the bayou country."

"That's much too expensive!" Jolie gasped. "I couldn't possibly let you do it."

"How could you possibly stop me?

Chapter 2

Every one of Jolie's arguments was brushed off with logical rebuttals until she found herself sitting down at a desk while her aunt began planning her trip.

First things first. Jolie's little Volkswagen would need to be checked thoroughly before the journey. The cost of gas, meals, motels had to be totaled up. She could use some new clothes if there was any money left in the budget. And so on.

She looked into accommodations in the town nearest the plantation of Cameron Hall. By the time Jolie's mother had come back from town, her itinerary had been figured out and it was presented to her mother by her Aunt Brigitte as a done deal.

Looking at the bottom line and that scary number with the comma in it, Jolie moaned, "You should at least come with me, Aunt Brigitte, and get your two cents' worth out of this."

"That's not the point. The idea is for you to get out in the world by yourself and have some fun. You're too young to be tied down yet. And you don't need a spinster aunt looking over your shoulder," Brigitte scolded her with fake severity.

Nothing could change Brigitte's mind. In no time at all, Jolie was seeing to every detail. And within a week her car was deemed ready for the long drive— the longest she'd ever taken.

She'd found out about places to stay but hadn't decided on any. Her suitcases were packed. When she pulled out onto the highway, the excitement of her newfound freedom finally hit her and she whooped with joy.

A passing trucker or two glanced at her curiously down the road and waved. She'd cranked up the radio and was car-dancing in her seat, singing along. She settled down when she caught a glimpse of a state trooper's car tucked under an overpass but even he waved at her.

After an hour or so, she grew more thoughtful, imagining what was ahead. The only thing that could spoil this trip was the possibility that Cameron Hall was no longer standing.

She'd gotten a letter from the people at the Chamber of Commerce—she'd written them first asking about places to stay—that said they had never heard of it. Her aunt had been quick to point out that it had been sold after the Civil War for taxes and most likely had been renamed.

Which didn't mean it wasn't there, she told herself.

Even though she wanted to hurry, Jolie took her time during the seemingly endless drive, breaking the journey into stages. She chose scenic back roads, avoiding the interstates for the most part.

When the little red Volkswagen crossed the state

line into Louisiana, her heart beat a little faster. It was almost as if she were coming home somehow.

By six o'clock that night, Jolie was less than a hundred miles from her destination. If she hadn't wanted to see the countryside during the day, she would have kept on going. As it was, she reluctantly stopped at a motel, as generic and forgettable as all the others she'd stayed in.

She could get an early start the following morning and allow herself to really see where she was.

After a breakfast of eggs and biscuits that would keep her going for a while, she unfolded a map and reviewed the last leg of her journey. She was going through the National Forest around Alexandria, down through Opelousas and Lafayette, to St. Martinville, the heart of Evangeline Country.

The map became reality as she finally stopped in front of a road marker in the center of town in front of the Evangeline oak tree, immortalized in Longfellow's poem.

Whew. She was *here*.

Almost three full weeks of sightseeing were ahead of her, but first she had to get settled in.

She parked in front of a restaurant, hoping that someone local could direct her to an inexpensive bed-and-breakfast or even a room to rent with a nice family. It sure looked like the kind of town where everybody knew everybody else.

The waitress who came with her coffee thought about it when Jolie asked and then suddenly glanced at a trio of men sitting at the counter. She turned back to Jolie with a wide smile.

"I may know a place. You don't mind if I ask the guys, do you? Known them since I was little, and their mommas and their daddies and their cousins and their dogs too."

Jolie laughed. "Go ahead then."

"Be right back," she said.

Jolie watched her walk over to the men, tap the dark-haired one on the shoulder, and with a look at Jolie, began speaking. Seconds later he was excusing himself from the others and coming over with the waitress.

"Miss, this is Guy LeBlanc. I think he can help you." She moved away to serve other customers.

"Pleased to meet you." Jolie knew his warm smile was meant to charm and it did.

"I'm Jolie Smith." She smiled right back at him.

"Denise said you were looking for a place to stay for a few weeks."

"That's right. Maybe with a kitchen I could use? I wouldn't be staying more than a few weeks," Jolie explained, brushing back a lock of her brown hair and feeling a little self-conscious. "Do you know where I could find something like that?"

"My home," Guy LeBlanc said calmly.

Her eyebrows shot up.

"Where my parents also live," he added reassuringly. "They used to rent to a college student, but she moved out after she graduated."

"Do you think they could be persuaded to let me stay?" Jolie liked the man's drawling voice, and noticed how different it was from other southern accents. Softer, for one.

"I'm sure so, but let me take you there and you can talk to them yourself. It's one large bedroom, real comfortable and clean. You'd be taking meals with the family, though."

He stood by as Jolie got up, and watched her reach in her bag to pay for her coffee. She put down a bill and waved goodbye to the waitress, who nodded and smiled.

As they left the restaurant, Jolie looked around—and at Guy.

He was in his early twenties, a year or two older than she was, maybe. He was less than six feet tall, but lean and athletic. His features were even and reflected his French ancestry, she supposed. A safe bet with a last name like LeBlanc. He could have some Spanish in him too—his eyes were a lustrous black and so was his hair.

He seemed confident, almost cocky. A young prince in this small town, she thought with amusement.

Guy nodded at a police officer, who hollered a greeting that made it clear they'd known each other since forever too.

"Where you going, Guy?" the young officer asked.

"Home."

"Can I come? I want a piece of your mom's pie."

"Sure," Guy said affably. "I was just going to show Miss Jolie here the way. We can all go. Unless you're supposed to be fighting crime."

"Ain't no crime to fight and you know it. Got two guys coming to replace me on the next shift, I'll radio them where I am." The officer looked at her curiously. "Miss Jolie, huh? You French? Not from around here, are you?"

"Yes to the second question, no to the third."

He nodded as if she'd just passed an important test. "Welcome to St. Martinville." He started his engine and swung out, waiting for them to get in their respective cars.

A police escort. Wait until Aunt Brigitte heard about that. It was all to the good. She wasn't in the habit of following men she didn't really know down unfamiliar roads.

Guy began to give her directions. "Half a mile that way. The white house on the corner when you see my turn signal. Just park in the driveway. There's plenty of room."

The little convoy traveled the ridiculously short distance, with the young officer in the lead.

She'd barely braked when Guy was out of his car, opening her door. His courtesy was a little overpowering, and she wasn't too sure how to deal with it.

Then she realized that his mother was looking out the window, the cop next to her. Probably dishing up pie and getting an advance explanation.

The officer came out with a tinfoil package to go. He waved a plastic fork at Jolie and wished her well, then drove off.

The room Guy led her into was some type of family room with white wicker chairs and more than one sofa. Plants thrived in green profusion. The atmosphere seemed almost tropical, but that wasn't surprising, considering the year-round heat and humidity of the Louisiana climate.

"Just wait here. Now where did my mother disappear to?"

Jolie nodded as he excused himself. She looked around the room again, liking what she saw. The immense size of the house told her it was old but it had been so well cared for that it was hard for her to guess its age.

"Here's Miss Jolie," Guy was saying to his mother.

"Just call me Jolie, please," she protested. "Miss Jolie sounds like a schoolteacher. Oh—hello."

By Guy's side was a petite older woman, barely five feet tall. Her hint of plumpness gave her a very maternal air, as did the wisps of graying dark hair in the bun atop her head. An open, beaming smile accompanied the small hand extended to Jolie.

"My son told me you're looking for a place to stay, Jolie."

"Yes." Jolie was warmed by a friendliness that had nothing to do with ordinary manners.

"She's so pretty," Mrs. LeBlanc said to her son playfully. "You didn't tell me that."

"Maman, we just got here," Guy said with a long-suffering sigh.

Jolie blushed a little. She really didn't want this nice lady thinking she was interested in her son. But at the sight of Jolie's discomfort, the small woman broke into a tinkling laugh.

"I was just teasing," she said. "Guy thinks he's irresistible to women, that's all. While you're staying here, you'd do well to ignore two-thirds of his compliments."

Jolie hesitated, and changed the subject. "Ah— you do have a room to rent. Right?" She realized she had no idea what it was going to cost.

The amount Mrs. LeBlanc named was well within her budget and Jolie was fine with it. And the quickness of the answer eased her mind about this proposed arrangement. Friendly as the LeBlancs obviously were, renting out a spare room was a business transaction they'd done before. Jolie preferred not to be treated *too* much like a member of the family just yet.

She now had a place to stay in a handsome old house with pleasant people. And she wouldn't go broke.

"So," Guy was saying, "what brought you out this way? Are you heading to New Orleans eventually?"

"Guy!" his mother scolded. "There's a million things to do right around here." She reeled them off with dizzying speed. "Our own Acadian House Museum and Craft Shop, and the Acadian Heritage Museum in Loreauville. The Shadows on Teche antebellum house in New Iberia. And what about Avery Island and its Bird City and Jungle Gardens? Don't listen to him," she told Jolie. "But New Orleans is not all that far," she added as an afterthought.

Jolie laughed. "I know I'm going to enjoy myself here, don't worry."

She was wondering, though, why she didn't come right out and tell them why she had come so far—to find the plantation home of her great-grandmother.

Mrs. LeBlanc was looking at her inquisitively.

Now or never, Jolie thought. "There was a reason I came here, though." She glanced from mother to son. "An ancestor of mine once lived on a plantation near here."

"Do tell," the petite woman said.

"I was named for her—she was Jolie Antoinette Cameron. The plantation was Cameron Hall. Have you heard of it?"

She held her breath as the two paused before replying.

Guy just shrugged, and shook his head. But his mother didn't give up so quickly.

"Do you know where it is from here?" she asked.

"I was told it was ten or fifteen miles from St. Martinville."

"That's not far," the woman said. Her soft voice conveyed a sadness. "But the years don't treat our old homes kindly down here, between termites, fire, hurricanes, and land developers."

"So it's probably not still standing." Jolie sighed. "Too bad." But she wasn't ready to give up without knowing for sure. There had to be old maps in the town offices and other records.

"Well, there are a few old derelicts still standing out in the countryside," Guy told her. He seemed eager to please.

She wasn't sure she wanted his help, but with his mother around to keep him in line, she guessed he wouldn't be too much of a pain.

"What did you say the name was again?" Mrs. LeBlanc asked.

"Cameron Hall."

"You don't suppose Etienne's old house—" She turned to her son. "But that was called the Temple, wasn't it? I confused the name of the plantation with his own. But we can ask him."

"Thanks so much," Jolie said. It was a beginning. Good enough.

"Now we must help you get comfortable." The petite woman began to bustle about, something Jolie suspected she did a lot. "Guy, you bring in her luggage."

Jolie made a move as if to help but Mrs. LeBlanc quelled her with a look. "No, no, no. You come with me, I'll show you the room."

As she motioned for Jolie to follow, chattering a

mile a minute, Jolie began to realize that the local accent was more French than Southern.

"Have you and your family lived here long?" She admired the handcarved wood of the balustrade her hand was resting on.

"All our lives, me and my husband Emile. We bought this big house a few years after we were married. Emile's been fixin' it up ever since."

"It's a gorgeous old house," Jolie said. "So did your original family come from France?"

"No, *cher*. We're Cajun. From Acadia in Canada, all the way to here. A few hundred years ago the English made the French settlers hightail it to the American colonies. Some of us just kept going. And here is where we ended up. We're really French-Canadian-Americans. Cajun is much easier to say, don't you think?"

Jolie had to smile. "Yes, it is."

They had climbed the stairs and were proceeding down a hallway. The petite woman flung open a door. "This is the room. What do you think?"

Jolie looked. "Wow. It's so big," she said happily.

She went into a huge, high-ceilinged room with two enormous windows that took up most of a wall. There was a desk and chair, a single bed with an antique frame and a large maple dresser. Throw rugs the color of a pale blue sky were scattered over polished wood floors, and the rest of the décor was in harmonizing pastels. It was spacious and cozy.

"I couldn't ask for anything more," Jolie said warmly.

"It was my oldest daughter's room before she was married."

"How many children do you have, if you don't mind my asking," Jolie said.

"I'd be insulted if you didn't. Family is everything down here." Her landlady was showing off the room's features, opening a concealed door to a huge, empty closet, to Jolie's delight.

"I'm getting that idea," Jolie said.

"Anyway"—the older woman put a finger to her lip thoughtfully—"I have five. Two of my older girls are married. Claudine, though, she still lives with us part of the year. My youngest, Michelle, teaches school here. And Guy's the baby."

Guy laughed, poking his head around the side of the open door to the room. "Safe to come in? I don't want to interrupt if you're about to sing my praises to Miss Jolie."

"I wasn't," his mother said briskly, winking at Jolie. Her dainty hand waved her son into the room. "Bring her suitcases in, Guy. Then I'm sure you have work to do, so our new guest will have time to settle in."

He did what his mother asked, carefully setting her luggage near the bed. He glanced at himself in the mirror when he straightened and ran a hand through his hair, fluffing it up a little.

"You look fine," his mother said. "Now shoo." He ambled away as the two women exchanged a look. "My son, the lover," Mrs. LeBlanc said, rolling her eyes. "Or so he thinks. I'll leave you to unpack. We'll be having a cold lunch around one o'clock. The dining room is to the right at the bottom of the stairs."

Chapter 3

"Don't you work somewhere, Guy?" Jolie half asked and half demanded.

"Would it be a crime if I didn't?"

They were strolling down the sidewalk on a fine day with nothing particular to do.

"It would be a waste," she said brightly, wondering why she'd bothered to ask the question in the first place.

"I guess it would disappoint you if I didn't have a profession."

Gee, what an ego. She honestly didn't think about him all that much or in that way.

She cleared her throat to keep from laughing. "Why should it disappoint me?"

"Hey, I gathered that you come from a hardworking family, so a man who lazes about would be considered a disgrace—"

"That's a strong word," she interrupted him, "and not what I meant."

"Well," he said proudly, "I happen to be an accountant with my very own small business."

Now that surprised her. Although he dressed better than a lot of the men in seven-days-a-week casual around here, she'd chalked that up to his mother, who liked everything to look nice.

And she had thought it had to do with his obvious vanity, she had to admit it. But somehow she just couldn't imagine him slaving over spreadsheets. His hair, yes. Tax returns, no.

"I have a select client list," he was saying. "Half the businesses in town and individuals too. That's why I can set my own hours. I'm my own boss."

"That's great, Guy," she said sincerely.

"And when I have free time, I spend it with the ladies." He smiled and his chest puffed up just a little.

Jolie thought of the boss rooster back on her parents' farm, who had pretty much the same agenda without having to do anyone's taxes. The lifestyle seemed to agree with both of them.

"I thought I'd show you our points of interest, Jolie, if you don't mind me talking like a tour guide."

"Sure. Thanks."

He winked at her. "And I promise to behave myself."

She suppressed a snort. "Uh-huh. Okay. I think you're trying to be more of a bad boy than you actually are, Guy."

He looked a trifle annoyed. "But women love bad boys. Plus they enjoy trying to reform me." Guy winked. "So I let them try."

"Really. Well, that's great."

"For the time being." He let their pace slacken. "I have a hunch you could be my undoing."

"Me?" Jolie laughed incredulously. "Why?"

"Because you could make a man want to change." Despite his smile, there was gravity in his gaze.

"After twenty-one years of looking at myself in a mirror, I know I'm not beautiful enough to make heads turn." Jolie smiled. "So your flattery won't get you anywhere with me, Guy LeBlanc."

"I'm telling the truth," he insisted. "If you were in a room with the most beautiful women in the world, yours is the face a man would remember. Soft brown eyes, pretty little freckles, and all the rest. A man thinks serious thoughts when he looks at you," Guy declared.

"Guess I'm the kind of girl you take home to mother," Jolie sighed. She was pleased by his over-the-top compliments, even though she wished she were the type that sent a man's heart racing and his head spinning with thoughts of anything but his mother.

"A girl he would be extraordinarily proud to take home to mother," Guy corrected her.

"Maybe." The conversation was becoming too personal, and the subject needed changing. "Getting back to you and the local ladies, so to speak, I bet you don't have much competition."

"Oh, I do. Formidable competition, in fact." The man at her side inhaled deeply.

"I have to meet him then," Jolie teased. "Who is he?"

"No, no, you aren't getting his name out of me," Guy laughed. "Besides, he's older and too experienced for you. You're much safer with me."

"Now why would you admit that?"

"Because I'm thinking of my sister who has him all marked out as her personal property, that's why."

"I see," Josie mused.

"And secondly, because your air of innocence wouldn't stop him. So consider yourself warned." His dark brows raised to make the point.

Jolie only laughed, a throaty sound. "Okay, okay. Hey, how far is it to the oak tree?"

"Just around the corner. I guess you know Longfellow's poem, *Evangeline*."

She nodded. "My elementary school stuck to tradition. We had to recite from it."

"Do you remember it?"

"Only the gist of it. Evangeline was separated from her fiancé Gabriel and searched for him until she found him dying in a hospital."

"It's based on a true story from the Acadian forced migration."

Jolie nodded. Around here, history might as well have happened a day ago.

His steps slowed and finally stopped. *"Voilà!* This is said to be the oak tree where the girl saw her true love again for the first time in years."

Jolie looked with interest at the spreading oak tree before them, its gigantic size dwarfing the tiny park that contained it. Beyond were the gleaming waters of a quiet stream, a scene of poetic melancholy right in the middle of town. So this was the famous *Evangeline* tree. She was impressed.

It was a monument to romance, in its way, even if the romance had been doomed.

"What is the river on the other side of the tree?" she asked.

"That's not a river, it's a bayou. Bayou Teche."

"It looks just like a river to me." Jolie gave him a

puzzled look. "I thought a bayou was more like a swamp or something."

"The first voyageur who saw that one called it Sleeping Water, because it didn't have a current that he could see," Guy explained patiently. "The water in a bayou does flow, though. But it sometimes changes direction and rivers don't do that—go in reverse, I mean."

"Okay, I get it. It just flows the way it wants to."

"That's about right."

"Teche is French, isn't it?" she asked. "What does it mean?"

"It's a corruption of an Indian word meaning 'snake.'"

"I'll keep that in mind," Jolie said, feeling her toes curl. She wasn't going to go wading in it, that was for sure. "Guess I have a lot to learn."

"Good. If you have a lot to learn, then you'll stay here longer." He turned his sexiest smile on her, one that looked like he'd been practicing it. "And I'd like that very much."

"Has anyone ever told you that you come on too strong?" she teased him. She caught him off guard but only for a moment.

"No. But that must be why all the girls fall at my feet." This time he made fun of himself.

"You wish." Jolie laughed and Guy could no longer keep a straight face either.

A car pulled up by the curb, and its driver, a dark-haired, pretty girl honked at them.

"Want a ride home?" she asked

"Now do you believe how popular I am? This happens all the time."

"Did you hear me?" the driver asked.

Guy turned to Jolie. "Should I say yes?"

"Do you know her?"

"Of course I know her. And it's a long walk from here. Would you rather ride?"

"I wouldn't want to make your fans jealous," Jolie teased.

"Oh, I can handle two women at the same time."

"Really. Okay, we'll ride home then. I'm dying to see you in action," she laughed.

"You sure took your time making up your mind," the girl said as Guy helped Jolie into the front seat and got in back. "You know that's a no-parking zone. I could have gotten a ticket."

"Just bribe the cop—a piece of pie will cover it," he joked. "We were debating whether we wanted to walk back," Guy replied. Jolie flashed him a gleaming smile. His finesse hadn't impressed the young woman at the wheel.

"In this heat? You've got to be kidding." She zoomed out into the main street, looking out for pedestrians, then casting an assessing look at Jolie.

This close, Jolie could see that her hair was darker than her own but not as black as Guy's. A pair of gold-rimmed glasses gave her dark eyes a luminous quality that added something to their childlike roundness.

"Since Guy hasn't introduced us, we might as well do it ourselves," she said. "I'm his sister Michelle."

"Aha." She looked over her shoulder at Guy.

"I forgot to tell you," he said blandly.

"I'm Jolie Smith," she said to Michelle. "I'm renting a room at your parents' house."

"You on vacation? Or are you planning to stay?"

"Vacation."

"And my dear brother was showing you the

sights." Michelle gave Guy a knowing look which he returned with an amazingly innocent expression. "How do you always find the pretty ones? But she's living with us. Makes it easier."

"No, I'm a chick magnet. They find me," he grinned. "And how were your brats today?"

"Bratty. But I have some nice kids too." She smiled at Jolie. "I teach in the local school. Would you believe that somebody let the chameleon out of the terrarium today? Not the first time. It always manages to pop up on a little girl's desk. I've heard enough shrieking today to last a lifetime. I think it was glad to be returned to its glass world where it's safe from females."

"Okay, you two, don't make fun of us defenseless males," Guy said.

"Oh, poor you," Michelle said bluntly. "Shut up, okay? And let me talk."

The conversation went on in the same vein, bouncing between the three of them, until they got back home. His mother appeared in the back door to welcome them, as if they'd been away in a foreign land for a decade.

It was an unusual experience for Jolie. She suddenly realized that she didn't feel in the least like a stranger to people she'd only met yesterday. They had opened their hearts as well as their arms, extending a precious gift of friendship.

"Well, what do you think of my sister?" Guy asked as Michelle let her mother help her carry her papers into the house.

"She's great," Jolie said. "I don't know why you warned me about her."

"Warn you? When did I do that?" He held open the door.

"You said she had your competition marked as her personal property."

"Competition? What are you talking about?" Michelle had overheard.

"Not you. I was talking to Jolie about Claudine," Guy said.

"Ahh!" Michelle's dark eyes rolled. "I can fill in the rest. I'm surprised you were brave enough to mention Steve to Jolie."

"He didn't, at least not by name." There was a laughing gleam in her eyes as Jolie looked at the disgruntled Guy. "So his name is Steve. I have to remember that."

"I'm glad Claudine isn't here," Guy said. "She'd claw your eyes out, Michelle."

"Don't be so dramatic," his sister told him.

"Well, if Guy won't give me more details, you're going to have to, Michelle." Jolie couldn't help but be intrigued by this unknown local Romeo.

"Fire burns and if you get too near Steve, you'll get scorched," Michelle said cryptically. "Give me my safe, solid, and comfortable Eugene any day."

Guy pounced on that. "She's in love with someone who teaches Ancient History," he said to Jolie. "Her only rivals are Socrates and Euripides."

"Now don't tell Jolie that ancient joke," Michelle warned him. "Not that I can stop you."

He turned to Jolie, laughing. "Thanks for reminding me, Michelle."

His sister gave a put-upon sigh and folded her arms across her chest.

"So, Jolie, what did the Greek philosopher say to his tailor? Knock, knock," he added.

"Uh—who's there?" Jolie said.

"Euripides toga and I'll kill you." He grinned as his sister began to pummel him. He dodged her before the sibling rivalry ended when their mother came in with a tray of glasses and lemonade, and they all helped themselves to it.

"I heard you talking about Claudine. I heard from her today," Mrs. LeBlanc said. "She's coming home this weekend."

"For how long?" Guy didn't seem too happy about it.

"I imagine until the holidays," his mother answered.

"Lucky her, being able to take off that much time. She must have a great job," Jolie said. A silence began to stretch out, a little awkwardly.

"My daughter's an artist, a painter," Mrs. LeBlanc explained. "She exhibits in New Orleans during the summer and again during the winter holidays and Mardi Gras. The rest of the year, she's here, painting away."

"What a cool way to make a living," Jolie said, glancing around at Michelle and Guy. "She must be really successful."

"*Oui*, she is," the older woman nodded quickly. "Practically all of the paintings you see in this house were done by Claudine."

Jolie had noticed the two in her room. Both were floral still lifes, done in sunny pastel colors. She would have asked Mrs. LeBlanc to tell her more about her daughter's work, but she was interrupted by the arrival of her husband.

Emile LeBlanc was short, although he towered

over his wife. He was only five foot six or so and fit. His hair was mostly silver and very thick, and it was easy to see it had once been as dark as Guy's.

After greeting his family and placing a fond kiss on his wife's proffered cheek, he turned to Jolie with a wonderful smile. She was in no doubt as to where Guy's charm came from.

"Who is this lovely young lady, Josephine?"

Mrs. LeBlanc explained, and Mr. LeBlanc listened to his wife with real interest.

"Jolie Antoinette are very French names to be attached to such a common one as Smith," he said. "No offense."

"None taken," she smiled. She told him the reason she'd come so far south and the name of the plantation her ancestors had once owned.

Emile LeBlanc shook his head. "I don't know of it. But it could be out there in the woods somewhere."

"I hope it's not too far in the woods," she said lightly.

"No, you don't want to go bushwhacking looking for it. You might never be seen again," he joked.

"Oh, she's not going to be devoured by an alligator, Papa," his wife said. "Don't put notions like that in her head."

"You mentioned alligators, I didn't," he pointed out.

They bickered fondly for a little longer, then something more important came to the older man's mind. "What's for dinner, *cher*?" he asked his petite wife. "We have to do right by our new guest."

"Just plain, good food. I don't want to scare her away with cuisine à la Cajun. Maybe she doesn't like too much spice."

Jolie tried to explain that she was up for anything and was fine with whatever they usually ate, adding that disrupting their routine was the last thing she wanted to do. But her protests were ignored as Mrs. LeBlanc vehemently denied that Jolie was causing her any inconvenience.

Jolie gave in, her hands raised in a gesture of mock surrender as the LeBlancs laughed. She enjoyed the warmth of this close-knit family too much to do anything but go with the flow of their lives.

Chapter 4

It was late the following morning before Jolie had said yes to enough food, drink, brochures, and directions to keep her going all day, thanks to her little landlady. But at last she was safely behind the wheel of the red Volkswagen and on her merry way.

Jolie really didn't think she could do it all and see it all, and she didn't want to. Just driving down meandering back roads in the flat countryside was pleasant, and it did generate a breeze. The air was warm and sticky, and the air-conditioning in the car had never worked all that well.

Traffic was non-existent. She was able to let the little car toodle along at any pace she chose.

Fields of sugar cane dominated the landscape. Some towered over her car while other, younger fields barely reached her windows. Occasionally she caught a glimpse of a stately mansion that might be the one she was looking for. But the signs she glimpsed as she drove by never said Cameron Hall.

Yielding to the sense of adventure that had come

back, Jolie turned off the dirt road onto one paved with . . . she slowed down for a closer look . . . seashells. Crushed. Which she would be if she didn't pay attention to where she was going.

More cane fields rose on each side of the car until Jolie felt like she was being swallowed up. Only the distant, much taller trees ahead promised a break from the endless cane.

Driving on, she was intrigued by her first glimpse of an honest-to-God swamp. Tall cypress trees rose gloomily out of stagnant water, their "knees"—really part of their roots—poking up everywhere. Spanish moss hung in long, trailing strands. Water hyacinths fought with algae for control of the surface, their clogging green leaves giving way only to the tiny islands of marsh grass and the spiky leaves of the palmettos.

Was there wildlife? There had to be, somewhere in there. Jolie slowed the car to a crawl. Except for an occasional flutter of wings, she didn't see a single critter.

She would have loved to see an alligator. Then it occurred to her that maybe an alligator would love to see her. It wasn't like she could fling Mrs. LeBlanc's picnic into its gaping jaws and hope for the best.

A few more feet and the bayou gave way to pastureland. The sight of cattle munching on the thick grasses seemed unnatural to Jolie, especially when they appeared to have been crossbred with Brahmans. Here were animals that should have been in the wild and woolly section of the western United States, not in Louisiana.

The road made a gentle curve around the pasture and she saw water that she realized was a bayou. Sunlight shimmered across its mirrorlike surface, emphasizing its calm serenity. A crane was feeding along in the rushes on the opposite bank where an oak tree's branches dipped low over the water. The trailing ends of the moss that hung from it were floating.

Now there was an idyllic place to eat. She spotted a turnoff to a gate where she could safely park her car and didn't hesitate to use it.

Gathering up the picnic things, Jolie crossed the road, managing to get across at a narrow place without dropping stuff or falling in.

It was worth it. She had walked into pure peacefulness. The heavy stillness from the heat of the day hung over everything. Every movement was as languid and slow as the stalking crane who raised and lowered his skinny legs in with care. The calls of the birds were muted, as if they were conserving their energy. There wasn't even the small sound of water lapping against the bank.

Without the breeziness of driving, her clothes felt sticky, clinging to her skin. She began to sweat and tasted the saltiness of it on her upper lip.

Kneeling on the short grass, she set out everything. Mrs. LeBlanc had put a wet washcloth in a plastic bag and she used it to wipe her face and cool down.

Might as well do her neck and shoulders, she thought. And the chafed spots where the elastic neckline of her peasant-style crop top had been irritating her. She slipped the short sleeves down until the neckline went straight across the tops of her breasts. Tilting her head back, she squeezed the cloth until droplets of water trickled over her shoulders, some finding their way down her cleavage.

She looked around absently at trees, the bayou, the faint traces of an ever-present warm mist that hung in the air—and then she saw him.

There was a man reclining beneath an ancient oak.

A rush of color stained her cheeks, because he was looking directly at her.

How long had he been watching? She pulled her flimsy sleeves back up.

The man rolled gracefully to his feet. He didn't look dangerous, but how exactly did you tell? He was coming over. Jolie shrank back.

"Seems like a shame to cover up such pretty shoulders." His drawling voice had a seductive softness that did little to slow the pace of her heart, beating rapidly with fear.

Jolie got busy collecting things. "Whatever. I was just leaving."

"Why? I'm willing to share this view of the bayou."

Something in his cultured voice seemed to demand that Jolie look up at him. So she did. And found herself staring into the darkest pair of blue eyes she'd ever seen.

She took inventory. Dark, curling eyelashes. Black hair and brows, black as a raven's wing. A healthy tan. Tall. Built. Wearing denim shorts that were decent but showed muscular legs. His rolled-up sleeves revealed a sinewy strength in his arms. Broad shoulders. Flat abs. Narrow hips.

Nice.

Her feminine assessment was made with lightning speed, but she had the feeling he was aware of it. He smiled, showing strong white teeth, and Jolie noticed the very masculine grooves that deepened on either side of his mouth.

"I promise I won't pounce on you."

What a thing to say. Her response was inane. "Good." Jolie longed to take a deep breath but she was just too nervous. "Sorry if I bothered you."

"You didn't." The man walked over to his place beneath the tree and resumed his reclining position. "I can't speak for the fish, though."

Then she saw the rod and reel propped up by a stick near the edge of the water. And a tackle box. How had she missed all that?

He had as much reason to be here as she did.

"Isn't it too hot to fish?" she asked out of the blue.

"Not according to my theory."

She stopped fussing with everything and sat back, taking that deep breath at last and letting it out through rounded lips slowly. "Let's hear it." She actually smiled as she spoke.

"The big fish are the smart ones. They know all the fishermen's tricks. So they eat when fishermen who follow the rules aren't fishing. And then they sit on the bottom, fat and happy, when the fishermen come back."

"Sounds plausible." A smile widened her mouth and brought out her dimples.

"It isn't," he said with a goofy grin. "But my worms are getting some exercise."

She laughed at his preposterous remark, but went totally silent when his rod bent suddenly. With breathless disbelief, Jolie watched him grab the pole and try to land whatever had taken the bait.

She saw something on the end of the line before

it plunked down into the grass. He reached down to pick it up as she scrambled over for a closer look.

"It's a crawdaddy!" she hooted.

"Down here we call them crawfish." He dodged its pincers as he picked it up and put it in a small pail.

"That's a crawfish?" Jolie stared at it, wonder creeping into her voice that this common creature, a larger version, was the famed crawfish.

"You know the legend, I suppose."

"No." She was feeling a bit giddy from the heat. "Tell me," she intoned. "I want to hear the tale of the River Dweller who pinches toes and loves cheeseball bait."

It was his turn to laugh. "Okay, you asked for it."

"I guess so."

"When the Cajuns left Canada, their friends the lobsters hated to see them leave. But there was no room on the bateaux taking them down the Mississippi. So the lobsters crept and crawled from Nova Scotia through the Erie Canal to the mighty Mississippi—okay, the canal wasn't built then and I forget how they did that part—and they finally arrived in the bayous of Louisiana where the Cajuns had made their new home. But they were tuckered out and a whole hell of a lot smaller. And that, girls and boys, is how Mr. Crawfish got here. He stayed here because it was just too damn hot to move."

She laughed and applauded. The sound made a crane fly away, its spread wings flapping and its skinny legs together, neatly extended behind it.

"Okay, so do you trust me now? Enough to have your picnic?"

She nodded a little shyly. "But will you share it with me?"

He seemed surprised at the offer. "Sure. Thanks. Whatcha got?"

She began to unpack while he propped his fishing pole again, coming over.

There were a lot of things about this stranger that appealed to her: his easygoingness, his ridiculous sense of humor, and yes, his handsomeness. And he was good at putting her at her ease, but that had its drawbacks. Jolie knew she was way out of her league with him.

But she couldn't not smile back at him.

She set out the main course: sliced roast beef on a roll that was crusty on the outside and soft on the inside, divided in half for two portions. Jolie handed him one.

"There's oranges and apples. Take your pick. There's two of each."

"This is plenty, thanks."

They were happy eating in silence, enjoying the savory sandwich. Jolie found herself relaxing. She didn't have to keep a witty conversation going, didn't have to answer personal questions. She could just be herself and enjoy life. As she reached for the thermos of lemonade, she realized there was only one cup.

"Oops—we have to share this."

He shrugged and smiled. "Not a problem."

He drank it down in one go and handed it back. "Ahh."

"You really enjoy yourself, you know that?"

"That's a Cajun thing."

"Are you Cajun?"

"No, but I believe in their philosophy."

"Which is?"

"Roughly, it is better to live than exist, better to sing than curse, better to make love than war. Or more simply, an Acadian loves strong coffee, laughing out loud, talking someone's head off, singing, dancing, rich food, strong liquor, and most of all, women."

"And what do Acadian women think of being last on the list?"

"They know last doesn't mean least. But they would probably add babies and husbands to the list."

"That's unfair!" she protested. "You just said that Acadian men get to love all women, but an Acadian woman is stuck with one—her darling husband."

"You have a point. But that's how it is. You know how Frenchmen are."

"Do I?" Jolie knew he was being provocative just to liven up the conversation, but what he said still irked her. "Always the great lovers, huh? All that sweet talk gives me hives."

"What's wrong with compliments?"

"Nothing."

He took the orange that was in her hand and started peeling it. "Women glow when you tell them they're beautiful."

"Try me," she said and instantly wished she hadn't.

"Here goes. Don't hit me, please. What if a man said your hair is so sleek and shiny he wonders what it would be like to get his fingers in it?"

"I'd wonder if he was straight."

He laughed at that. "Okay, what if he said your freckles remind him of sun-drenched summer days and he wants to count them all?"

"Oh, please."

Thinking for a moment, he gave a heartfelt sigh. "Or this . . . your soft brown eyes remind him of a wary doe wondering if she should enter a strange meadow?"

His blue eyes locked on hers. The peeled orange was in his hand and he tore off a section, carrying it to her lips. Not thinking too clearly, she parted her lips to accept it. Forbidden fruit? Sure seemed like it. She felt a laugh bubble up, and then realized that she could just as easily cry.

"I'm glad that Frenchman isn't around," she said. They gathered up what was left. "He's just too poetical for me."

"Oh?"

"Too flattering is what I mean."

He chuckled. "Are you always critical of yourself?"

"Well, I know I'm okay-looking. Let's leave it at that." She felt an ache in her chest for no apparent reason. "I'm no Helen of Troy."

"Hm. A man wants to make love to a woman, not go to war over her. A beautiful woman isn't so beautiful if you have to constantly fight off rivals to prove your love."

"That's deep. I think." An unexpected anger showed in her eyes as she packed up the basket and got up. "Is that a reverse compliment? Downgrade beauty and upgrade plainness?"

"No, I was saying that inner beauty is much more attractive than outer beauty."

Ready to go, Jolie made sure she had everything. For some reason he was making her feel inadequate. He had an overpowering personality and way too much sex appeal for her peace of mind.

Nothing doing. She wasn't going to fool around with him.

"I hope you don't think I just eat and run, but I really have to be going."

She hoped he wouldn't make her have to come up with more excuses. *Keep it simple, Jolie,* she told herself. *Wave. Get in car. Drive away.*

"I'm sorry—it's early yet." His tone was persuasive but his words were vague.

"You know how it is." Regret crept into her sigh.

He helped her with all the things, making her feel worse about leaving when the afternoon was still so beautiful. It put a dent in her ego that he gave up so easily. Irrational, she knew. But that was how she felt.

Once everything was stowed in the back seat, Jolie turned to say goodbye.

"You should paint spots on the car to match your freckles." A finger brushed her cheek in emphasis. "Then you would both be ladybirds ready to fly away home."

"Interesting image." She was unable to meet his compelling eyes. "Well, thanks for sharing your secret fishing place with me."

"Thanks for the lunch."

"Goodbye." The single word sounded artificially bright to Jolie's ears.

"Not goodbye. *Au revoir.* Until we meet again."

Not much chance of that, Jolie thought as she drove away. How could they possibly meet again? He didn't know her name or where she lived and vice versa. And that was a depressing thought.

Chapter 5

Guy and his father were attending a meeting of a local men's club. Mrs. LeBlanc was visiting an older relative who was confined to her home. Michelle was sitting on the green plaid cushions of the wicker sofa, school papers spread around her with more that she was correcting on her lap.

There was an airy instrumental playing on the stereo, filling the room with its lighthearted sound.

Jolie was in a matching wicker chair trying to finish a letter to her Aunt Brigitte, but she couldn't match the jubilant enthusiasm in the previous missives. A strong, tanned face with raven black hair and contrasting deep blue eyes was on her mind. It was frustrating that a stranger she would never see again kept coming back to haunt her. It wasn't as if she had never been around great-looking guys, because she had.

Why was this one so different? Jolie knew that he'd fascinated her with all that Louisiana lore, his sense of humor, and lack of ego. He'd been confident, but not arrogant, teasing without mocking and knowing without revealing what he knew.

But still. She couldn't fantasize about a man whose name she didn't even know. Jolie didn't realize she'd sighed until Michelle looked up.

"Writing to the boy at home?"

"If I had an ounce of brains I would be," Jolie grimaced. "But I'm writing to my aunt instead."

"Now I know two things," Michelle chuckled. "That there is a boy at home—"

"He's not a boy. He's a very serious man. Maybe too serious."

"That would be the second thing. You broke up with him?"

"Right on both counts."

"Miss him?"

"No, except every now and then when I get an attack of conscience," Jolie admitted.

"He loved you but you didn't love him. That never feels right." Michelle tapped the papers on her lap into a neat stack and set them with the others on the couch.

"John had it all—he was gentle, responsible, and good-looking. I cared about him a lot but nothing happened when he kissed me." Jolie laughed at herself, realizing how immature that sounded. "So I guess I'm still looking for Prince Charming." She wished she could get the face of the stranger out of her mind.

"*Lagniappe*," said Michelle, nodding her head.

"What?"

"*Lagniappe* means 'something extra.' You see it a lot in travel ads for Louisiana. I guess it says a lot about us."

The word suited her longing, but didn't give Jolie any more of a clue as to what exactly she was looking for.

Maybe time would tell. If she was listening. She was just so distracted and unsure.

"Something extra, huh?" Jolie sighed again. "I guess I can find out what that's all about. I thought I would drive to Opelousas tomorrow, tour the Jim Bowie museum, then stop in Lafayette."

They chatted about more sights to see, and then went their separate ways.

Later, when Jolie was under the covers of her bed, sleep was slow in coming. And when it did, she was too restless to derive much benefit from it as she fell into a tossing, fitful slumber.

Jolie had set out to exhaust herself mentally and physically on her jaunt to both cities. She succeeded to the point where she couldn't remember if she had seen that odd Steamboat Gothic house with the widow's walk in Opelousas or Lafayette and realized it had been neither. The house was in a smaller town called Washington.

Now, the following morning, she practically had to force herself out of bed. Her sleep had been heavy and she awoke feeling awful all over. Her mouth felt dry and cottony. Still sleepy, she went down the stairs to the first floor.

"Good morning," Mrs. LeBlanc's lilting voice called cheerfully.

Jolie saw her by the kitchen door. Dragging her feet, she walked that way as her little landlady chuckled.

"There's fresh-squeezed orange juice in the jug," the woman told her. "Glasses, in the right-hand cupboard above the sink. What would you like for breakfast?"

"Just some toast and coffee, thanks." Jolie got herself a glass. Stifling a yawn, she poured some orange juice, eager to refresh her mouth with its sweet, tart taste.

"So, what are your plans for today?" Mrs. LeBlanc set a plate of toast in front of her and returned to the counter for the coffee.

It was nice to be mothered so far from home. Jolie smiled up at her. "None, really. I was thinking about going out to the state park."

"Good. You remember me speaking about our friend who owns an old plantation?"

Jolie struggled for his name. "Etienne?"

"Yes." The older woman smiled brightly. "He called yesterday while you were gone. I mentioned you were staying with us and wanted to see the sights around here, and he very generously offered to show you around his place today."

"Today?" Jolie echoed. She really wasn't in the mood to spend time with a talkative, elderly Frenchman. For some reason, she just assumed he was ancient.

"He said you could stop by around ten this morning, before the heat of the day. I never thought to ask him, but he might know something about the plantation you're trying to find."

"Cameron Hall?" She perked up. That was the reason she'd come all this way. She wasn't going to pass up a chance to talk to someone who might know about it.

"I told him you'd most likely go."

"Oh, yes. Definitely." Jolie nodded vigorously, shaking the last of her sleepiness away in the process.

"The Temple, Etienne's plantation, is several miles from town." Mrs. LeBlanc bustled around and found a pen. "I'll write down the directions."

"Thanks so much. I really do appreciate it."

She picked up her plate, glass and cup as Mrs. LeBlanc told her with a wink to leave all that in the sink and get going.

At nine-thirty Jolie set out for Etienne's plantation. Her dull mood had come back. And the imaginary clouds didn't disappear when she discovered that the directions took her the same way she'd been going when she met the stranger. When the asphalt road finally took a turn she didn't know, she felt better. She didn't want to go back to where those blue eyes would haunt her again.

A narrow dirt road branched off to her left, bearing the sign *Private Road—No Trespassing*. This was it.

Jolie sighed, a flicker of interest piercing her boredom now that her destination was near. A ramshackle fence with wires long since parted from its posts ran parallel with the road.

No chance of getting onto the property that way, she thought. A dense tangle of vines, escaped shrubs growing wild and free, and spiky palmettos grew too thickly under pine trees for that.

No matter how hard she tried to see through it all, she was only able to catch glimpses of white. It had to be the plantation but it was invisible from the road.

Two crumbling white pillars marked the entrance where a grand gate had undoubtedly been, now blocked by padlocked, utilitarian sections of metal fencing.

It was obvious to her that prosperity had long ago turned its back on this place. Still, it was intriguing. She was beginning to wonder what kind of eccentric character this Etienne would turn out to be.

Parking her Volkswagen, Jolie got out and walked to the gate, looking through it. Everything seemed deserted. She knew there were critters in all that green, though. Birds. Maybe muskrats. Snakes.

She shivered, even though she was warm.

Then she noticed a bell suspended on the side of one of the pillars. She pulled the rope attached to it and the strident ding-dong rang shrilly in the stillness. That harsh, unmelodic sound had to rouse someone, Jolie thought.

She moved to the front of the padlocked gate thing to see.

There was a sudden rustle of brush, followed by a whirlwind sound coming right at her. Suddenly she was staring at the bared, snarling fangs of a dog, his front paws on the gate, eye level with her.

She was rooted to the spot and hoped that the chain and lock would hold. He was a big German shepherd, black as a midnight sky without moon or stars, hardly the greeting or greeter she had expected.

She took a tentative step when she realized the animal wasn't going to burst through and bite her. She didn't intend to stick around to see what Mr. Etienne Whoever was like. Heading straight back to town was a much better plan.

Just as she turned toward her car, a voice rang out, clear and commanding. "Black, heel!"

Jolie looked back to see the dog's snarling mouth change into a canine grin as he came down heavily on all fours. With a wagging tail, he raced to the man just coming into view. She stared incredulously as he patted the dog before continuing toward her. It was the stranger from the bayou.

"I hope you'll forgive Black. He's a great guard dog. And much nicer when he's been properly introduced."

"Maybe some other time." She wanted to go, but that audacious twinkle in his blue eyes kept her there. "Hey . . . are *you* Etienne? Holy cow. You must be."

"At your service, Miss Jolie Antoinette Smith." As his head dipped in a bow, his dark hair shone as blackly as the dog's.

"But how—I mean—how did you know?" She was stammering like a schoolgirl.

"I thought I recognized that picnic basket you had with you and Josephine's touch with the food. A phone call confirmed it."

The gate was unlocked and swung open to admit her. A heady feeling overtook Jolie when she realized he had sought her out. Her own pleasure in seeing him again shone in her eyes. Then a question suddenly occurred to her.

"Why didn't you tell Mrs. LeBlanc you'd already met me the day before?"

He was so near to her when she stopped to ask that it almost took her breath away.

"Why didn't you?" he countered smoothly. Jolie had an idea that he already knew the answer.

"I didn't have your advantage of being able to deduce where you were staying." A faint blush rose in her cheeks before she stepped away from him. "Besides, how would it have sounded if I'd told her about that afternoon?"

He made a wry face. "I don't know."

She played out the scene, pretending to talk to Mrs. LeBlanc. "Say, I shared my picnic lunch with this man today. He had dark hair and really blue eyes—I guess he's in his thirties. No, Mrs. LeBlanc, I never got his name."

Etienne was suppressing a smile.

"Now don't you think that would have sounded a little strange to her?"

"No." He shook his head and the smile finally appeared. "A bit bold, maybe. For you. Which is why I almost didn't call."

"Didn't call? Why?"

He began leading her simply by walking himself down the narrow path to the plantation.

"Oh, I have a policy of staying away from Sweet Young Things. Even if they're over twenty-one, they're still wet behind the ears. I don't need the aggravation."

"Thanks a lot," she said indignantly. But she did kind of fit the description, especially after a shower with no makeup. Squeaky clean and much too young.

"You're welcome."

"But wait a minute," she said, looking at the path, which was overgrown, and not at him. "You did bother. Why?"

"I'm not sure. On an impulse, I guess," was his laconic reply.

He stopped for a second to push several long, supple branches out of the way and hold onto them,

waving her ahead and through. "Don't want you to
get switched."

"Every inch the plantation gentleman, aren't
you?" she said crossly. She sauntered, taking her
sweet time. After all, she was a certified Sweet Young
Thing and entitled to drive him crazy.

"I try."

They went on a little ways further before he spoke
again. "Anyway, Jolie, I'm glad that I gave in to that
impulse."

She wanted to say that she was glad too, but that
would have been too revealing of her budding feelings for this man. So she said nothing.

"Are you sorry you came?" he asked.

She didn't bother to lie, not with him looking
right at her. "No."

A ghost of a smile touched his mouth. "You're
really something."

Jolie walked quickly on, too conscious of the man
beside her.

"Hey, slow down. I think we're going to have a very
enjoyable day, Black." His teasing words were addressed to the German shepherd padding beside him.

She looked away from the man and his dog, forcing her attention ahead of her. The dense growth
began to thin out. Her steps faltered as an amazing
view spread out before her. Dominating it was a
mansion of such colossal proportions that it took
Jolie's breath away.

Immense pillars surrounded the square building
and supported a second floor balcony. Jolie couldn't
begin to guess how high the house was. A few details
became more clear. It needed paint. Some bits were

falling off. But the palatial effect it had been designed to give was still very powerful.

Adding to its grandeur, the plantation was surrounded by oak trees of a size and girth that astounded Jolie, even though she'd seen ones like them before. Their branches were the size of trunks of regular trees, here and there dipping so close to the ground that a person could sit on them as if they were in a gigantic chair. As always, their leafy limbs were draped with green-gray Spanish moss, turning the gnarled giants into picturesque wise old men with flowing gray beards.

Jolie finally tore her gaze away from the impressive scene, her dazzled expression turning toward Etienne. He was smiling at her gently.

"The Temple always affects a stranger that way," he said.

She just didn't have words.

"It is like a temple," she said after a little while. "How lucky you are to own it."

"This place owns me." Etienne smiled ruefully. "It—well, I don't call her it and I don't mind saying so."

Jolie gave him an encouraging smile.

"A house like this is a demanding mistress. She has moods and she likes to be seen in her best light—does that sound crazy?"

"Not at all." Jolie loved his imaginativeness.

"I saw her for the first time four years ago. A year later I gave in and bought her."

"I thought the Temple was your family home, passed down through generations." Jolie glanced at him in surprise.

"If it had been, I never would've allowed her to

get into this dilapidated state. She was being used as a cattle barn until I bought her."

Jolie didn't have to see his expression to know that anger was just below the surface. And she agreed with him. History mattered, this old house mattered. Complete disregard for an architectural marvel that men and women had labored for years to make beautiful upset her too.

Five steps led to the wooden porch and the enormous double door leading inside. Jolie noticed new sections of planking replacing rotting boards below her feet. Good thing. She didn't care to fall through and say hello to nine billion termites happily munching.

But he wouldn't have let her walk anywhere unsafe. Etienne opened one of the doors and waved her through. The inside was dim and it took a while for her eyes to adjust.

"Nice and cool," she said, surprised again.

"The walls are really thick and the temperature tends to stay right around seventy-four degrees year round."

She shivered slightly.

"You're turning into a Southern belle right before my eyes," he laughed.

"I have gotten used to it being so warm all the time. Nice change after South Dakota, you know. Although we do have broiling days in the summer sometimes."

He nodded, taking her through various rooms, some grand, some not, most with no furniture.

"All the floors in the downstairs were destroyed by the cattle," he said. "I just had them replaced." His eyes were shadowy. He took carelessness like that personally, she figured.

Jolie followed as he pointed out details that she might have missed—that room was the butler's pantry, that, the office of the plantation owner where business was conducted.

He explained that the carved fireplaces in each room had been vandalized and were beyond restoration. New ones were being constructed, but she sensed his indignation that the beauty of the originals was gone forever.

"Good thing that cattle won't go upstairs." Etienne led her back that way. "Because these are magnificent." He pointed out what he loved about it. "This is a self-supporting oval spiral. The steps are cypress and the balustrades are mahogany. No nails—check it out. Each post is individually fitted into the whole."

The wood still had a luster and was satiny smooth to the touch. Jolie let her hand trail along it as they climbed the steps to the second floor.

Here the fireplaces in the bedrooms were untouched, although somewhat neglected. Etienne pointed out one that he had cleaned, stained, and revarnished. Most of the furniture was original but just too layered with dirt for its beauty to be seen. Then he led her back into the hallway and took her through an upper gallery to where she could see out huge windows to a breathtaking view of the rear lawns.

A ribbon of shining water winked at her beneath more giant oaks and magnolias.

"Is that a pond down there?"

Etienne shook his head, gazing over his land with a lordly air. "That's Bayou Teche. Roads didn't exist in the old days, so these houses were always built near navigable water," he explained. "The waterways were the roads in early-day Louisiana."

Jolie nodded, realizing the logic of it. Then something else occurred to her.

"You didn't show me the kitchens. Where are they?"

"Not part of the house, believe it or not. The danger of fire was just too great."

"Oh. That makes sense."

"I found some foundations," Etienne went on, "that I think were probably the kitchen outbuildings and smokehouses."

"They were really self-sufficient," Jolie said.

"Yeah. In a way, every plantation was its own little world."

"Hey, where do you live?" The look in his eyes flustered her for a second. Maybe she shouldn't have asked. "I mean, you obviously can't . . . well, live in the house. Not yet, anyway."

"C'mon." He reached out and took her hand, the warmth of his touch sending tremors through her. "I'll show you where I live."

Chapter 6

Etienne led her back downstairs and out the same door they'd entered. Then he turned to the left, instead of taking the path leading to her car. As they rounded the mansion, Jolie spied a much smaller version of the Temple.

"It's just like the big house!" she exclaimed in delight.

"Commonly known as the *garçonniere* where the younger or unmarried men in the family resided. *Garçon* is the French word for boy."

He released her hand to open the screen door, then brought it back to her shoulder as he escorted her inside.

It was only one large room with stairs leading to the second floor and a lace grillework partition sectioning off the kitchen area. The décor and furniture were simple, with a masculine look that befit the term for the small house.

"Would you like a cold drink?"

Of course she would. But nothing with alcohol in it. Etienne's voice had a seductive quality and a caressing softness. Or was that only her imagination, always looking for that something extra her heart longed for?

"Lemonade, please."

He nodded and went to the fridge, pouring some in a glass and handing it to her. His dark, curling lashes shadowed the blueness of his eyes.

In this much smaller space, the chemistry between them seemed a lot stronger. This was where he lived. The air seemed imbued with his essence.

"Want to sit outside?"

Had he read her mind? She only nodded.

"You might be more comfortable there," was all he said.

Jolie went with him, finding herself a lawn chair and settling down a little primly with her lemonade. Etienne seemed content to gaze at the mansion under renovation, his eyes occasionally straying around the lawn of this one.

She took the opportunity to study him covertly. Since their previous meeting by the banks where he'd been fishing, he seemed changed to her. He wasn't quite the same person she had met that day, or thought she'd met.

There was still the same litheness of movement and the instinctive grace of an athlete. His dark blue eyes still gleamed in the same way and his smile was just as ready to trigger the deep grooves around his mouth.

But before Etienne had given her the impression of indolence, even laziness, a devil-may-care approach to life. And today—today Jolie had seen something else. The purposeful set of his jaw, the chiseled, slightly aristocratic nose that could flare with distaste, the blue eyes that flickered with burning anger, and the overwhelming strength that emanated like an aura around him. But she was struck not only by his born-and-bred dignity, but also his iron-willed determination that hinted at an occasional ruthlessness.

"Have you decided whether I can be trusted?" His face was turned away from her, his strong profile etched against the trees. Yet he had been completely aware of her scrutiny.

"I think," Jolie fought back her embarrassment, "that if you put a gold ring in your ear, you would make an excellent pirate."

"From some women that might be a compliment." Now he turned to study her. "What a pity I'm only a poor plantation owner."

"The best things in life are free." Jolie almost squeaked out that old cliché. Seriously, she didn't know what else to say.

"Don't you believe that." He made a sound somewhere between laughter and disdain. "You pay for everything in one way or another."

The cynical tone in his voice startled her. "And what is the price for love?"

"Only the most precious thing a man has—his freedom."

"Right. You must watch a lot of John Wayne movies," she said. Talk about talking in clichés. He'd gone off the deep end. She wasn't altogether sure he'd meant to sound that movie-ish, though. "Or else you're just a confirmed bachelor."

"How about you?" he asked. "How would you define yourself?" He looked at her for a beat. "Of course, you're young to be doing that. You're probably still figuring the world out."

"Yes and no." Her chin tilted up in defiance. "I believe happiness begins in love and continues in marriage, but I'm a dyed-in-the-wool romantic. Should I apologize for it?"

"No," he said quietly. "I think you're telling the truth." A quirk of his mouth revealed his amusement. "So define love for me then."

Jolie took a breath, then slowly exhaled it, looking up at the house, and noting absently how the bright sunlight bathed it in a deeper yellow glow. It was a magical place. She wondered about the people who'd lived and loved in it all those years ago.

"I don't know. I've never really been in love. What about you?" she asked.

"Many times."

Trust him to say that, she thought unhappily.

"Which is why I don't believe in it," he went on.

"If your freedom is so precious to you, why did you tie yourself down to this plantation? You said yourself that it's more demanding than any woman."

He didn't speak to that, only said, "You actually listen to what a man says. That's another rare trait." His gaze moved slowly over. "I was tired of traveling, of not having any roots. And this place literally had my name written on it."

"I don't understand."

"Let me show you," he laughed, setting his glass on the tiled porch floor of the *garçonniere*. Jolie did the same.

His arm slipped around her waist as he assisted her down the narrow steps of the porch. Jolie felt herself tense at his easy intimacy. She couldn't match his seeming indifference to save her life. Etienne puzzled her. Basically, he was an enigma. She had no idea what had happened to make him so wary of women—and so attentive to her nonetheless.

"If you felt the need to settle down, then haven't you ever wanted kids?" Jolie asked, trying to be as blunt and bold as he was.

He looked down at her, his eyes on her lips a little too long for her peace of mind. What was worse, Jolie wanted him to kiss her.

"I'd have to be married. Guess I am a traditionalist when it comes to that. But there's more to marriage than procreation, or there should be."

"You're kind of contradicting yourself. I would guess you're not all that sure about what you want either." She held her breath, waiting to see what he'd say to that.

He halted their strolling pace. "Stay here a second." He walked to a flowering shrub and broke off a large white bloom. He walked back to her, bringing the petals to his nose to sniff the fragrance before offering it to Jolie.

As she took it, his fingers didn't let go of the stem and she had to touch them.

"Something beautiful for a beauty," he said, in a husky, drawling voice that enveloped her in virility. A rosy hue stole over her face when he finally let her take the flower. She tried to hide her blush in a silent appreciation of the velvet smoothness of the petals. Moving on, she stole a glance at him. He seemed to be smiling, and it hurt her that her lack of sophistication amused him.

His arm was around her waist again, guiding her closer to the shining mirror of water.

A pillar, aging and pockmarked, stood forlornly near the water. Its mate lay in a heap of rubble, mostly bricks and stucco, in the tall grass. Here along the bayou was the front entrance to the plantation that had once matched the gates Jolie had entered, but had now fallen to ruin. Etienne led her to the one standing pillar.

"This is what led me to my final decision to buy. Seemed like fate somehow. I had to have the house."

At his odd statement, Jolie followed his solemn gaze to the standing pillar. Despite the ravages of time, she could just make out the worn letters that had been carved into it. But they were so faint and so old-fashioned she couldn't quite read them.

She gasped when she realized the name they spelled out.

"Cameron!" she breathed so softly that it was barely audible, blinking hard to make sure that the name wasn't a figment of her imagination.

It wasn't.

She stared back at the mansion, standing in all its regal glory amidst the giant oaks before turning to Etienne, tears of exultation in her brown eyes.

"I've found it!" Her voice squeaked with emotion. "I've found Cameron Hall!"

Her delight bewildered him and she managed to control herself long enough to tell him the details.

Jolie practically threw herself into his arms, not thinking.

"Can you believe it?" she exclaimed, looking up at him. "I thought I would never find it." Her voice was a little shaky. "And it's your home. That's just totally amazing!"

Her face was radiant with the thrill of her discovery. Etienne caught his breath as he looked down at her.

And then . . . she became conscious of the pressure of his thighs against her, the muscular hardness of his chest, and the firm caress of his hands on her back and shoulders.

Fate had played a part—and brought them together in this unlikely place. The connection between them was more powerful than ever.

She felt Etienne's arms tighten around her. The sensuous curve of his lips moved nearer.

There was nothing wrong with a kiss to celebrate, she thought confusedly. Jolie felt as if she were on the brink of another discovery.

Then his lips were on hers, soft and gentle, like the flower he'd given her that she had dropped in her excitement—she didn't think of it now as his lips moved persuasively against hers.

The way she yielded only intensified the passion in his kiss. When he stopped to let her breathe, his hands cupped her face. Jolie felt cheated. She wanted more. She wanted all the kisses he cared to give.

"I've wanted to do that from the first moment I saw you," he said raggedly. His face was only inches away from hers.

She had moved her hands from his back to rest against his chest. The roughness of his thumb caressed her lips, parting them slightly before he claimed them again.

This time there was no gentle exploration as her arms wound around his neck in abandonment, and she succumbed to the desire to let her fingers run through his black hair.

The flame that blazed within her seemed to be in him too. His arms encircled her body, arching her against him as if he wanted to fuse them together.

A moan escaped her lips when his mouth deserted hers to nip at her earlobe and the pulsating cord in her neck. The longing to have his lips on hers became too much to bear. Then his hands moved to her arms, firmly drawing them from around his neck to hold them tightly against his chest.

Jolie couldn't bring herself to meet his gaze. He'd given her that something extra she craved so deeply—and she suspected there was much more.

"That was quite a kiss for a Yankee girl," he said quietly. "Were your Southern ancestors that passionate?"

"Maybe so. I was told they had lots of little ancestors—"

"And then came you." He kissed the top of her head.

Looking up at him, Jolie saw the sensual glitter in his eyes. What did it mean? She just wasn't sure. She fought a surge of feeling. After one embrace, it was idiotic to tell a man you were falling in love with him.

"That was my lucky day," he whispered. "And today was yours. So—"

He straightened away from her and she felt foolishly bereft.

"Stay to lunch with me?"

The matter-of-fact question crushed her and he noticed it. He seemed about to sweep her into his arms again just to make up for it and she hesitated, not sure if things were happening a little too fast.

"Jolie," Etienne murmured, and she sensed his body straining toward her. Her vulnerability was too great. Another passionate embrace like the last and she might agree to anything.

"I'd like to stay." She swallowed hard as she looked into his face.

The expression in his eyes told her she'd been right in thinking he would have had his way in one manner or another. She hadn't realized the tenseness that had been between them until Etienne relaxed, catching her hand to brush its palm with a kiss.

"At the moment, food is the last thing on my mind." He nestled Jolie under his arm and held her so closely against him that it made walking tricky but she didn't mind.

They went back to the plantation. Jolie couldn't help thinking that the big house was looking down at them with satisfaction. She breathed in deeply, drinking in every scent and sound that surrounded this happiest of moments in her young life. Not only had she discovered Cameron Hall, but Etienne as well. A smile as golden as the sun radiated from her face.

When they entered the smaller version of the house, Etienne pulled her into his arms again.

"Is it really necessary that we eat right now?"

Jolie felt warmth spreading through her at the lean hardness of his body against hers. Her resolve to remain level-headed was nearly swept away with the fiery desire for his kiss.

"We—we should, yes." Her breathy stammer wasn't too convincing.

"Guess you're right."

Jolie caught a fleeting glimpse of emotion in his eyes that she didn't quite understand.

"Etienne?" Her hand touched his arm to stop him when he moved away from her. He stared down at her puzzled expression and she couldn't understand what she'd done to upset him.

"Don't look at me like that." There was no softness in his face. She was aware that he had to be the kind of man who didn't settle for chaste kisses. Unless she wanted to totally frustrate him, she'd do well to keep a little distance.

Something in her expression must have given away her wavering confidence, because Etienne lifted her chin and planted a kiss, not such a scorcher as the others, on her lips.

He smiled. "I forgot to tell you that you have to help fix lunch."

"Oh, I'm very good at that." Jolie adopted his lighter mood quickly. "I got an A in home economics in high school."

"No kidding. We have to put that training to use." Etienne walked to the fridge and opened the door. "What would a home ec queen make out of romaine lettuce, leftover ham, hardboiled eggs, and big fat tomatoes? That's all I have—wait, there's a box of fossilized croutons too."

"Give those a minute in the microwave." She laughed easily now. "If you're able to conjure up some oil and vinegar and dried herbs, I might be able to make us a chef's salad."

"That's my specialty," he assured her. "Leave the dressing to me."

Jolie never did discover exactly how he made it, since she was busy with her own tasks. But it turned out to be delicious.

As they were eating, Etienne turned the conversation to his plans for further renovation of the plantation. Although of course she was interested, she found herself just enjoying looking at him, studying the gleam of his black hair in the sunlight and the sharp contrast of his gorgeous blue eyes to his coloring. Doing that meant she only caught bits and pieces of what he was saying. She was reeling inside, not willing to believe that he was really attracted to her.

". . . on rainy days, I've been refinishing the wood on a Victorian sofa and two matching chairs," he was saying, swirling the white wine that accompanied their meal. "One more application of varnish after I hand-sand the last coat I put on, and they'll be done. Except for the reupholstering, which I can't do."

"Listen to you," she teased. "Sometimes I'm not sure if you're a wicked pirate or just a worried Joe Homeowner."

He grinned. "The second at the moment. Upholstering pieces that old can cost a fortune, you know."

"Well, it was sort of a hobby of mine back in South Dakota. I learned how when I wanted to save a vintage rocker that I loved."

Etienne glanced up sharply, making her blush. She hadn't meant to ask for the job, but she wouldn't mind helping him with it.

"I'm pretty good at it," she said quickly. "In fact, I used to pick up extra money when I was in college with redos of our neighbors' oldies but goodies."

"I don't doubt that you're capable," he replied. "But you're here on vacation. It just occurred to me that you'll be leaving."

Joy swelled in her heart as she realized his slight frown had nothing to do with his opinion of her skill at upholstering, but her eventual departure. So he did care for her.

"I planned to stay for three weeks." It was hard keeping her voice calm. "Or until my money ran out."

"I could pay you for your time." A dangerous light came into his eyes. "Anything to keep you here longer."

"You might regret that offer." Julie laughed and toyed with the stem of her glass of wine.

Etienne hesitated before replying. "It would be a shame if you had to leave when you just found Cameron Hall."

"And you? What about you?" Jolie wondered why he'd chosen his words with such care.

He obviously didn't want to commit himself. He was a man like any other when it came right down to it and love wasn't all that necessary to any of them when it involved making love. Or at least not to the same degree that it would be to a woman. Besides, he'd already told her he didn't believe in love.

Nervousness showed in her hands. She gave herself something to do by stacking the dishes to carry to the porcelain sink. She knew Etienne was watching her intently but she didn't know what to say.

Stick to the middle of the road, she told herself. Stay safe.

"I'm glad Cameron Hall hasn't been restored." She kept her voice light as she carried the dishes to the sink. "It has the atmosphere of how it was long ago, more so than if it were freshly painted and filled with expensive antiques."

He made a noncommittal sound in response.

"Well, that does sound contradictory, I guess," she went on, feeling confused.

She turned to glance at Etienne, whom she'd left still sitting at the small table, only to find that he was standing directly in back of her, making her feel insignificant. This close, he towered over her. The feeling was intensified by the enigmatic expression in his eyes.

"My, my, you're domestic." His blunt words caused her a flicker of pain. She couldn't believe his eyes could be so cold. "Marriage has never been part of my plans, Jolie."

"What am I supposed to say to that?" She swallowed the tears trying to flow.

"Nothing." The single word was clipped. "I just want to be sure we understand each other."

"What?" She felt suddenly blindsided. "I'm not stupid and I'm not a child!"

A corner of his mouth lifted in a half smile. "No, you're not. You're all woman—I've already discovered that."

That powerful, magnetic charm of his put Jolie under his spell again. She started to move around him to get the rest of the dishes, but his arm shot out and blocked her way.

"And in spite of a common-sense inclination to get you out of here, I keep thinking of reasons for you to stay."

His voice was a hot whisper against her hair as he moved closer, getting her back against the sink.

Jolie felt her knees go weak, and knew that if her hands let go of the countertop, they would find their way around his strong neck. She forced herself to turn around and focus on the dirty dishes in the sink, always a good reality check.

"Did you know Jolie means 'pretty' in French?" he asked huskily.

"Yes," she gulped, stalling for time. "But not what Etienne means. Translate, please."

"Steven." His mouth found the hollow between her shoulder and her neck. Jolie moaned a little and moved away so swiftly that he was unable to stop her.

"You mean I don't even know your real name?"

"Around here it's one or the other, since they mean the same."

A sudden stab of something akin to fear pierced her heart. Wild panic made her tremble as she remembered Guy and Michelle speaking of a man named Steve.

A womanizer. Guy's competition. Was he *that* Steve?

He was looking at her with puzzled wariness. "Didn't Mrs. LeBlanc tell you who I am? My full name is Steve Cameron."

"She only called you Etienne," Jolie said quietly, realizing there could not be another man around here who fit Michelle's warning phrase so well. *Fire burns and if you get too near Steve, you get scorched.* And . . . the LeBlanc family considered him Claudine's property. He was definitely off limits to her.

"Well, she always called me that," was all he said.

Chapter 7

Pieces of the puzzle were coming together, forming a picture Jolie wasn't sure she could figure out. Guy had referred to Steve as a formidable opponent. That was an understatement. Steve Cameron was all that and more. No wonder the name Cameron on the pillar had persuaded him to buy the plantation.

Her thoughts racing, Jolie looked at Etienne, who was really Steve Cameron. How could she not have realized that this ultra-masculine man had to be the one Guy and Michelle had described? He was watching her, showing only slight interest in her bewilderment.

"I feel like a fool." An embarrassed laugh accompanied her words. "Guy and Michelle mentioned you as Steve, but when Mrs. LeBlanc talked about Etienne, I pictured an elderly man. Even after I met you, I just didn't put two and two together."

"I can understand Guy wanting to protect his claim, but what about Michelle?" Although he asked the question, Jolie had the feeling he wasn't all that interested in the answer.

"Guy has no claim on me." She didn't like the

look in Steve's eyes. He knew that already. "I only asked Michelle about you because she was there when Guy mentioned you. She described you—not physically, though."

"Don't tell me Michelle thinks I'm dangerous." He chuckled, leaning back against the counter in a relaxed way.

"Not to her."

"Am I dangerous to you?" The blue eyes looking at her held the same charm as his seductively soft words.

Danger meant possible harm. Did he have the ability to hurt her? She was so close to falling in love with him for no reason. He'd given no indication that he cared for her. Yes, Steve Cameron was dangerous to her, but she wasn't going to reveal her own feelings and admit it.

"Oh, please. Don't be silly." The casual-seeming reply came easily as she began gathering the rest of the dishes on the table. "Did Mrs. LeBlanc tell you that Claudine was coming home this Saturday?"

"She mentioned it." He took the dishes from her and put them in the sink. "Leave them," he ordered. "I want your opinion on the furniture I'm refinishing."

Jolie's lips tightened at his adept shift away from anything personal. She knew no more about his relationship with Claudine than she had before. Well, she herself might be inexperienced by comparison, Jolie thought determinedly, but she wasn't a shy country mouse who could be put off that easily.

"I understand you and Claudine are really close."

He led her out of the area. She'd expected him to be taken aback by her directness, but he wasn't. If anything, Steve was amused.

"You can thank Claudine for me being here," he said cryptically.

"What do you mean?"

"I met her in New Orleans and she invited me to visit her parents, which I did. With her. She brought me out here for a picnic while she did some sketches of the plantation. Later I bought the place."

She didn't have the nerve to ask if it was because of Claudine. "What do you do for a living, anyway?"

He shrugged. "I live." The grooves around his mouth deepened at Jolie's wide-eyed expression. "Okay, there's more. I raise sugarcane which pays the mortgage and for some improvements to the house. There's a year-round vegetable garden and I have a milk cow that faithfully gives me a calf to butcher each year. No particular ambitions otherwise. Wealth and power are not that important to me. Does that disappoint you?"

"No. You just seem like the type who could succeed at anything."

"What type is that?"

"The commanding type."

Her answer hardened his expression, especially the hint of ruthlessness around his mouth and that piratical gleam in his eyes.

"The furniture is in here," was all he said.

Another sidestep, she thought. He was good at them.

He opened the door of a weatherbeaten building, and threw a lot of technical questions at her that made it clear he knew what he wanted. Jolie was thankful that she could reply intelligently. She wanted him to think well of her, after all.

When they'd gotten through an overview, they

strolled out of the building. Steve had given Jolie the go-ahead to pick out materials and order swatches they could go over together.

She felt somewhat bereft. The intimacy that had encircled them just wasn't there anymore. There seemed to be nothing personal about his attentions. And despite the pleasure she felt at being in his company, Jolie wanted to go back in time to the way it had felt before.

No matter where they walked, the plantation house dominated the landscape, rising majestically before them. As Jolie and Steve paused near one of the giant oaks, her gaze was drawn to it again while her restless fingers played with a lacelike bunch of Spanish moss on a low-hanging branch.

"Do you really think they lived as luxuriously and grandly as we've heard?" Jolie sighed. "And were they that wealthy?"

"Some were. But not all. And it wasn't all mint juleps and house parties, if that's what you mean. Not if the family wanted to prosper. They had to contend with everything from yellow fever to hurricanes. Two crop failures in a row would mean ruin. And turning a profit depended on a lot of things, one of which was slavery. That had to end and so did the plantation way of life."

She nodded, not wanting to make small talk about that. The long-ago evil still haunted this beautiful country and its people on both sides of the color line.

"But it was a unique world. You've probably heard some of the better stories."

"Tell me what you know," she murmured.

"All right." He thought for a minute. "In one

household, it was customary to stop all the clocks when a guest arrived so that time would stand still in the joy of that moment, and the clocks wouldn't be started again until that guest had left, whether it was a day, week, or month later."

"I like that." She smiled.

"Outdoing each other was like a game to plantation owners, with opulent homes and a liking for hospitality. For example, a breakfast tray for a female guest would be brought in while she was sleeping and a full-blown rose placed on the pillow beside her. If the woman didn't open her eyes, the servant would hold the rose under her nose until its fragrance did the trick. Then the woman would be served a *petit noir* of coffee to wake the body. The host believed her spirit would be awakened by the rose."

"That's really beautiful."

"Probably one of the best tales happened right near here."

She looked up at him eagerly.

"Okay," he said with an indulgent smile. "A Monsieur Charles Durand owned a plantation on Bayou Teche a few miles outside of St. Martinville. He was quite a colorful character. His first wife had twelve children and he swore on her grave that he would never marry again, but within a year he did. He wanted to be completely fair to his second wife, so they had twelve children."

"Oh my. Sounds like a Southern fairy tale. I hope it ended happily."

"Interesting you should say that about fairy tales. When two of his daughters were betrothed to men from Louisiana, the locals expected something very fancy for the double wedding and they got it. He had boys go to the woods and trap large spiders. A few days before the wedding he had the spiders set loose in the avenue of trees leading to the main house."

Jolie shuddered and gave him a doubtful look. "Really?"

Steve laughed. "I'm just getting to the good part. Southern spiders spin seriously big webs. The trees became a network of lacy webs and on the morning of the wedding, the servants were sent out with bellows filled with silver and gold dust which they sprayed on the webs, turning the avenue into a shimmering canopy for the bridal parties."

Jolie's eyes widened. "Is that true?"

"It's a great story, if it isn't."

"What if it had rained? Or the wind kicked up?" She bit her lip at the thought. Weddings had a way of attracting wild weather, in her experience. Jolie had been a bridesmaid more often than she wanted to count.

"Mother Nature didn't mess with Monsieur Durand, apparently." He laughed again at her obvious concern, but Jolie didn't mind.

"I'm glad she didn't." She sighed wistfully, trying to imagine the massive oaks surrounding Cameron Hall glittering with gold and silver tracery.

"Do you realize it's after three? Actually, almost four o'clock," he said gently.

Jolie turned toward him, feeling a little awkward. It didn't seem possible that the time could have gone by so swiftly.

"Oh. Well, I—I'd better be going."

She brushed nervously at her skirt, averting her face from his amused eyes. But when she was about to head down the tangled lane leading to the car, he caught her wrist and pulled her to him.

"I don't care if you stay all night." The fire in his eyes sent her pulse leaping. "As a matter of fact, I'd prefer it. But I wouldn't like to get on Josephine's bad-boy list."

Jolie was more flustered than before. "No. I mean—does she keep a list?"

He just grinned. "Maybe."

"Anyway, I'm sure she expects me back for dinner." She just couldn't meet his gaze or deal with his virile vibe. "Thanks for reminding me of the time."

"You're welcome." He gave her a wink. Then Steve intertwined his fingers with hers. "C'mon, I'll walk you to your car."

Minutes later, when she was behind the wheel of her red Volkswagen, he leaned down and brushed her lips in a fleeting kiss.

"This time you can believe me when I say *au revoir,* Jolie."

Then Steve went back to the gate where the black German shepherd sat, ears pricked and bright eyes studying the scene. Jolie waved goodbye and reversed the car into the dirt lane. It was only when she was on the main road that she realized Steve hadn't said when he would see her again. But there was a new, warm, enveloping glow in her heart. Jolie felt none of the doubts of their first meeting.

As she walked into the LeBlanc house, the questions began. Mrs. LeBlanc wanted to know how her afternoon with Etienne had gone as Guy stood in the doorway, broodingly watching her. She disguised her elation by just announcing that the Temple,

Steve's plantation, was Cameron Hall. Mrs. LeBlanc seemed happy with that as an explanation for why Jolie had stayed out so long.

She didn't bother to correct the assumption, excusing herself as soon as she could to go to her room.

"You didn't tell us your impression of Steve Cameron. Maybe you forgot," Guy said. He'd followed her to the staircase. Her hand gripped the banister tightly before she relaxed a little.

"Hmm. Well, *you* could have told me that he was devastatingly handsome." She kept her tone light so Guy wouldn't guess the impact Steve had made on her. "And you really should have told me that Etienne and Steve were the same person. I thought I was meeting an elderly French gentleman."

Guy dismissed that complaint without saying a word. "So were you devastated?"

Since she hadn't confided that she'd met Steve before, there didn't seem to be a compelling reason to admit it now. Jolie settled for a reply that was half true.

"I guess stunned would be a better word. I don't know why I didn't connect him at first with the Steve you mentioned. Of course, it's a common name, and I also didn't know that Etienne is Steve in French."

The way Guy was looking at her mouth was disconcerting, as he knew about the kisses that had started a fire in her.

"Was I right about his experience?"

Jolie turned to continue up the stairs. His prying questions were irritating her. "What do you want, Guy? A blow-by-blow account of his attempt to seduce me?" Her voice was threaded with annoyance.

"I never thought Maman would send you out there to his place," Guy muttered.

"Oh, come on," Jolie sighed. "Do you really believe what I just said?"

"No. Steve's too smart to play his cards like that."

Jolie stiffened. "I'm not a prize in some game, okay?"

"To him you might be. He probably really likes your, uh, wholesomeness."

"Hey." Her tone was crisp. "I was raised on a farm, so I guess I am guilty of wholesomeness, as you call it. But it also means I know about the birds and the bees. And a whole lot more. One little kiss is really not going to rock my world, Guy." That may have been an outright lie, but Jolie was now too angry to care.

"Then I was right—the game has begun." His smile was a cross between sarcasm and smugness.

"Mind your own business. I can take care of myself."

"Listen, Jolie." Guy's voice changed to a pleading tone. "I just don't want to see you get hurt. I've seen Steve in action before."

"So? Keep it to yourself. Isn't that a requirement of the manly code of honor?"

Jolie didn't feel like sparing the sarcasm either. But it did hurt to hear even a hint of other women Steve had chased. Too much had happened today for her to think clearly. She wished she'd never gotten tangled up in this conversation with Guy. She was only becoming more confused.

"Look," she told him, "I guess you're trying to look out for me and I appreciate it. Sort of," she added a little more truthfully. "But I'm an adult and capable of forming my own opinions, right or wrong. I thought Steve was fascinating, if you really want to know."

She didn't give Guy a chance to reply, going up the stairs two at a time to make sure of that. But he was bound to have the last word. And it carried up to her.

"He's fascinating, huh? So is a cobra!"

Steve didn't contact her the following day, Friday. Jolie almost despised herself for puttering around in town with stops at the LeBlanc house to see if he had.

Not that she asked outright if there were messages from him. She didn't know if the family was on to her pathetic ruse or not. A part of her didn't care.

But when Saturday dawned, most of her faith that he would contact her had vanished. She didn't want to believe that Guy's hints were true or that she was one of many.

Guy suggested that they spend the day together with a group of his friends and she said yes in a hurry. They got through several sets of tennis, and segued to a relaxing afternoon beside a swimming pool.

The exercise and the enervating warmth of the southern sun melted most of her inner tension. Jolie was feeling better about life when they returned to the LeBlanc house. She hadn't bothered to change out of her red-flowered bikini, deciding instead that the long-sleeved matching red blouse covered it up well enough.

No one seemed to mind her lounging around the

sun porch dressed like that as far as she could tell. The whole family was in a laid-back mood anyway.

Then Michelle dashed upstairs to shower and change for her date with Eugene, her teacher boyfriend. Mr. LeBlanc got a phone call that involved a lot of friendly, endless mumbling on his end of it. Mrs. LeBlanc was making dinner. And Guy got busy online looking for movie theaters within driving distance to find one for him and Jolie to see that night.

Which left her alone. She didn't much mind.

She was the only one who saw the car pull up the driveway and come to a stop by the back door. A young woman hopped out.

Uh-oh, Jolie thought. Here came her competition. She was gorgeous. Masses of black hair, amazing figure, cute clothes, pouty lips. The color drained from Jolie's face when Steve got out on the other side of the car and a memory clicked in her mind. Claudine was coming home today, the same Claudine who considered Steve Cameron her private property.

And there he was with her, calmly unloading bubblegum-colored duffel bags and print-patterned suitcases from the trunk of her car.

Double uh-oh. Jolie just didn't trust women with adorable luggage and this one had a mountain of it. Not only that, Steve looked like her personal bellhop with the duffels under his arms and the suitcases gripped in his strong hands.

Jolie was ready to turn away from the window so that when they entered the house they wouldn't know that she'd been watching. But the scene hadn't played itself out yet. She saw Claudine move to stand closer to Steve. With a pang, she watched the other woman's long, artistic fingers spread themselves on his chest, pushing open the shirt a little to actually touch his skin.

Steve was looking down at Claudine and although Jolie couldn't see his expression, she knew he wasn't fighting her off.

She felt a little—no, a lot—sick as she watched Claudine pull Steve's face down to hers. Like a fool, she thought he would break free of the clinging embrace but he didn't.

He accepted Claudine's kiss. Even though his arms were filled with her luggage, he even returned it.

Smooch, smooch. No big deal. But why did it make her eyes cloud with tears? Jolie turned away from the window.

She wiped her eyes with the back of her hand. She wasn't about to give him the satisfaction of seeing her cry. It was just as well she'd seen them arrive. There was little doubt anymore as to just how foolish her hopes were. She had been warned, even if she'd been ready to shoot the messenger, that she wasn't anything more than an interesting diversion for Steve Cameron.

There was no way she was going to stand there in the room when those two walked in. Jolie hurried into the hallway. She saw Guy in the alcove staring into the computer monitor, looking at capsule movie reviews.

"Find anything worth seeing? Two thumbs up? Hey, one thumb up will do." Jolie forced cheerfulness into her voice, a complete contrast to what she was really feeling.

"Come and take a look. I don't know what you've seen and what you haven't."

Jolie stared at the monitor as if her life depended on it. "Scroll down. Now up. Not that one. Scroll down again."

"Don't make me crazy," Guy complained, but he did as she asked.

The sound of laughter and opening doors heralded the arrival of Claudine and Steve. Guy sighed as he pushed back his chair from the monitor, giving Jolie a resigned look.

"The queen bee has arrived at the hive," he said. He took Jolie's hand and led her toward the hallway.

If his lack of enthusiasm was noticeable, his parents more than made up for it. They noisily welcomed their daughter home.

Jolie and Guy were standing behind the group. She was grateful for the extra few minutes to put on a look of unconcern.

The instant Guy had seen Steve with Claudine, his hand had tightened on Jolie's. She actually didn't mind. She even let him pull her a little closer.

Jolie was sure it would be a while before they were noticed. Yet, with sort of a sixth sense, Steve turned from the commotion around Claudine to look behind him.

There was a hint of amusement in the depths of his blue eyes as his gaze caught Jolie's—and flicked down a bit to her side, where Guy was holding her hand, a clasp that was growing a little moist for her liking, truth be told.

A betraying flush of pink crept into her cheeks as Steve looked at her face again, but she boldly returned his glance, as if daring him to comment.

Steve didn't seem to pick up on the challenge in her eyes. He chose instead to let his gaze roam over her scanty attire until she felt nearly naked under it.

Damn him anyway.

Before Jolie could get over her annoyance at the way Steve's gaze was taking liberties, Emile LeBlanc greeted him in French. His reply was in the same language, which continued for several exchanges. Not once did Steve hesitate for a correct word, proving himself as fluent as the LeBlancs. Jolie admired his ability and understood why Mrs. LeBlanc had referred to him by the French equivalent of his name. She refused to allow herself to wonder how he knew the language so well.

"Is this your new girlfriend, Guy?" Steve asked.

There was a bite to the question that drew Jolie's gaze from Steve to the young woman now facing her. Dark, dark brown eyes were inspecting her with contemptuous thoroughness. Jolie's self-confidence was deflated by the strikingly beautiful Claudine.

The other woman was the personification of all Jolie's dreams of the glamorous good looks she'd never had. Claudine's skin was a flawless shade of ivory, a perfect contrast to her black hair, raven brows and long, curling lashes that owed nothing to mascara. Large gold hoops hung from her delicate ears, giving her a gypsy appearance. Claudine was definitely an orchid and Jolie felt like a field daisy beside her.

Vaguely she heard Guy explaining her presence as a guest, somehow omitting the fact that she was a paying one. But Guy's attempt to give importance to her status did little to boost Jolie's ego. The sheer futility of attempting to compete with anyone as gorgeous as Claudine for Steve's attention was a lead weight on her heart.

That, coupled with the fact that Claudine had turned away from Jolie, dismissing her as unworthy of her attention, to direct herself to Steve, made Jolie tug at Guy's hand. He looked down at her apologetically.

"I think I'll go and change," she whispered, noticing out of the corner of her eyes the way Steve was listening to Claudine with intense interest.

"We'll eat out somewhere," Guy said. Jolie couldn't stop the smile of relief from curving her mouth.

"Are you two leaving?" Claudine suddenly seemed interested in them now that it looked as if part of her audience was departing.

Jolie let Guy make the explanation and escaped.

Chapter 8

By the time Guy and Jolie returned late that evening, the house was silent. There was no way of telling whether Claudine was home or out with Steve and Jolie wasn't about to voice her speculations to Guy. After church on Sunday morning, Guy arranged a jaunt with Michelle and her boyfriend for the four of them to drive down to Jean Lafitte's famous pirate stomping grounds, Grand Isle on Barateria Bay. Claudine was still in bed asleep so there was no reason to suggest that she accompany them.

On Monday, Jolie chose to go to Baton Rouge, taking the interstate through twenty miles of swamps, driving on a road above it all, thanks to cranelike legs of concrete pilings. On her return to the LeBlanc house that evening, Claudine was missing from the gathering. But Jolie didn't ask where she was, because Claudine was bound to be with Steve.

Sleep eluded Jolie for much of that night, and she awoke late the next morning. She almost walked out of the kitchen when she saw Claudine seated at the table with her mother. But Jolie had never let envy for another woman's looks stand in her way and she wasn't about to be intimidated by them now. So, helping herself to a cup of coffee, Jolie joined them at the breakfast table as nonchalantly as she could.

"Good morning." She smiled brightly at Claudine and Mrs. LeBlanc. The former barely glanced her way but the older woman returned the greeting.

"What are your plans for today, Jolie? I was just suggesting to Claudine that she might show you around."

"There's no need for that," she replied quickly, noting the bored look on Claudine's face. "I was thinking of driving to Jefferson Island and touring the gardens there, but I feel too lazy for that today. Besides, I wouldn't want to interfere with Claudine's plans."

"I was thinking of going into the country today and doing some sketches. The watercolors of Steve's plantation sold quite well." The smile that flitted across the crimson lips made it clear that Claudine had more important things to do than act as a tour guide for Jolie. While Jolie couldn't help thinking, a little cattily, how convenient it was that Claudine's work would take her to Steve's home.

"I've seen some of your paintings. I thought they were really beautiful." It wasn't easy not to respond with coldness but Jolie succeeded in sounding pleasant.

"Well, they are meant to sell." There was that saccharine smile again. "Few people see my more serious work, but then few people would understand it."

Jolie felt like she'd been tagged as a hopeless peasant when it came to art appreciation. If she had been a dog, her hackles would have been rising about then. As it was, she sipped her coffee and smiled.

"Did I tell you, Claudine," Mrs. LeBlanc said with her usual exuberance, "that Jolie discovered that Etienne's plantation was once owned by one of her ancestors?"

"No. How interesting." Dark eyes turned to Jolie, reassessing her. "How did you find that out, Jolie?"

Something told Jolie that she should tread very softly in her explanation.

"One day last week, Thursday I think, Mr. Cameron"—she secretly thought the formal reference to him was very clever—"invited me out to tour his plantation. He showed me the old pillar with the name Cameron etched on it. My ancestor's name was Cameron and they had called their plantation Cameron Hall."

"Your ancestor was an American?"

Jolie had already learned that in antebellum Louisiana the landed French considered mere Americans uncivilized, even barbaric. Doors opened very slowly to what the gentry considered Yankees, even those from south of the Mason-Dixon line. And she was from well above and far to the west of it. Claudine's question betrayed the same snobbery.

"As a matter of fact, she was from a very old Creole French family. Robert Cameron, her father, was the son of Scottish immigrants. He was killed in the Civil War, fighting for the South. A few years after the war was over, her mother remarried, this time to an officer in the Northern Army. Cameron Hall had already been sold for back taxes," Jolie concluded.

"Fascinating," Claudine murmured.

"It's quite a coincidence that her Cameron Hall is once again owned by a Cameron," Mrs. LeBlanc commented brightly.

"Personally, I wish Steve didn't own it." Her daughter scowled. "He would be much better off if he didn't."

"How can you say that?" her mother exclaimed. "It's a beautiful place."

"Then the National Historic House organization should do more than put up a plaque on the porch," Claudine retorted. "Why don't they fund the restoration? That broken-down mansion costs a fortune in upkeep. Steve would be close to rich if he didn't pour money into that place trying to fix it up enough to live in it. It's a decaying monstrosity. Even if it were new, it would still be outrageously expensive to run."

"He could open it up, or part of it, to tourists once it's restored," Jolie said, not liking Claudine's cold practicality. "He could recoup some of his costs that way."

"Old plantation houses are two for a penny in the South. The Temple, or Cameron Hall or whatever you want to call it, isn't all that different from the others," Claudine answered caustically. "He can't even boast about hoof prints where Union soldiers rode their horses up the stairs."

"I would think that being an artist, you'd want to see it restored." Jolie kept her voice steady and calm as she stirred her coffee, hoping not to show her dislike for such a mercenary attitude.

"I don't think much of the starving-artist lifestyle. Kind of a cliché, isn't it? I just can't see myself in a garret. I'm not even sure what a garret is." A touch of malice sparkled in Claudine's dark eyes. "Give me totally modern every time—a new house or apartment is much more my style. Not a cold, damp, halfway restored plantation house." She shuddered theatrically.

"Always, she talks like this," Mrs. LeBlanc protested with a Gallic wave of her hand. "She lets her head rule her heart."

"Aspirin can cure a headache, Maman." Claudine rose from the table and carried her coffee cup to the sink. "But what is the cure for heartache?"

Jolie was curious to know the answer to that rhetorical question. She just might need a remedy herself if she didn't get Steve Cameron out of her system in a hurry. Claudine's departure from the kitchen caused a sudden bustle of activity by her mother. Jolie drank up her own coffee and went back to her room, trying to summon up enthusiasm for the long day ahead.

Sunlight flooded the bedroom, its golden beams illuminating the sleeping figure in the bed. A bird trilled a wake-up call outside the window, causing Jolie to stir slightly, not liking the brilliant glare trying to penetrate her sleep. A fresh, beguiling floral scent teased her nose.

She sighed, blinked, and started to snuggle into her pillow. But those few, barely focused blinks had let her see something that shouldn't have been there.

A line creased her forehead as Jolie opened her eyes wide and stared at the pillow beside her head. An enormous, full-blown rose lay on it, its rich pink color contrasting with the white pillowcase. Slowly, she inched her hand from underneath the covers, half expecting the rose to disappear before her eyes. But when her fingers touched the stem, Jolie knew it was real. She pushed herself upright, burying her nose in the tender petals.

Two things clicked in her mind. Steve's reference to an old plantation custom of awakening guests with a rose, and the feeling that she wasn't alone in the room. Her hand reached out to grab the tangled covers and pull them up to hide her skimpy pajamas even as she turned to look around.

Steve was in the room, studying her with quiet concentration from where he sat in the armchair. He smiled and got up.

"How did you get in here?" Jolie felt like the breath had just been knocked out of her.

"Through the door."

He leaned against the bedpost at the foot of the bed, not showing any remorse for the way he was looking at her or the embarrassing position she was in.

"You shouldn't be in here. What if Mrs. LeBlanc finds out?"

"She isn't here. I found a note downstairs. Seems she'll be gone all morning."

"But why are you here?" Jolie was beginning to feel a little ridiculous with the bedcovers clutched around her neck and a pink rose in one hand. The blood was no longer pounding in her temples, but a trembling had taken over her body.

"I had the feeling you were trying to avoid me."

"That's just silly." But Jolie couldn't meet his gaze.

"Glad to hear it." A very male and very charming smile spread across his face. "You look good enough to eat first thing in the morning. Did you know that? All rumpled and soft."

She blushed furiously, not knowing how to reply to such a personal comment. The soft chuckle from Steve didn't help. It annoyed her a lot that he found the situation so funny.

"Ah, now that you know I'm not trying to avoid you, I think you should leave my bedroom."

"Why? Are you afraid I'll crawl into bed with you? Sounds like fun, I have to say." His blue eyes danced over her.

"You wouldn't dare!" Jolie whispered, aware of the betraying leap of her heart.

Steve just smiled again and reached for her robe, which was draped over the end of the bed. Walking closer, he handed it to her—but not before looking down at her for what felt like an eternity.

"You have fifteen minutes to meet me in the kitchen. Or I'll come back up to get you."

Jolie spluttered indignantly as Steve walked calmly out of the room. She was down in ten minutes, still fuming. He was so damned sure that she would fall in with his wishes and also angry with herself because that was exactly what she was doing.

But she knew he would have come back. She tried to console herself with that to keep her self-respect.

"Well, here I am," she said defiantly as she entered the kitchen.

"Made you some coffee." He handed her a mug. "Milk, sugar, over there, as you undoubtedly know by now."

His blue eyes checked her out from head to toe, taking in her blue jeans and polka dot top with approval. But Jolie refused to react and allow the warmth of his gaze to melt her defenses. It was hard, especially when her nerves were jumping at the slightest sound.

"Did you find any fabric you like?" Steve asked when the silence threatened to last.

"Fabric?"

"To recover the sofa and chairs," he prompted.

Time for a fast fib. "I'd forgotten all about it."

"Did you?" His astuteness brought a flash of color to her cheeks that quickly receded. "I thought we might do some shopping together today. If you're still interested in helping."

"Claudine probably has a much better eye for color and all that than me." Jolie shot him a cold look. "Why don't you get her to help you?"

"I asked you."

"Well, I know that," she retorted before controlling her impulse to be sarcastic. "But that was before Claudine returned."

"What you're really trying to say is that you don't trespass on other people's property, isn't it?" There was a hint of a smile on his face, enough for her to know that Steve was mocking her.

"Something like that," Jolie replied carefully.

"Just to set the record straight, I belong to no one. Claudine and I have known each other for a long time and we have a lot in common. But I don't run her life and she doesn't run mine. Now do you want to spend the day with me or do you want to be alone?"

"Claudine seemed really fond of you and you acted as if you liked her. That's why I assumed you two were close." Jolie sprang to her own defense. "I'm not the only one who thinks that way. So do Guy and Michelle."

"I think you're reading too much into what Michelle says. As for Guy, he's just covering his butt." A knowing gleam came into his eyes as Jolie shifted uncomfortably in her chair. Steve rose and walked around the table. "Come on, let's go."

"I didn't say I would," she protested as he pulled her chair away from the table, an action that meant she had to get up. Taking her arm, Steve guided her to the door.

"After making a fool of yourself, I bet your pride won't let you give in, so I'll just bully you into coming with me." The wide smile as he looked down at her took her breath away. "What would Guy call it? The masterful touch or the iron hand in the velvet glove?"

"He'd probably call it kidnapping," Jolie retorted, hearing the door slam shut behind them.

"Mwahaha. Then I'll have you at my mercy all day." Steve opened the door of his SUV and helped Jolie inside.

"And will you?" she asked quietly.

"Will I what?"

"Be merciful," she said in a small voice.

Steve paused before turning the key in the ignition, regarding her in intense silence for a moment. "If you promise not to turn the force of those soft brown eyes on me, sure. Just one look from you is incredibly effective."

Jolie turned away, wondering if he knew just how susceptible she was to his true blue gaze. Still, it was exciting to find out that there was something about her that really got to him. But was it a weapon or a liability, considering her own weak defenses?

When Steve turned in the direction away from the

downtown business district of St. Martinville, Jolie looked at him curiously.

"Where are we going?"

"New Iberia." Steve glanced reassuringly at her. "I thought we'd find a bigger selection of upholstery fabrics and we could take in some of the sights, too. Have you been there?"

"Just to the plantation called the Shadows on the Teche. I went yesterday." She couldn't help thinking of how difficult it had been to enjoy the day after talking with Claudine in the morning.

"Did you like it?"

"Oh, yes. It was beautiful, especially the lawns and the little gazebo along the bayou," Jolie was able to admit honestly. She hadn't noticed much about the beautiful interior décor of the grand old house, but she'd wandered the walled lawn at her leisure, delighting in the chameleons that abounded in the shrubbery. "I did notice that the front of the house faced the street instead of Bayou Teche."

"That's because the Old Spanish Trail passed there, so it was sort of built backwards, if you know what I mean," Steve explained. "Did you go out to Avery Island?"

"No." Jolie shook her head.

"We'll drive out there after lunch." He turned his attention back to the road.

Jolie found herself settling back in the seat with contentment. It seemed natural for Steve to be behind the wheel, his strong hands firmly guiding the car. It was great just sitting there beside him and knowing they were going to spend the entire day together. Steve would never know how important the time he spent with her was to Jolie. It was too important, considering the uncertainty of their relationship. Even if she was just a passing fancy to him, she didn't feel that way and she couldn't ignore the depth of her own emotions where he was concerned.

At the second store where they stopped in New Iberia, they found the exact material that Jolie had in mind for the sofa and chairs. It was crushed velvet, in a very light shade of moss green, a perfect complement to the dark walnut wood. Unfortunately there wasn't enough of it left on the bolt to do all three items. The clerk assured them that he could get another bolt shipped from the manufacturer in the same color.

"I think we should wait until the other bolt comes in," Jolie said to Steve in a confidential tone. "Sometimes the colors are a little different, unless they're from the same dye lot and have the identical lot number on the selvage. You really have to look and make sure."

"I think you're right." Steve turned to the clerk to tell him what they'd decided.

After determining that the new shipment would arrive in less than a week, Steve walked with her back to the SUV. Glancing at his watch, he said, "It's still about an hour before lunchtime, but since you didn't have breakfast, why don't we eat now?"

"I am getting hungry," Jolie admitted.

"Do you like Mexican food? I know a place that makes insanely great tacos."

"Sounds wonderful. Let's do it."

Rafael's turned out to be a small restaurant on a side street. Its décor was a mix of simplicity and elegance, with a classic Mexican-Spanish atmosphere.

They'd barely seated themselves at a table when an older man entered the dining area from one of the back rooms. The moment he saw Steve, his face broke into a gigantic smile.

"Esteban!" That was followed by a torrent of Spanish that Jolie couldn't keep up with. She figured out the man greeting Steve was the owner, and it was obvious that Steve was a regular.

"Rafael, this is Jolie Smith," Steve said. "She's vacationing here in Louisiana." Turning to Jolie, he continued, "I'd like you to meet Rafael Alvarez, a very close friend of mine."

"*Buenos días, Señor* Alvarez." She extended her hand to the older man,

"Ah, do you speak Spanish, *señorita?*" The man bowed graciously over her hand.

"Of the hello-goodbye-how-are-you variety, sure," Jolie admitted.

"What a pity!" *Señor* Alvarez smiled ruefully. "It is a beautiful language for lovers. You must have Esteban teach you." Dark eyes glanced at Steve, who was regarding her with amusement. "He is a real *hombre,* eh?"

Steve staved off further personal remarks by asking Rafael what he recommended for a light lunch. Jolie didn't pay too much attention to the suggestions offered, letting Steve choose for her as she let her thoughts wander.

"You're in a daze," Steve said when Rafael left the table. "What's on your mind?"

"I was just wondering," Jolie said. "You speak French fluently and now Spanish. A lot of people know one or the other but not both. That's not that common."

"So now you're curious."

"Yes. I mean, I know that now you own a plantation, but before that . . . what? You must have learned to speak those different languages before you ever moved here. I was wondering what kind of work you did before."

"I was an officer on a tramp ship for about eleven years."

"What's a tramp ship?" Mentally Jolie pictured a derelict old hulk.

"Despite the name, she was a respectable vessel." Steve grinned. "It's just a term for ships who don't have a regular port of call. They might take a load of grain from New Orleans to, say, Japan, and from there they might take cargo to India and so on. Sometimes it's two or three years before they ever return to the same port."

"Which was why and how you learned different languages." She smiled as understanding dawned.

"Yup. Actually, I speak four languages besides English. Italian and German as well as French and Spanish."

"You said eleven years. You must have been very young when you started." Jolie looked at him with interest. Steve didn't strike her as the type to be completely open about his past.

"Seventeen. I was an orphan and had no close relatives. Going to sea seemed so adventurous and different, and at the time, I was living in Boston. I dreamed of running away to a South Sea island and I haunted the wharves for months before the captain of this tramp took pity on me and agreed to sign me aboard. He was kind of like a father figure to me, being without a family himself. I sailed with him until he died about five years ago."

"That's when you came back here?"

"I came back to the U.S. and finally ended up in New Orleans, where I met Claudine. By then wandering had lost most of its magic, although the sailing life was good to me." His eyes gleamed at her from across the table. "So, do you want to hear any more about my sordid past?"

"Well, you did omit all the girls in different ports." A teasing smile curved the corners of her mouth. "You must have left a string of broken hearts all over the world."

"The type of women I met . . ." His face hardened only for a moment before softening with cynical amusement. "I kinda doubt their hearts were broken. No nice girls go to the places where sailors are looking for fun."

"I guess I was partly right, then, when I thought of you as a buccaneer. So you were once a sailor." Jolie smiled as a waiter approached with their lunch.

"Remind me to give you my gold earring," Steve joked. "It would look much better on you than it ever would on me."

"I don't know about wearing just one earring. Maybe you'd better keep it as a souvenir," she laughed easily.

"Wouldn't you like a memento of our time together?" Steve asked quietly just as Jolie started to pick up the steaming taco from her plate. The question caught her off guard.

"No," she replied sharply, knowing how vivid her own memory of Steve would be without a tangible reminder. She tried to laugh away her sharpness, but it sounded nervous and fake. "You'd better keep it for another girl who would look good dressed as a gypsy."

"Whatever you say." Steve shrugged indifferently, turning his attention to their meal.

Chapter 9

"Have you read anything about Avery Island?" Steve asked after they had crossed the small bridge over the bayou and paid the toll.

"Not a thing."

"Bet you noticed how flat it is here in Louisiana, though."

"Sure," Jolie said. "It's basically a gigantic delta this far south, as I remember."

"That's about right."

Jolie looked at his strong profile. "So go ahead, tell me all about Avery Island. Is it a real place? Or is this going to be like the legendary lobsters that crawled all the way from Acadia?"

"No," he laughed, "this is for real. Anyway, Avery Island literally sticks out. It's a salt dome, and its highest point is nearly 199 feet above the marshes and bayous that surround it."

"My, my."

He gave her a wry smile. "Guess I'm boring you."

"No, I like facts. Sometimes."

"Okay, here come a couple more. Avery Island

was a salt mine for about three hundred years. And it's the birthplace of Tabasco sauce. The end."

Jolie had to laugh. "A salt mine? Really? Now when people groan about their jobs and say 'back to the salt mines' I'll know what they're talking about. Cool."

The tour turned out to be interesting. The ceilings towered sixty feet into the air, supported by crystal pillars. Yet she couldn't forget that the surface was five hundred feet or so above where she was. Despite the immensity of the mine, she was just beginning to feel claustrophobic when they started to go back up.

"Feel better?" Steve asked when Jolie inhaled deeply once outside.

She gave him a startled look. "How did you know?"

"You look a little pale." Steve smiled. "That's the last time I take you to the center of the earth."

"Thanks." His sense of humor really was disarming, but she was still determined to keep her feet on the ground. But she pretty much forgot about being determined to do anything but give in when he gave her a few more tender kisses in the car before they drove away to another sightseeing destination.

"Mayward Hill." Steve pointed to the mansion a few turns in the road past the entrance gate. "It's the focal point of the Jungle Gardens and the former house of the late Edward Avery McIlhenny, founder of Tabasco."

"Sacred ground," she breathed.

"Well, to a Louisiana native it is. I hope you like to walk."

"The road doesn't end here," Jolie observed as Steve pulled into one of the lots. She could see where the narrow road continued on and even branched off into other directions.

"No, it doesn't, but to really appreciate the beauty of the place you should walk. Besides, it's the only way down to Bird City."

"I enjoy walking." Jolie scrambled out of the car to join Steve. "I only said that because the road went on."

"Got it. Anyway, this place is huge, about two hundred and fifty acres."

Jolie smirked. "No problem. If I get tired, you can carry me."

"Okay, princess."

The path they were on led them past giant stands of bamboo to a pier and lookout tower over a large lagoon with hundreds of waterfowl. It was such a serene place that Jolie hated to leave it, but Steve convinced her that there were other things well worth seeing.

Back to the car, and on the road they went, magnolia trees and giant oaks on each side, then, under them lofty stands of more bamboo or low, flowering azaleas. Towering trees, some with historic markers, gave way to junglelike growth that reminded her a little of the wilder country around Cameron Hall.

"Should I be scared?" Jolie asked. "Any tigers running around loose in there?"

Steve shook his head. "Not as far as I know."

She gave him a narrow look. "There better not be."

"Watch your step right here," he instructed her. "This path isn't used very much so it's bound to be overgrown and a little slippery."

In places the concrete was covered with moss and it was chipped and broken in others. Steve helped her over the worst parts, although his touch by itself was unsettling. They came to a small lagoon and at a bend in the path, two white swans came into view, swimming slowly. Invisible propulsion moved them with regal elegance, causing only the slightest ripple in the mirror-smooth water.

Jolie was so intent on watching them that she didn't pay attention to the uneven ground ahead of her. Her toe hit a jutting piece of concrete and she stumbled forward, as graceless as an awkward duckling. But Steve's arm was there preventing her from falling in an ignominious heap. Breathless embarrassment reddened her cheeks as she stammered her thanks. He didn't let go.

"You hurt?"

"Just my pride."

Whispering softly into her hair, he said, "It was inevitable, you know. You had to end up in my arms one way or another."

Almost before Jolie could turn around, they were sharing a very hot kiss. All the longing to be in his arms that she'd tried to suppress burst free as his hands caressed her body, crushing her against him with urgency.

It was a good thing they were completely alone on the path. Steve pushed the collar of her blouse away so his mouth could explore the hollows of her shoulder and a little lower. Jolie fell into a kaleidoscope world that had her reeling at every touch from his lips, his hands, his body. While she lacked Steve's expertise, she was more than willing to enjoy it fully.

The sounds of people not too far away put a stop to the delicious embrace, and she sighed, adjusting her blouse and hair to more or less the way they'd been. He didn't quite stop, though, gently stroking the nape of her neck. That public display of affection was perfectly respectable. Jolie didn't make any attempt to hide the radiant lovelight in her eyes. There was no need to hide from Steve what he must have already guessed.

"I underestimated you, Jolie," he whispered. "You know how to start a fire."

"I'm of age," she retorted. He could make anything he wanted out of that information.

"Don't remind me," he replied as he followed her. She stopped short, trying to avoid another stumble, and their bodies collided. He groaned almost comically. "Please, baby, please. Not here."

"Shut up," Jolie giggled.

"We're being watched, you know."

"What?" Jolie glanced over her shoulder to see what he was looking at. On a small hill in a glass-enclosed temple sat a large golden Buddha, above a small pool that reflected him in the late afternoon sun. She only needed a slight nudge from Steve to continue along the path to the base of the temple.

The Chinese Garden was a popular place, so there was no way they were going to be alone in it. After entering the temple and getting a closer look at the Buddha that had sat in the Shonfa Temple of Peiping eight hundred years ago, they walked back to the car, sticking to the public path.

Under the arched wisteria vines, past the cactus gardens and the camellias, completing the loop at Mayward Hill, they drove on toward the exit gate. The sun was hovering near the horizon, casting rich, golden-orange rays that began to turn to the crimson hues of sunset. She wanted the day to go on forever.

"Have dinner with me tonight," Steve said. It was something more than a request.

"I'd love to."

They decided on a seafood restaurant and ordered a feast, beginning with fried oysters and progressing to stuffed shrimp and then soft-shelled crab. It was impossible to eat any of it neatly, but it was all fresh and flavorful. He was still thoughtfully sucking on a crab leg, when Jolie was scrubbing up with a lemon-scented wet wipe, laughing when she looked at him.

He took the leg out of his mouth and looked at her. "What's so funny?"

"You. Somehow you remind me of a raccoon devouring a crawdaddy."

He grinned. "Crawfish, down here. Remember the legend?"

"Oh, right." She handed him several paper napkins and he put down the crab leg to get cleaned up.

"So how come you like seafood so much?" she said teasingly.

"I spent a lot of time at sea and, contrary to what you might think, the bill of fare featured frozen fish sticks every damn day. I like mine fresh."

"Me too," she smiled. "So if you were at sea, how did you learn so much about agriculture and renovating old houses?"

"You know it all because you grew up on a farm, right?" Steve said.

"Well, yeah. Want the short version?"

He nodded, chuckling, looking at his watch. "I'm timing it, okay?"

"Okay." Jolie launched into a two-minute, all-inclusive discussion of farming, including her 4-H projects and membership in Future Farmers of America, and how she could pretty much fix every problem under the sun, from a stuck-in-the-mud tractor to a teacup with a broken handle, and her personal secret for coaxing a balky cow into a stall, and a whole lot more. She wrapped up by saying that she'd learned all of it mostly by just following her parents around. She hadn't expected him to appreciate it as much as he seemed to. He was cracking up at her pithy descriptions of life on the north forty, but he really was impressed.

"I never had your advantages, Jolie."

"If you can call them that," she said wryly. "Anyway, your turn."

"Well, it didn't take many long days at sea before I discovered reading. The ship had a fairly good library and what they didn't have, I could find online. Once I bought that house and all that land, I learned by doing. And I made about ten million mistakes."

"You?" she asked mockingly. "Make mistakes?"

"I sure did. And I know I'll make ten million more."

"Well," she said, laughing, "farming is a really unpredictable way to make a living. And it's hard work."

"Don't you think I'm capable of hard work?"

"I was just remembering the first time I met you and you were telling me what a devoted follower of the carefree Cajun philosophy you were." Jolie smiled impishly.

"That has its merits. Life can be taken too seriously. I do admire their sense of humor and the way they accept things they can't change."

Jolie was thoughtful for a minute. "That's probably

easier to do once you've lived for a while. I'm still really impatient."

"Hmm. I'm not sure if I want that to change." He gave her a friendly but faintly wicked wink.

Smiling, she stared at her cup, the salt shaker—anywhere but at him. "I'm not even going to ask why you said that."

A companionable silence stretched between them, until he spoke again. "What are you thinking about now?" Steve asked.

"*Lagniappe.*" There was a touch of wistfulness in the smile she gave to him. "That's the kind of day it's been for me. A day with something extra."

"And your escort, was he something extra, too?"

"Yes. Totally."

Steve chuckled. "You can be glad we're in a restaurant and there's a table between us."

The mock threat was accented by the sensuous curve of his mouth, sending her heart racing at the thought of Steve raining kisses on her. His hand reached out to still her fingers, which were playing with her empty coffee cup. At once rough and caressing, his hold on her had an electric effect, sparking the safely banked glow of desire.

"Have I told you today how gorgeous you are?"

"Freckles and all?" she asked with a shaky laugh. She was too used to regarding herself as only attractive not to joke about a compliment like that.

"There are supermodels with freckles, Jolie. And I won't let you dismiss a compliment that I really meant." Steve's voice was gently scolding. "If anything, I envy the sun for planting so many little kisses on your face. It made you radiant for always."

"You're too much." She looked at him fondly. No, not fondly. That word was just too tame.

"I'm not sure that applies to me," Steve said.

"What do you mean?"

"I'm generally the one left with the task of fighting the fires you start, as if you didn't know." His intelligent eyes raked her thoroughly, leaving her in no doubt of what he meant.

It was pitch black outside when they began their drive home. There was only a sprinkling of stars in the sky and the moon was nowhere in view. Wispy traces of fog drifted over the road, occasionally sending out gossamer veils that swirled around passing cars, including theirs. To Jolie, the light fog was a part of the ethereal enchantment of the moment.

It seemed too soon when Steve stopped at the curb in front of the LeBlanc house. The silence between them came back until the crickets chirping outside sounded too loud to Jolie's ears.

He turned to look at her, his face shadowy but his masterfulness clear in his body language. Then in one more second she was captured in an embrace like no other. His kiss was so devastatingly sweet and possessive that she heard nothing but the pounding of her heart . . . and felt his heart beat in the palm of the hand that she pressed to his chest.

The kiss had to stop. He said only one word. "Wow."

Jolie nodded, buttoning up the blouse that he'd made short work of, knowing she looked a lot less respectable than she had on the path he'd led her down before. That had been a very hot kiss. This one, well . . . the only way to describe it was extremely hot. It was the kind of kiss you thought about over and over again. He'd *meant* it.

"You'd better go in—now," Steve added with growly emphasis. "I'll call you tomorrow."

"Okay," she managed to whisper, glancing over at him before she swung her legs out. Jolie saw the hunger in his eyes and wondered what her own looked like. She very nearly slammed the car door and dove toward him for a repeat performance, but discretion and common sense took over. She hurried toward the house. Once there, she opened the front door and stood in its shadow to watch Steve drive away.

Jolie blew out a breath when his taillights winked as the car went over a distant bump in the road. She whispered an endearment under her breath as well as a final goodbye, and went inside.

The house wasn't exactly quiet. An exuberant zydeco medley was playing on the sound system, but softly. Whoever had put it on hadn't stuck around to listen to it, and the plaintive accordion and gut-bucket bass drowned out the lyrics in Cajun French. Jolie didn't care. She was too giddy with excitement over that once-in-a-lifetime kiss to understand them anyway.

She wanted to savor that for a little while longer, so she tiptoed upstairs to her room, leaving the door open as she crossed the floor to switch on a lamp. As she turned to go back and shut the door, she saw Claudine standing there.

Her dark hair was loose and tumbling around her shoulders like a black cloud, its sheen heightened by her milky-white complexion. She was wearing a robe with an exotic blue-green design that reminded Jolie of peacock feathers, and beneath it, a matching nightgown. Suggestive and seductive—not what Jolie would wear in her own mother's house but then she wasn't Claudine.

"So you're back. Did you have a good time? With Steve, I mean."

"I had a very good time."

"I suppose you dragged him around to every tourist trap within fifty miles of New Orleans," Claudine drawled.

"We took in a few sights, sure," was Jolie's calm response. "It was fun."

"Steve can be a lot of fun," the other woman said in an insinuating voice.

"Uh-huh. I enjoyed myself." Jolie picked up her brush and stood in front of the mirror to brush her hair, hoping Claudine would take the hint to go away and mind her own business.

"He's been to all those places so many times, it's a wonder he wasn't bored to death." Claudine studied her fingernails and extended them. It was such a feline gesture that Jolie half expected to hear a meow when Claudine looked up.

"I don't think he was bored, as a matter of fact." The secret smile on Jolie's face was revealed in the mirror and Claudine saw it. A fire of anger lit in her dark eyes.

"I hope you don't take his attentions seriously," Claudine said pointedly. "You could get hurt, you know. Women have."

"I think I'm old enough to take care of myself." The brush didn't miss a stroke.

"Oh, okay." Claudine curved her mouth into

something resembling a smile. "I was just trying to give you a little friendly advice, that was all."

"Thanks."

"If all you want is a harmless vacation flirtation, then he's the right guy. But he isn't about to be tied down."

"That must be very frustrating for you." Jolie could not resist that little dig.

Claudine drew in her breath with a very soft hissing sound. Again Jolie was reminded of a cat—a very annoyed cat whose favorite catnip toy was dangling just out of her reach all of a sudden.

"Let's get this straight." The pseudo-polite act was abandoned and Claudine's real opinion of Jolie became all too clear. "Right now, your innocence amuses him, but that won't last long. He'll either seduce you—bye-bye, innocence!—or he'll get tired of trying and drop you. And back you go to South Dakota. Give my regards to the cows," she said with contempt.

"You could be right," Jolie said, not afraid because Claudine was so clearly scared underneath that Steve was no longer her personal property. "And you could be wrong. We'll see."

Claudine's hand raised threateningly in the air. For a moment Jolie thought the other woman was going to strike her. Instead Claudine quelled her impulse by folding her arms tightly over her chest. She tossed her hair in a defiant, princessy way.

"You're making a very big mistake," was all she said to Jolie.

"Am I? Well, it's mine to make, isn't it? So, if you'll excuse me, I'm busy right now."

Claudine exited in a huffy swirl.

Well, Jolie thought. *I won the first battle but now it's war.* Claudine had dragged their rivalry out into the open but it just wasn't in Jolie to back down from anyone.

The next breakfast she shared with the LeBlancs was just plain odd. Mr. and Mrs. LeBlanc were cheerful as ever and unaware of the tension between Jolie and their daughter Claudine, who kept referring to Jolie with exaggerated politeness as "our paying guest."

Guy had either been filled in by his sister, or eavesdropped on the conversation in Jolie's bedroom. He kept on making dumb jokes about love being cruel and indulging himself in insinuations as he glanced from his sister to Jolie, who could practically see the wheels spinning in his head as he figured out how he might spin the simmering conflict to his advantage somehow.

God save her from local-boy Lotharios, she thought, feeling a lot more sure of herself since the golden afternoon she'd just shared with Steve.

The phone rang. Claudine stabbed her serving of ham with a fork and sawed off a piece, drowning it mercilessly in red-eye gravy. Jolie knew the other woman knew who was calling—and that he wasn't calling for her.

Guy jumped up to answer it, but Jolie could hear that Steve wasn't letting him find out much. He called to Jolie and handed her the receiver with an inquisitive look. His mother, bless her heart, ordered him right back to the table.

"Good morning, sweetheart. How'd you sleep?"

His husky voice managed to transmit little tremors that tingled through her.

"Really well."

"That's nice. I didn't sleep a wink." A wry note crept into his voice—she loved, just loved the sound of it.

Guy went by, carrying plates like a waiter, on his arm. She willed him to disappear and stay disappeared.

"I called to tell you that I'm going to be tied up today," Steve went on. "One of the tractors broke down and I have to go into Lafayette for parts."

"I can help," she said eagerly.

"No, but thanks. You're a lot prettier without being covered in axle grease, you know."

"You've never seen me that way."

He laughed. "Maybe some other time, Jolie. Besides, it's going to take the better part of a day to get the damn thing running again."

"I understand," she said, feeling kind of crushed anyway. She barely noticed the racket Guy was making in the kitchen, except to be glad he couldn't hear her side of the conversation or the disappointment in her voice.

"I'm disappointed too, Jolie," Steve was saying. "So what are you going to do today, without my company?"

"Miss you, mostly," she said pertly.

"Mostly? You mean there's a slight chance you could be happy without me?" he asked jokingly.

"A very slight chance," she joked back. "But I'll be fine. I can find something to do on my own or with a friend."

"Hm. Any more comments like that and I'm likely

to say the hell with the tractor," he growled with mock fierceness.

"Promise?" she said boldly, then hurried on before he could take her seriously. "I take that back. I'm a farmer's daughter and I know that broken machinery can't wait for a rainy day to be fixed."

"Thanks, ladybird. Maybe tomorrow."

"You bet."

After he hung up, Jolie turned to the sound of footsteps entering the hall. Guy again. He stared at her, his brown eyes showing hurt and uncertainty.

Oh, please don't start, she thought wildly. It wasn't as if she'd led this man-puppy on or anything. But, well, he'd followed her home because this was his home. It made avoiding him really difficult.

She dodged his nosy questions by agreeing to go out and play tennis with him and his friends, and worked off her nervous tension by making most of the winning points in set after set.

When the sun called it a day, the sweaty group said their goodbyes and she got into Guy's car, hoping and praying again that he wouldn't spout any juvenile nonsense to her, or defend his sister's pride, or try to hold Steve to a non-compete clause in an imaginary contract.

He did all three. She ignored him as best she could.

Later, in her room, she began to think. Even being apart from Steve for a single day was more difficult than she could have imagined, once she wasn't tearing around a tennis court.

Slowly but surely, as if seeded by Claudine's malevolent looks at breakfast and thrown off balance by her efforts to tactfully dodge Guy's ridiculous maneuvers, she realized that it was Steve himself she wasn't sure of.

He'd knocked around the world, done all kinds of things, whereas she'd grown up thinking Yankton, South Dakota, was a big place and hadn't done anything at all.

Their time together had been so brief. They knew so little, really, about each other. One or two sun-washed, lazy, teasing afternoons plus three or four scorchingly memorable kisses did not make a relationship.

As the hours of night ticked by, she made the mistake of lying in the dark making lists of what could possibly go wrong. They were long lists, that boiled down to one essential word: everything.

What if he wasn't in love with her, after all?

Chapter 10

When Steve called the following day, Jolie had left the house to run into town on a personal errand. He'd left a message that he would call Jolie that night. She'd misplaced the charger for her cell and it never had worked all that well down here anyway, so they mostly communicated on the LeBlancs' good old-fashioned land line. While she regretted missing his call, Jolie felt better than she had last night after sleeping some. She still had something to look forward to even if she had a whole day to wait.

She might as well sightsee on her own, she thought, and decided on the Rip Van Winkle Gardens west of New Iberia. It was a short drive and an interesting place, although the stately, English-style gardens seemed too restrained after the tropical exuberance of the Jungle Gardens at Avery Island. But then, Steve wasn't with her. Jolie was sure that had a lot to do with her relative lack of enthusiasm. The day was extremely hot and humid, so when Jolie drove back through New Iberia, she decided to stop for a cold drink.

Maybe it was a coincidence, maybe she subconsciously wanted to go back again, but she happened to park her Volkswagen on the same block where Steve had ordered the material for the sofa and chairs. Obeying an impulse she knew was foolish, Jolie entered the store. The salesclerk who'd waited on them recognized her immediately.

He explained that the shipment had come in that morning, and said how lucky it was that Jolie had come in when he was about to contact Mr. Cameron. Since it had been paid for, he asked if Jolie wanted to take it today. She hesitated, disliking the idea that Steve might think she was being bossy by picking up the material for him, with the rationale that she was only saving him a side trip to New Iberia.

It took some maneuvering to get the extrawide and rather stiff roll of upholstery fabric into her little car, but she managed. Not until Jolie was sitting in the restaurant two stores away did she realize how long she'd been in the store. After a few sips of lemonade, she decided to head out, not wanting the LeBlancs to hold supper for her the way they had last night, when she and Guy had been late.

Jolie arrived in time for dinner but too late for Steve's call. Frustrated with herself for being gone so long, she was barely able to eat anything. What if Steve thought she was playing some kind of girl game? He hadn't said he would call again. What if he didn't? All the while she was helping Mrs. LeBlanc carry dishes to the kitchen, Jolie obsessed over it.

She debated calling him herself, but didn't really

want the family to overhear and comment, even good-naturedly. There was only one way, she decided. She would drive out to Cameron Hall that very night no matter what.

And she had the convenient pretext of delivering the upholstery material.

She didn't tell Mrs. LeBlanc anything except that she was going out and would be back later that evening. Dusk had already given way to night when Jolie slid behind the wheel of her car. Michelle had just driven in after returning to the school for papers she'd left there and Jolie had to wait until her car was parked and the driveway was clear.

"Are you going out?" Michelle called on her way to the house.

"Yes," Jolie answered without explaining further.

"The fog is a little thick. Be careful." Michelle waved to her and entered the house.

Once Jolie left St. Martinville and began to drive through the countryside, Michelle's comment began to seem like a radical understatement. The fog swirled around her so thickly that she had to drive with extreme care and slow way, way down. Her headlights barely revealed the ditch alongside the road, let alone illuminate the road more than a few feet ahead of her. Moisture condensed on the windshield to add to the difficulty of seeing, and the air vents didn't make much of a difference. It was partly by chance that she found the correct crossroads, and then the road that would take her to the dirt lane leading to the plantation.

Time inched by as slowly as her Volkswagen. And the more time that went by, the surer Jolie became that she was going to miss the final turn. Her fingers ached from clenching the steering wheel so tightly. A throbbing headache bothered her and her eyes hurt from the strain of peering into the gray shroud that surrounded her.

She was almost ready to give in to tears when a small white sign glistened near the side of the road. It was impossible to read, though, as the fog thickened around it. She stopped the car and stepped out, leaving the motor running while she got a closer look at the sign with the flashlight from the glove compartment.

Private Road—No Trespassing. Unwelcome words that nonetheless brought a sigh of relief. By some miracle, she'd made it. The plantation was a quarter mile farther. The only trouble was, the closer she got to it and the bayou on the opposite side, the denser the fog grew. There was no chance at all she would be able to see the iron gates of the entrance. The only alternative was for her to guess at the distance and then explore on foot, relying on her flashlight to reach her destination.

Four steps from the Volkswagen and she could barely make out its familiar egglike shape. The fact that it was red did help, even at night. Taking two steps forward, Jolie inhaled deeply, knowing that the fog had closed in around the car and hidden it completely. She inched her way along the ditch looking for the culvert leading to the gates while she tried to rid herself of the fear that she was only going to end up getting lost in this mess.

In the murky darkness, she nearly missed the entrance. As before, it was padlocked. The beam from the flashlight barely penetrated beyond the gates. Hesitantly she touched the cold, dripping-wet sections of fence, giving them a shake to see how sturdy they were. The bell hanging from the pillar seemed oddly muffled.

Jolie decided only a foghorn could pierce this. Still she waited before attempting anything so rash as climbing over to the other side. The last thing she wanted was to encounter Steve's very protective dog, even though Black had met her. But the animal didn't appear.

Okay. On to Plan B.

The gate proved easy to climb over, especially for a former tomboy. On the other side, the trees and shrubs loomed ominously on either side of the narrow lane. Any minute she expected Black to spring from the darkness, white fangs flashing in the night. Her flashlight picked out branches of the giant oaks, the Spanish moss taking on a ghostliness that spooked her more than a little. Jolie couldn't help thinking it was a perfect setting for a Gothic romance.

A small patch of light winked dimly at her from the *garçonniere*, and her already jangled nerves were set on edge when a low, rumbling bark sounded from the narrow gallery. Jolie was close enough to make out the light shining from the screen door and the dog standing guard in front of it.

"Steve!" she called out. The dog growled in answer although he didn't come any closer to her. Jolie called again, her voice sounding strange in the silence. If he were inside the *garçonniere*, he surely would have heard her.

The dog, fortunately, seemed to consider her no threat when she stepped onto the porch. Still Jolie hesitated to walk past him to the door.

"Where's Steve?" she asked him.

His tail wagged in a friendly way and Jolie took a courageous step toward the door. Instantly the dog's lip curled and a threatening growl came from his throat. When she halted, his tail wagged again. Evidently he'd decided she could be where she was, but the *garçonniere* was forbidden. She wasn't going to argue with him.

"Is it all right if I wait here for Steve?" It was silly asking the dog since he couldn't reply, but the silence of the fog was really beginning to get on her nerves. The sound of her own voice was comforting and at least she wasn't talking to herself.

The dampness had seeped into her clothes, sending its cool fingers into her bones. She shivered and rubbed her arms briskly while she glanced around. There was no sign of Steve at all. The thought of finding her way back to her car and then back to the LeBlanc house was frightening.

"What are you doing here?" She jumped a foot when Steve materialized at the far end of the narrow gallery.

"I came to see you." Her heart jumped too—she willed it to be still. "I'd just decided you weren't here."

As Steve walked closer, Jolie could see an emotion she was tempted to call anger in his eyes. It upset her. She'd expected surprise, even gladness, but she hadn't thought he would be angry.

"The fabric for the sofa and chairs arrived today. I was in New Iberia and happened to stop in—" She broke off, still feeling compelled to fill the uneasy silence, avoiding his measuring gaze. "I left it in my car, in case you're wondering." She added all in a rush, "I didn't have anything special to do tonight, so I thought I'd bring it out."

"How did you get here?"

"I drove," she answered weakly under his glowering look. "Crazy, I know. But I didn't realize the fog was so bad until I got out in the country." She shivered again but not from coldness. "I was practically here by then or I would have turned around. The fog sort of swallowed me, though."

"Why didn't you just go into the house and warm up?" He opened the screen door and moved her inside at last.

"According to Black, I'm not allowed any farther than the porch." Jolie felt hurt by Steve's unwelcoming behavior.

Steve glanced at the dog sitting outside as if he'd forgotten Black was there. He raked his fingers through his hair, curling slightly from the dampness.

"Sit by the fire and get warm while I get the pickup," he ordered, gesturing to the fireplace and the tiny flames licking at a solitary log. "It has fog lights and I can get someone to drive your car back in the morning."

"Thanks for being so overjoyed to see me!" Jolie tossed sarcastically after him as he started for the door. There was a betraying trembling in her chin as tears burned the back of her eyes.

"What's that supposed to mean?" Steve glared at her.

"I drive all the way out here and I don't even get a hello? Why do you want to hustle me home?" She had to shout or she would cry.

"Whoa." Steve took a deep breath, trying to control himself, Jolie guessed. He studied her silently with his hands on his hips.

"I don't understand," she murmured, finding it harder and harder to meet his accusing eyes.

"That's obvious," he said. "How many cars did you pass on the way here?"

"None." Jolie felt herself growing smaller.

"That's because anyone with an ounce of sense wouldn't be out in this fog."

"Michelle had just come home when I left. She didn't seem concerned."

"I bet you didn't tell her where you were going." Steve sighed with exasperation when Jolie shook her head. "If you had, I'm sure she would have told you to stay where you were."

"Well, she didn't and I'm here! You don't have to be so awful about it!" She had to cover her mouth to keep a little choking sob from making itself heard.

"Jolie, you could have run off the road upside down into a ditch or crashed into a telephone pole." A short laugh followed his admonishing words as he shook his head. "And I'm not supposed to be upset by that?"

"Maybe I didn't think you cared," Jolie whispered. She knew it was an overemotional answer, but the chill-inducing walk and the shock of his even chillier behavior kept her from thinking straight.

Steve covered the distance between them in one fluid movement and lifted her up on her tiptoes. "Cared?" he groaned. His words were muffled by her hair.

"Don't," she protested, put off by his moodiness.

He relaxed his hold a little without letting her go. "You can be glad that I can't make up my mind whether to turn you over my knee or keep you in my arms."

"If you feel that way," Jolie gazed into his face, thrilling to the fire she saw in his eyes, "then why do you want me to leave?"

"Would you rather stay here until the fog lifts? When it's this thick, it's doesn't burn off until morning. You can't honestly expect to spend the night with me without something happening, can you?"

"No, no, of course not," Jolie murmured, gently pulling away from him. "It's just that . . . well, I haven't seen you for so long." She looked at him wistfully. "I missed your call this morning. And again in the afternoon." His gaze didn't waver from her upturned face. "I just wanted to see you."

"I wanted to see you too." Was it her imagination or were his hands trembling as he held her? "But not here."

His response puzzled her. "What difference does it make?"

"If I have to explain that to you," Steve said in a low voice, "then you're more innocent than I thought."

"Damn it!" Jolie's temper suddenly flared up. She looked around desperately for something to throw to relieve her tension and found nothing. "Why does everyone seem to think I was born yesterday? I'm not all that innocent!"

"You don't know what you're talking about," Steve said flatly.

"What, are you a Boy Scout all of a sudden?" she asked sarcastically, before quicksilver tears sprang into her eyes. "I can't help the way I feel about you.

Don't you see? I just want you to hold me right now. I can't help it."

"You're talking nonsense, Jolie."

"Oh, go to hell. I'm talking to a brick wall," she sniffled, wiping away a tear that did escape before she regained her self-control.

Before she had a chance to apologize for telling him off, she was yanked into his arms, knocked breathless as she came to an abrupt halt against his hard chest.

"I wish I was made of brick," Steve growled before covering her mouth with his in an utterly passionate kiss. "Then you couldn't get to me the way you do sometimes—" He broke off and kissed her again.

Their mutual desire burst forth with volcanic intensity as he kissed her mouth, her neck, anywhere he could. The strength of his embrace rendered Jolie essentially powerless—but she wanted to be right where she was.

Then he was sweeping her off her feet and taking her bodily into his arms. Overwhelmed with wonderfully pleasurable sensations, she wasn't really aware of where he was carrying her. His stride changed and Jolie realized that he was climbing the stairs.

"The couch is too small and the floor is too cold." He was answering a question she hadn't asked.

Then he set her down on her feet, and Jolie thought uncertainly that she wasn't quite ready for this.

"What's the matter?" Steve whispered huskily as his hands ran over her. "Don't you want me to make love to you, Jolie?"

A startling, sudden icy-cold numbness spread over her. "N-no," she breathed unhappily. "Not this way."

"What do you mean?"

There was a catch in her voice. "This just happened a little too fast, that's all. I mean—no, that's not all."

"What the hell is the matter?"

His frustration and her fear were a volatile mix. But she didn't have to give in if she just wasn't ready. He would live—one of her aunt's pithier sayings about the male sex.

"I don't know," was all she said.

"Okay. But I want you, Jolie," he sighed softly and traced her cheek with just his fingertips. "I won't deny it."

"Why?" She needed to know the truth—and more importantly, needed to know the depth of his attraction to her.

"Because you're a woman and I'm a man. Is there ever any more to it than that?"

"Yes, Steve, there is." Jolie answered slowly, lifting her head up to see his masked expression. The overpowering nature of her feelings for him proved that.

"You say that because you're young." There was a faraway smile on his lips. "You don't know yet how damn contrary humans can be. And fickle."

"What? Are you trying to warn me off?"

"Maybe not completely." He was looking at her as if he was memorizing her down to the last freckle. "Jolie, you're something totally special. Natural, honest, and giving—"

"Gee whiz. Thanks."

He picked up on the bitterness in her voice, judging by the sad look in his eyes. After a painfully long moment, he shook his head. "You know something? I don't ever want to hurt you."

Suddenly, there seemed to be an ever-widening gulf between them, even though they were in exactly the same place they'd been when he set her down. She didn't understand it. At all.

"I'm taking you home."

A flash of fire brightened her brown eyes, but it didn't take away her puzzlement. "I'm getting the feeling that you feel sorry for me," she snapped. "Don't."

"Whatever you say. But you deserve to be loved, don't ever forget that."

"Really? You think so?" Her sarcastic tone was edged with misery. "My Aunt Brigitte told me once that real love is incredibly rare. Few people ever find it because most of them are too selfish. They can't give of themselves, except superficially." She wished she hadn't said that when she looked into his shadowed eyes.

"Are you quoting her or are you accusing me of being one of them?" he asked coldly.

Not the last. Jolie had to admit to herself that she hadn't described him or accused him. She'd just been ranting because she was confused, tired, and upset. He could have been more understanding.

"And now I'm getting the silent treatment," he said, raking his hand through his hair. "Tell you what. How about you stop jerking my chain and we go back to the point in this discussion where I still had some brains left and was going to take you home."

She shook her head in bewilderment. "I don't understand you. One minute you act as if you really care for me and the next you're, like, trying to prove how cold and unfeeling you can be. Listen, Steve, I'm convinced."

The narrowing of his eyes made Jolie aware once again of the length and thickness of his lashes. For a moment she felt almost hypnotized by the blue depths of his gaze.

"This isn't the time or place for the discussion you want," Steve said, brushing past her and walking down the stairs. Halfway down, he turned to look up at her. "C'mon. I mean it about taking you home."

Jolie hesitated. Another thought had surfaced, an irrational one. But she *had* to know. "Are you still— I don't know how to say this."

"Just spit it out," he said wearily, not coming after her.

"What about Claudine?"

He scowled. "What about her? How'd she get into this conversation?"

"Well, I heard . . ." She paused, not wanting to mention that Guy was her source of information on that subject for fear that Steve would ridicule her.

"Can we talk some other time? I feel like I'm going to end up sleeping on the stairs tonight, what with everything."

"But—"

"Claudine is someone I've known for a while. No law against that, is there?"

"N-no."

He took a deep breath. "You didn't tell me every detail of your love life and I don't even want to know. Same goes for me. But don't assume what you don't know, Jolie."

"I think I get it."

"Maybe. But right now you're testing my patience. For the last time, I'm taking you home. Now get down here."

Steve's bad mood had clearly gotten worse. She couldn't fault him for that—he'd been all alone when she showed up unexpectedly and whatever it was he'd wanted hadn't happened.

So be it. The spontaneous, fiery passion of those moments had vanished in a heartbeat and Jolie wasn't about to keep on talking when he was making it plain that he wanted none of it.

It was obvious to her that his feelings toward her were ambivalent. She wondered if he even knew how he felt. She certainly didn't. He was too complex for her limited experience to fathom. And Jolie was sure he knew that too.

She went down the stairs with him well ahead of her, scooping up his keys, muttering a few words to his dog, and ushering her out and to his truck without another word.

The fog lights on the pickup effectively increased the visibility. For all the attention he paid her, she could have been an inanimate object in the seat beside him. When they pulled up in front of the LeBlanc house, Steve left the motor running.

She got the message. No lingering goodbyes.

"I'll drive out with someone to bring your car back in the morning, probably before you get up. Thanks for bringing the fabric, by the way." His unemotional tone stung her and Jolie reached for the door latch, but a hand on her arm forestalled her. "I have to go to New Orleans tomorrow on business. I'll be gone a couple of days."

"Why are you telling me?" Jolie knew her question had a belligerent tone, but Steve's coldness had hurt and she wanted to strike back.

"I don't know." Steve gave an angry sigh and reached across her to open the door. "Good night, Jolie."

Chapter 11

"Where have you been?"

Jolie had raced all the way into the house and was halfway up the stairs when Claudine's demanding question brought her up short. All Jolie wanted was to be in her room where she could cry. The tears were scorching her eyes.

"On an errand, if it's any of your business," she retorted.

"It must have been a convenient errand since it meant Steve brought you back," Claudine jeered. Jolie wanted to flee up the stairs, but the raven-haired girl went on, "Too bad you didn't invite him in. There was something I wanted to talk to him about, but I guess it'll have to wait until tomorrow."

"It will have to wait longer than that." Jolie made her voice sound as quietly sarcastic as Claudine's, although she didn't trust herself to meet the other woman's gaze. "Steve is going to New Orleans tomorrow for a couple of days."

"How fortunate for you!" Claudine called after as Jolie finally made her escape.

The little red Volkswagen was parked in its former place behind the house the next morning when Jolie arose and looked out the window. The awkward roll of moss-green velvet had been taken out. She wondered what he would do with it, now that she wasn't going to be redoing his sofa or doing anything else with him, or for him.

She hadn't slept well and there were dark circles under her eyes. She had tried hard to make herself see how illogical she'd been, but there was no room in her heart for logic, only Steve. What did it matter that she had known him for less than two weeks? Love was love.

If only she understood him better. It wasn't as if they could talk it out face to face. Knowing that Steve was in New Orleans made the day stretch ahead of her with incredible emptiness. Even if he were here, she might be just as discouraged. Jolie remembered how things had ended with John Talbot before she left South Dakota—her conflicted emotions had seemed so all-consuming at the time and now, very minor. Compared to her love for Steve.

Jolie knew she couldn't hang around the house all day. Mrs. LeBlanc had been awfully curious about her morose expression at the breakfast table, but heading out to some tourist spot to distract herself held no interest for Jolie whatsoever. So much for sightseeing. But there was one thing she did want to do. It would probably be foolish and a big mistake, one that she might really regret, but she wanted to take pictures of Cameron Hall so that she could show her family what their ancestral home looked like. The thought of returning to South Dakota and never seeing Steve again filled her with despair.

Wandering around the plantation grounds with the ever-watchful German shepherd at her heels did little to improve her low spirits. It seemed so final to be taking pictures of the place, as if she were leaving tomorrow. She had at least a week of her allotted vacation time left.

She knew she would never be able to look at the pictures without thinking of Steve, imagining him against the backdrop of flame-pink azaleas and towering pillars.

Jolie returned to the LeBlanc home at the same time that Guy and Michelle did. It would have been rude to retreat to her room, although that was what she wanted to do, but Michelle had issued such a friendly invitation to join them for cold drinks that Jolie hadn't been able to refuse. It was too bad that the ringing phone two minutes later was for Michelle, who left her with Guy, the one person Jolie had wanted to avoid.

"Cheer up, Jolie," Guy said, glancing over at her with a smile that was part amusement and part sympathy.

"What do you mean?"

"You're sulking. It isn't as if you weren't warned this was bound to happen."

"I don't know what you're talking about. What was bound to happen?" On the defensive, Jolie rose to her feet and walked over to look out the window, not seeing the red cardinal flitting about the magnolia tree.

"Claudine and Steve being together. You know what I mean."

"Steve's in New Orleans," she said. But something in Guy's complacent statement made her turn around. "Isn't he?"

"You honestly don't know, do you?" Guy shook his head in amazement. "Claudine went to New Orleans with Steve."

"No," she breathed in disbelief. "No! That's not true!"

She held back a hysterical sob. Now she understood what Steve had said. He'd been tactfully trying to tell her that he didn't care for her. He had to have guessed how she felt and was trying to make her see that he didn't feel the same. He'd even hinted that he might use Claudine to make his point.

"You really fell for him, didn't you?" Guy asked. She couldn't trust herself to speak without crying so she just nodded. "Hell. Claudine always wins."

"She didn't," Jolie answered in a shaky voice, raising her tear-filled eyes to meet his. "Don't you see? Steve doesn't care about either one of us. That's what he was trying to tell me last night."

"Last night? Did you see him last night?" Guy asked in an accusing voice.

"Yes, for a little while." She wasn't going to tell him what happened. "What am I going to do, Guy?" she whispered. "I can't face him again. I just can't."

"He had no business playing around with you," Guy declared.

"Too late now." She was saddened and amused by the avenging-brother look on Guy's face. "And it isn't Steve's fault that I made a fool of myself." She gave a huge sigh. "I think it's time I went home."

"To South Dakota?"

"Yes. I ran away from one problem there right into another." Determinedly she wiped the tears from her cheeks and squared her shoulders. "If a change of scene was the cure before, it should be effective again."

"But you planned to stay another week. You told Maman you would."

She sighed with resignation. "I know what I planned, but . . . but I think it's better that I change those plans."

Jolie made the announcement to the LeBlanc family that evening at the dinner table. She used the pretext of getting a letter from her parents, which she had, and adding that a close relative was ill, which wasn't true, and summed up by saying both had led to her sudden decision. If she packed tonight and loaded the car in the morning, she could be on the way home before Steve and Claudine returned from New Orleans.

But Jolie hadn't counted on the fuss kicked up by Emile LeBlanc, who insisted in his paternal way that she shouldn't start the long trip until her car had been checked out by a local garage. She tried desperately to reassure him on that score, even offering to show him the maintenance log and the receipt from the Yankton shop.

He was just as adamant that she do things his way, and said that since she was now practically a member of the family, he wouldn't sleep at night worrying about a breakdown and her by the side of the road in some desolate place at night.

Non. He would not permit it. Then Mrs. LeBlanc chimed in that tomorrow was Saturday and everyone knew the interstates were choked with speeding truckers, who would run right over the *p'tite auto*.

Finally Jolie was forced to agree to have the Volkswagen checked again, but she refused to wait until

Monday. She would leave Sunday morning regardless of the traffic.

By late Saturday afternoon Jolie had all her suitcases packed and ready to load into the car. Guy gave her a lift to the local garage to pick up the Volkswagen, which had required only a few minor adjustments. As Jolie settled the bill, she gazed over at the young man who had become her silent supporter.

"When do you think they'll be back?" she asked quietly, knowing she didn't have to spell out that by "they" she meant Steve and Claudine.

"He probably won't drive after dark because of the fog, so they'll be home anytime between now and sundown."

As it happened, when Jolie and Guy returned to the LeBlanc house, it was to learn that Steve had just dropped Claudine off and left. It was a relief to know that she wasn't going to run into him accidentally.

Fate had been kind to send her to the garage at the right time to collect her car, thus saving her further embarrassment. Nor was Claudine around. She was monopolizing the bathroom after a muggy trip from New Orleans. Jolie had something to be at least a little happy about in that she didn't have to look at the older girl's smirk of triumph.

Jolie and Guy were outside wrestling her suitcases into the diminutive car when Michelle came to the back door and told Jolie she was wanted on the phone.

"Okay. Do you know who's calling?" Jolie asked Michelle as she looked apprehensively at Guy.

"I didn't ask but it sounds like Steve," Michelle answered, letting the screen door shut as she walked back into the house.

"Do you want me to tell him you're too busy to come to the phone?" Guy asked.

Jolie brushed her hair behind her ears and breathed in deeply. "No," she said, while she wondered what kind of fool she was. "He's not likely to try to change my mind."

Her words sounded brave, but that was far from the truth. She picked up the receiver of the hall phone. "Yes?"

"Hey. It's me, Steve."

Like she wouldn't have recognized his voice.

"Your car was gone when I dropped Claudine off," he went on.

How could he be so offhand about it? Jolie made a noncommittal reply. "Yeah. Well, I heard you were back from New Orleans. What's up?"

"There was a football game, so the traffic was pretty heavy or we would have been back sooner."

"Look," she couldn't stand this small talk, "I'm glad you called, but I was going to give you a ring later on," she lied, "to let you know I was leaving tomorrow to go back to South Dakota."

"What?" It was said so quietly that she almost didn't hear it.

"Yes, something happened. An aunt of mine is in the hospital and my folks wrote and suggested I return home. It happened kind of suddenly, I guess, and she needs this operation." Why was she rattling on like this, as if she had to give him a good reason for going? She ought to just go.

"It does sound very sudden," Steve said dryly.

"Yes, well, I still wanted to say goodbye before I left, which was why I was going to call you later."

"I want to talk to you, Jolie." He spoke slowly and very distinctly.

"I'm sorry. I just have so much to do before I leave—packing and so on—that it's really impossible for me to—"

"Is that Steve on the phone?" Claudine's voice brought Jolie's hand over the receiver so the sound wouldn't carry to Steve. Claudine was looking down at her over the stair railing, dressed in a short terrycloth robe that stopped at her knees.

"Yes, it is." Jolie asked Steve to hold the line a minute before she turned back to Claudine. "Was there something you wanted to talk to him about?"

"Uh-huh," Claudine said with wide eyes. She gave a theatrical sigh as she came the rest of the way down the stairs. "I can't find my blue and green silk nightgown and the matching kimono. I've looked everywhere—I think I must have packed it with Steve's stuff. Damn," she swore softly.

"Here." Jolie thrust the phone into Claudine's hand. "You ask him."

Rigid with anger and jealousy, Jolie remembered the blue-green outfit that had reminded her of peacock feathers in all its seductive glory. Claudine shrugged at Jolie's irate face and calmly took the receiver.

"Steve? It's Claudine." She smiled a little too sweetly at Jolie. "You remember my blue-green gown—yes you do, I know you do. I can't find it and I was wondering if it got mixed up with your clothes . . . oh, okay, that's what happened. No, that's not necessary. I can pick it up tomorrow . . . Jolie?"

A perfectly outlined eyebrow arched questioningly

at her. Jolie spun around and stalked from the hallway back outdoors.

The closed expression on Jolie's face stopped Guy from asking any questions as she went about the last of the loading up with a vengeance. In less than half an hour she had everything stowed in the car, including the maps showing her route. And the beginning and end points of the trip were entered in the GPS, even though the thing generally drove her nuts. She decided to mute the little voice and just use the screen to start out.

A purpling dusk was disappearing into the dark of night when she locked the car door, everything in readiness for her morning send-off. Guy had gone into the house minutes before to leave her to it.

As Jolie wiped the sweat from her forehead, she turned toward the back door to join him. She'd only taken a couple of steps when the screen door slammed shut and Jolie glanced up to see a tall man standing in her path—Steve.

Pausing, she thought about running, but where would she go? There wasn't any place to hide around here. This wasn't her real home or her real family.

She walked toward Steve and he walked toward her.

As she drew closer, she could see the lines of tiredness etched on his face, but she refused to allow compassion to weaken her resolve. In the half light, his eyes seemed even a darker blue as he watched her approach.

"You didn't have to drive all the way in," she said coolly, stopping a few feet away from him.

"Really, Jolie?"

"We said our goodbyes over the phone."

"Our conversation was interrupted," he reminded her.

"By that time everything that was important had been said. And Claudine was oh-so-anxious to talk to you."

"I just gave her back that blue-and-green thing. She stuffed it in my duffel bag when I wasn't looking."

"It isn't a thing," Jolie pointed out. "It's a slinky nightgown and matching kimono. But it's considerate of you. I'm sure she'll appreciate it." Jolie continued to answer him calmly.

"What made you decide to leave in such a great big hurry?"

"I told you. My aunt's ill."

"I don't believe you."

"Hey, she's my favorite relative in my extended family, whether you believe it or not," Jolie said heatedly. "If not for her, I wouldn't even have made it to Louisiana—she financed my trip. We've always been very close, so if she's ill, that's that. Too bad if you or anyone else doesn't like it."

Her genuine feeling for her aunt threw him, even if he doubted the particulars of Jolie's reason for leaving. She could see the struggle in his eyes—he wanted to keep right on not believing her. Tough luck, she thought mulishly. Here was her chance to leave and not look back, maybe even have a crumb or two of dignity left into the bargain.

"I have this feeling there's something you're not saying." His quiet statement made her stop trying so hard to look busy.

"I don't know what that would be." Jolie swallowed,

her mind racing to find a loophole in her story, if she'd left one. "I—I didn't thank you for the insider tour of the local sights, I guess. You really went the extra mile and it made my trip very special."

"Right. The *lagniappe*—so you liked that?" His bitter, questioning smile made her breath catch. Something extra. The very phrase she'd first associated with him. "I'm glad," he went on. "I wanted to make Louisiana come alive for you."

She didn't know how to tell him that he'd made *her* come alive. And made her connect with powerful and very womanly emotions she'd never experienced until Steve Cameron held her in his arms.

For what it was worth, she told herself. Now it was . . . over. Time to go home, sadder but wiser. She hated the idea. From somewhere deep in her heart, Jolie summoned a smile.

"It's such a romantic place," she said. "It's in the air in Louisiana—no escaping it, I guess."

"Works well for a fast fling, doesn't it?" he said mockingly. "All you have to do is breathe it in."

"Yes," she said quickly, fighting off pain she didn't want him to hear in her voice. "And now I have to get my head out of the clouds."

"Not a problem, I don't think, Jolie. Nothing much happened. No embarrassing scenes, no vows of undying love that have to be taken back." There was a look of contempt in Steve's eyes that made her glad she'd pretended not to care. "Aren't you glad now that you didn't get swept away by your emotions and do something you would live to regret?"

Of course he was referring to their previous encounter on the night of the fog, but Jolie could only compare it to her silence in not actually declaring her love for him. She couldn't have stood his pity.

"Yes," she whispered, grateful the light had faded and Steve couldn't see the shimmer of tears gathering in her eyes.

"Now you'll be able to gossip with your girlfriends about the man you met by the bayou."

Jolie turned her head away. "It almost seemed like something out of a story, how you turned out to be Etienne and Etienne turned out to be Steve Cameron, the owner of Cameron Hall," she agreed in a tight voice. She would never be able to tell anyone the whole story just as idle gossip.

"I guess you were right when you said there wasn't any more for us to talk about. I was beginning to think I would regret the day I invited myself to your picnic." Steve sounded as if he was talking to himself, but even in the dark she could tell he was looking at her. "What the hell. We had fun. But I guess this is goodbye."

His hand was extended toward her. She hesitated to take it, knowing the touch of his hand would only intensify the desire to throw herself into his arms. Her self-control didn't fail her as Jolie placed her hand in his, feeling the warmth of his strong grip spread up her arm and through her body. But it didn't ease the cold, throbbing ache in her chest.

"Goodbye, Steve," she said softly, feeling as if the words condemned her to heartbreak.

"Ladybird, ladybird, fly away home," Steve murmured sardonically before he let go of her hand. "Maybe I'll see you again sometime, Jolie. You never know."

The light from inside the house made everything

outside seem darker. The trees were cobwebby shapes against the first twinkling stars. Steve became a dark shadow before he was lost to the blackness and out of sight.

Only now could Jolie admit why the crack in her heart had not split the rest of the way. She'd been hoping against hope that Steve would brush aside her lame story and sweep her into his arms, telling her that he loved her too much to let her go. But instead he'd offered a flat *maybe I'll see you again.*

Steve was glad to see her go. He felt better that she only thought of him as a friend with benefits, a vacation fling, nothing special. That was the reality—with all the shattering results of a broken heart.

Jolie shivered. She suddenly felt so cold. So very cold. And alone. And empty.

Chapter 12

Several months later . . .

Jolie hadn't returned to her parents' farm. Her destination instead was her Aunt Brigitte's apartment in Sioux Falls. After the strain of the long journey to South Dakota, during which Jolie had refused to give vent to her grief, it was natural that the floodgates had burst open the second she saw Brigitte.

In her practical way, her aunt took over after that, declaring what Jolie had been unable to, that it was impossible for her to return to her parents' home. Within only a few days Jolie had been hired as a dietitian at a private nursing home. The salary was minimal, but money didn't mean much to her so long as she had enough to live on. She needed to do something to fill in those awful, memory-filled hours.

Her aunt had insisted that Jolie take the second bedroom at her place, at least for a while, until she could get on her feet, emotionally and financially. It was just as well that Jolie had gone to her aunt since it was Brigitte who made sure she ate, got to work on time, and made the decisions that Jolie was beyond caring about.

The first week set the pattern for the following weeks. Jolie got up in the mornings, went to work, came home, ate the dinner Brigitte prepared, helped with dishes, read a book or watched TV, ignored everything online, and went to bed.

At Christmastime Jolie made her first attempt to join in with the holiday spirit and shake herself out of her stupor. She made a real effort to pick out the most appropriate and personal gift for each member of her family. The hardest one was her father, because every time she walked into the men's department of a store she visualized what Steve would look like in a denim shirt or a cable-knit sweater or whatever was on display.

Aunt Brigitte encouraged her, indulging herself in buying sprees for Christmas decorations that she'd considered frivolous in previous years. She planned to celebrate with Jolie, who only had Christmas Day off from work.

Sometimes Jolie actually seemed cheerful. Then she would exchange a look with her aunt which was always followed by silent sighs on both sides. She wasn't kidding herself or Brigitte. Steve still occupied the only place in her heart.

There'd been a small Christmas party at the nursing home for the patients, all of them elderly, and Jolie volunteered to stay late and help with the cleaning up. She was feeling more depressed than usual, considering that Christmas carols were still ringing in her ears—probably because so many of the patients were without families or had families who conveniently forgot them. It intensified her dread of the future.

Stepping out of the nursing home, Jolie held the collar of her coat around her neck to keep out the biting cold of the north wind. Snow crunched beneath her boots and the flurries in the air promised additional inches before morning. She patted the dashboard of the little Volkswagen affectionately as it started with the first turn of the key. In weather like this, Jolie was glad her aunt's apartment was so close to where she worked.

As always, once away from the demands of her job, her thoughts strayed back to Louisiana and Steve. She had hoped, prayed, that time would lessen the vividness of her memories but it hadn't.

Parking the car in front of the ground floor apartment, Jolie fixed a smile on her face before scampering into the building. It was a game she played to lift her spirits. Maybe one day it would become natural and that was as far as she allowed herself to think.

"It's just me!" she called brightly, closing and locking the apartment door behind her, before hanging up her coat. "I think we might be in for a storm tonight."

She rubbed her arms briskly just thinking about it as she walked into the living room. Her aunt was sitting in her favorite chair just inside the door, her brown eyes dancing mischievously when she looked up at Jolie.

"It's about time you got home," she said. "You have a visitor."

The living room stretched out to Jolie's right. She followed her aunt's gaze in that direction. Steve stood near a small table that held a nativity scene.

Jolie was caught all over again by his vivid blue eyes and imprisoned in their depths. He was, if possible, even handsomer than she remembered.

"What are you doing here?" she demanded hoarsely, unconscious of her aunt quietly slipping from the room to leave them alone.

"I had to see you," Steve answered quietly in his drawling velvet voice as he took a step toward her. There was a tenseness and noticeable strain in his face.

"Get out of here! I don't want to see you!" Her hand came up to her throat to choke away the sobs that were rising.

"There are some things I've got to tell you," he continued determinedly.

"I don't want to hear them!" She turned swiftly around and would have fled to her bedroom if his hands hadn't closed over her shoulders and stopped her. It was hard to fight the desire to melt in his arms.

"I'm going to say them anyway," Steve muttered above her ear. "And after I've said them, if you still want me to leave, I will."

"Oh, please, Steve, let me go." Jolie closed her eyes tightly, hardly able to bear his nearness. "Words just don't mean anything anymore."

"Not even . . . I love you?"

She was drawn back against his chest and she felt his lips moving with caressing roughness. "I never meant to fall in love with you. Lord knows I tried not to, just as I tried to forget you. But you haunted me even before you left Louisiana. All those things I said about never marrying and not believing in love were just a way to give myself some breathing room. You were the one—the only one, Jolie. I was just too scared to admit it."

Waves of pure rapture swept over her but she refused to give way to them. She had been through too much in these last months. There had been too many tormenting memories. Even as her heart swelled with love for him, her mind fought back.

"Even when you took Claudine to New Orleans with you?" Jolie asked.

Steve turned her around in his arms so that he was looking into her face. "I knew you believed that's what I'd done. Maybe I even wanted you to, I don't know. She called me and asked to ride along, but I swear to you, we stayed in separate hotels. And that damned gown she was yapping about was planted. She really had it in for you. I had no idea of the extent of it, but we got into a huge fight about it the day after you left."

"Why didn't you tell me that?" Jolie whispered. Some of the fight went out of her as she gazed into the face she adored.

"You were so ready to believe the worst." He smiled ruefully, deepening the grooves near his mouth. "And so ready to have me believe that I just didn't matter to you."

"Never," Jolie said heatedly.

"Are you sure, Jolie, very sure?" Steve demanded, the fierceness coming back into his eyes. "Because these last few months without you have been hell."

Her arms slid around his neck and pulled his head close to hers. It was like coming home after a very long time. Steve's soft kiss changed into a hungry embrace that left her in no doubt as to the depths of his feelings.

Much later, they ended up on the small sofa and Jolie was cradled in his lap where he could kiss and caress her as much as he wanted. His will was strong and she was more than willing.

"Do I give you a few minutes or just walk in?" Brigitte called from just outside the living room door.

Jolie started to struggle upright but Steve held her in place. "Come on in," he called back. "Your niece really needs a chaperone. Things are getting out of hand here."

Aunt Brigitte entered, looking everywhere but at them, just in case. Jolie fixed her disheveled clothes and gave her tousled hair an ineffectual pat or two. When Brigitte finally glanced their way, there was a twinkle of happiness and approval in her understanding brown eyes.

"And now, sweet Jolie," Steve said, planting a kiss on her lips, "the time has come to say what I have to say—"

"Just ask," she breathed.

"If you'll let me get the words out!"

She picked up a sofa pillow and pummeled him with it until he begged for mercy. "Okay," he said, laughing, "I may never get to ask you, but we're going to be married just as soon as we can get a license and a minister. Cameron Hall is in need of another Jolie Antoinette Cameron as mistress, and so is the master."

"That was a proposal in front of a witness, Mr. Cameron." Jolie gazed adoringly into his face. "And in front of a witness, I accept."

"I don't think Steve intended to give you much of a choice." Her aunt smiled. "I don't have any champagne for the celebration, but I could make some cocoa."

"Do you want some help?" Jolie offered, disliking

the thought of leaving Steve's side even for a moment. She didn't have to worry, because her offer was firmly refused.

"Before I forget," said Steve, addressing himself to her aunt as he put an arm around Jolie and drew her closer to him, "Jolie told me that you made her trip to Louisiana happen. I want to thank you for that, from both of us. If Jolie has no objections, I thought we might name our first girl after you."

The older woman's eyes became starry bright with tears as she smiled and said, "Only if I can be her godmother."

"Absolutely," Jolie said, feeling a happy tightness in her throat.

"Well, I'd better make that cocoa." And her aunt hastily left the room.

"I hope you didn't mind," Steve said, gazing down at her with unbelievable warmth.

"I think it's a wonderful idea." A shy blush covered her cheeks. "Of course, we could have boys."

"We'll just have to keep trying until we get it right," he said, laughing at her open-mouthed expression. "Honey, I don't care if we have two, ten, or twenty kids. All I want is you. Anything else is a bonus, although a boy and a girl would be nice."

"Oh, Steve, I love you so much," she said breathlessly, gazing into the face she had been so afraid she'd never see again.

It was an invitation he couldn't resist. And neither could Jolie as she offered her lips to his.

"And I love you," he whispered against her mouth.

THE
IVORY CANE

Chapter 1

Overhead a seagull screeched. The blustery wind off the Pacific Ocean swirled around the boats docked at the yacht harbor of San Francisco. Distantly, Sabrina heard the clang of a cable car, the one climbing the steep hill of Hyde Street.

The light blue luxury car she was in was wheeled expertly into the parking lot in front of the harbor. The driver, a beautiful redhead in her mid-thirties, braked precisely between the white parking lines and switched off the motor. As she reached for the door handle, emerald green eyes flicked to the silent young woman in the passenger seat.

"It's chilly outside, Sabrina. It would probably be best if you waited in the car while I go see if your father is back." It was a statement, not a suggestion.

Sabrina Lane opened her mouth to protest. She was tired of being cosseted. With a flash of insight, she realized that Deborah wasn't interested in Sabrina's well-being so much as spending some time alone with Sabrina's father.

"Whatever you say, Deborah," she replied grudgingly,

her right hand closing tightly over the handle of her oak cane.

The silence following Deborah's departure grated at Sabrina's already taut nerves. It was difficult enough to deal with her own physical restrictions without having her father's girlfriend invent a few more, regardless of the motive.

Her father's girlfriend. One corner of her mouth turned up at the phrase. Her father had had many female friends since her mother died when Sabrina was seven. But Deborah Mosely was not just another woman. If it hadn't been for Sabrina's accident some eight months ago, Deborah would have already been her new stepmother.

Before the accident, Sabrina had thought it was great her father had found someone he wanted to marry. Deborah wouldn't have been Sabrina's choice, though she liked her well enough, but it hadn't mattered, not so long as her father was happy.

Back then, Sabrina had been totally independent, with a place of her own. Small. But hers. She had a career, not a lucrative one, but she supported herself.

Now—the word screamed with a despairing wail. It would be a long time, if ever, before Sabrina could say any of that again.

Why me, a sobbing, self-pitying voice asked silently. *What did I ever do to deserve this?*

Her throat tightened with pain at the unanswerable question. There was simply too much time to think about what-might-have-beens and if-onlys. The damage was done and irreparable, as specialist after specialist had told Sabrina and her father. She would be sightless for the rest of her life and there was nothing, barring a miracle, that could ever be done to change it.

A seed of rebellion stirred to life. That she might forever sit in cars or stay at home while someone else decided what was best for her . . . just the thought made her angry.

A sickening idea came to her. What if Deborah's wish to be alone with her father wasn't about getting romantic? What if she was trying to persuade him to send her away to that rehabilitation home? Rehabilitation— the word always made her feel like a criminal.

Please, God, Sabrina prayed, *don't let Dad listen to her.* She didn't want to go to that place. There had to be some other alternative.

She felt guilty praying to God for help. It hurt to have to have anyone to help her. She'd always been so completely self-sufficient. Now she was constantly depending on someone. At this very minute, Deborah might be persuading her father to send her to another school and here Sabrina was, sitting in the car, accepting her fate by the very fact that she was not participating in the discussion but allowing someone else to talk for her.

Thousands of times Sabrina had walked from the parking lot of the harbor to the slip where her father tied his boat. If she stayed calm and took her time, there was no reason why she couldn't traverse it again.

Her long fingers tightened the cord of the striped tunic and adjusted the rolled collar of the dark turtleneck she wore underneath. The wind whistled a warning outside. She ran a smoothing hand up to the back of her head to be sure her mink-brown hair was securely pinned in its knot atop her head.

Taking a deep breath to still the quivering excitement

racing through her, Sabrina opened the door and swung her long legs on to the pavement. With the car door closed behind her and the cane firmly in one hand, she moved slowly in the direction of the harbor fence. The icy tendrils of fear dancing down her spine added to the adventurous thrill of her small journey.

Made bold by her initial success, Sabrina unconsciously began to hurry. She stumbled over a concrete parking stop and couldn't regain her balance. The cane slipped from her hand, skittering away as she sprawled on the pavement.

Excitement disappeared immediately, leaving only black fear. Her shaking fingers reached out for the cane, but it was out of her grasp. Except for the shock to her senses, there was no pain. She wasn't hurt, but how was she going to make her way to the dock without the cane?

"Damn, damn, damn!" Sabrina regretted her own foolishness for making the attempt in the first place.

If her father found her like this, it would only confirm the validity of Deborah's opinion that Sabrina needed more professional help. Propping herself up on one elbow, she tried to check the rising terror that was leading her toward panic and think her way out of this predicament rationally.

"Are you all right?" a low, masculine voice asked with concern.

Sabrina's head jerked in his direction, embarrassed red surging into her cheeks that a stranger should find her, and feeling so humiliated that she was forced to seek his help.

The feminine line of her chin, tapering from high cheekbones, tilted to a proud angle. "I'm not hurt," she asserted quickly, then grudgingly, "My cane, would you get it for me?"

"Of course."

The instant the cane was retrieved, Sabrina reached out to take it from him, not wanting to endure the mortification of his pity and hoping a quick thank-you would send him on his way. As her outstretched hand remained empty, her cheeks flamed more.

A pair of strong hands slipped under her arms and bodily lifted her to her feet before she could gasp a protest. Her fingers touched the hard muscle of his upper arms, covered by the smooth material of a windbreaker. The salty tang of the ocean breeze mingled with spicy aftershave and his virile, definitely masculine scent. Sabrina was tall, nearly five foot seven, but the warm breath from his mouth stirred the bangs covering her wide forehead, making him easily six inches taller than she was.

Her cane, hooked over his arm, tapped the side of her leg. "Please let me go," she said crisply while her fingers closed over the cane and lifted it from his arm.

"Nothing hurt but your pride, is that it?" the man said gently, loosening his grip on her slim waist and letting his hands fall away.

Sabrina smiled tautly, keeping her luminous brown eyes averted from the man's face.

"Thank you for your help," she murmured unwillingly as she took a hesitant step backward.

Turning away, she waited for interminable seconds for him to continue wherever it was that he was going. She could feel his eyes on her back and guessed that he was waiting to be sure she hadn't hidden an injury from the fall.

Afraid that he might feel compelled because of her need for the cane to help her even more, Sabrina stepped out boldly. The shocking blare of a horn simultaneously accompanied by the squeal of car brakes paralyzed her. A steel band circled her waist and roughly pulled her back.

The husky male voice was still low, but there was nothing gentle in its tone as he growled in her ear. "Were you trying to kill yourself? Didn't you see that car coming?"

"How could I?" Sabrina muttered bitterly, unable to tug the steel-hard arm from around her waist. "I'm blind!"

She heard and felt his swift intake of breath a split second before he turned her around, her upper arms now prisoners of his hands. His eyes burned over her face. Sabrina knew he understood that she was gazing sightlessly back. For once she was blessedly glad she couldn't see. The pity that would be in his expression would have been unbearable.

"Why the hell didn't you say so?" There was an edge to his voice that caught her off guard. She hadn't expected that. "And why isn't your cane white?"

Stung, Sabrina retorted in kind. "Why, is there a law that says I have to have a white cane? And dark glasses?"

"No, but—"

"Should I run around with a little tin cup and sell pencils?"

"You shouldn't run anywhere—"

"Damnit!" she exploded. "Why does being blind make me that different from everyone else? Why do

I have to be singled out? I hate when parents point their fingers at me and tell their children to let 'the blind lady' go first. My cane isn't white because I don't want any special consideration or pity!"

She paused, out of breath, her chest heaving.

"Have it your way," the man said after a beat. "But you nearly got yourself killed. If that driver had seen a white cane in your hand, he might've slowed down or given you the right of way or at least honked his horn to let you know he was there."

"You and that driver can go to—"

He snorted. "Go right on being a proud fool. You won't live long. Just keep on stepping in front of cars and sooner or later one of them will hit you. Maybe it won't trouble your conscience, but I'm sure the driver who ultimately does run you over won't get why you didn't carry a cane that could've saved your life."

"Hey, it's not that difficult to understand," Sabrina replied in a choked voice. "If the driver lost his sight, he'd know what it feels like to advertise your blindness."

"Uh-huh. It's kinda obvious why you reject pity from others," the man said. "You're much too busy revving up your own."

"Meaning I pity myself?" she asked, incredulous. "You—" She didn't bother to add the word *arrogant* and something even more choice as she instinctively judged the distance between them and his height before connecting with a resounding slap against the man's jaw.

Her hand fell and she sensed that he had raised his in the next instant. She half expected a slap but instead he stroked her cheek for the briefest possible second.

Her shock at his action magnified her reaction tenfold.

"How dare you!" she exclaimed in an outraged whisper.

"Sorry," was all he said. "I wasn't thinking straight. A hard slap will do that to you."

"Poor baby," she mocked. But she half wanted to touch her cheek where he had touched it.

"Do you think you have a right to treat people like that when they try to help you?"

Sabrina gasped, caught in a trap of her own making. He had tried to help. She didn't know why she'd lashed out at him and struck him. Even so, she was angry.

"Who do you think you are?" she yelled as she turned away.

"Not so fast." His hand took her shoulder and effectively halted her steps. "You're acting like a little kid. Do you hear any cars coming now? Do you know where you're going? Got your directions straight?"

"Just leave me alone!" Sabrina demanded. "I can take care of myself just fine!"

"Again, I really am sorry." There wasn't a whole hell of a lot of apology in his tone. "But I was raised to believe that we are all our brother's keeper, or sister's, as the case may be. So, whether you like it or not, I'm going to see that you arrive safely wherever you're going. Go ahead and walk away."

Sabrina could sense his shrug of indifference but didn't deign to respond to it.

"I'll be right behind you."

She wanted to scream her frustration, but the stranger's determination made it clear that it would be a waste of energy. She could not go on the docks, not with this man as an unwanted bodyguard. The last thing she wanted was to have her father feel that it wasn't safe to leave her alone even for a few minutes. The second he saw this man at her side there would be a barrage of questions and the entire humiliating story would be told.

Reluctantly she turned back in the direction she'd come. "Don't go to any trouble," she said. "I'm only going to the car."

"And drive it?"

Sabrina chose to ignore that. Embarrassment and anger had all but erased her sense of humor. She tried to step past the tall stranger but he moved to block her way.

"Which car?" he asked softly.

"The Lexus behind you in the next row."

"That isn't where you were headed when I first saw you."

She gritted her teeth. "I had intended to go out on the docks to meet my father and Deborah. Since you insist on accompanying me, I prefer to wait for them in the car." There was an overly sweet quality to her carefully enunciated words.

"They went out sailing and just left you here in the car?" His tone seemed to indicate that her father and Deborah were somewhere on a spectrum between a little dim and completely clueless.

"No, my father went sailing and Deborah came down to pick him up. She's somewhere out on the dock now and I was going to see what was keeping them," Sabrina retorted.

"Deborah is . . . your sister?"

At least it was a statement and not another question.

What a pleasure it would be to tell him off *and* tell him he was wrong.

"You seem determined to pry into my personal life," she sighed impatiently. "Not that it's any of your business, but Deborah is my father's one and only. Meaning my potential stepmother."

He took in that information for a beat before he spoke. "Not the wicked kind, I hope."

"No, she's just annoying. Like you."

He ignored the insult as his hand closed over her elbow, the firm hold guiding her steps in the direction of the car. Several steps later, the end of the cane clunked against the side fender.

"Which slip does your father dock in? I'll go see what's keeping him for you," the man offered.

"No, thank you," she refused curtly. "He's already practically convinced that I need a permanent babysitter. If you go and tell him everything, I'll never be able to persuade him that I don't want anybody wiping my nose for me." Exasperation filled her voice. "If I give you my word that I won't leave the car, will you go away and leave me alone?"

"I'd love to oblige, but I'm afraid it's too late to keep our meeting a secret from your father," the man said.

Sabrina scowled. "What do you mean?"

"Is Deborah a redhead?"

"Yes."

"Well, there's an older man walking toward the harbor gates with a redhead at his side. He's looking this way with a frown on his face," he replied.

"Please go quickly—before he sees me," she pleaded.

"Since he's already seen me, if I were your father I would be very suspicious if a strange man was talking to my daughter and left when he saw me coming. It's better that I stay," the man said.

"No." Sabrina whispered her protest. With this guy, words didn't do much.

She heard the clink of the fence gates opening and closing. Time had run out.

"Stop looking as if I'd tried to hit on you. Smile." The sound of the man's low voice held a smile of his own, warm and a little amused at her obvious discomfort. Her reluctance was obvious as the corners of her mouth stretched into a slow smile.

"Sabrina." Her father's voice hailed her, an undertone of concern in the otherwise warmly happy way he said her name. "Were you getting tired of waiting?"

Nervously she turned, trying to keep the faltering smile in place, knowing how discerning her father could be.

"Hello, Dad." She forced a casualness into her voice. "Did you have a good sail?"

"What else?" He laughed the rhetorical question.

Sabrina sensed almost the exact instant when her father's inquisitive gaze was turned on the man at her side. She had been so busy trying to get rid of him that she hadn't thought of a single excuse to explain his presence.

The problem was taken out of her hands.

"You must be Sabrina's dad. She was just asking me if I'd seen the *Lady Sabrina* come in while I was at the docks. I have the ketch down the way from yours, *Dame Fortune.* My name's Bay Cameron."

"Grant Lane," her father countered, the vague wariness leaving his voice at the introduction.

Unconsciously Sabrina had been holding her breath. She let it out in a silent sigh. The stranger, now identified as someone called Bay Cameron, could think on his feet, she decided with relief. Of course she was sure there wasn't another boat in the yacht harbor named *Lady Sabrina*, but the man had been quick to put two and two together simply from her father's use of her name. And it sounded like such a plausible reason for her to be talking to him.

Her father's hand touched her shoulder and she turned her face to him with an easy smile. "You weren't worrying about me, were you, Sabrina?" he teased.

"Not a bit. Not an old salt like you. Of course, you were minus the best deckhand you ever had," she laughed.

"Yes, well—" His stumbling agreement made Sabrina wince. She hadn't meant to remind him of the many hours they had spent together sailing these very same waters before the accident that had left her permanently blind.

The stranger named Bay Cameron filled in the gap. "Women always worry when their men are at sea."

"It's our nature," Deborah spoke up in her best purring voice. "You men wouldn't like it any other way."

"That's right, Deb," her father agreed. "Mr. Cameron, this is my fiancée, Deborah Mosely."

"It's a pleasure. But I shouldn't keep you any longer. I'm sure you all have plans of some kind," Bay responded.

"Thanks for keeping Sabrina company." There was sincere gratitude in her father's tone.

"Yes," Sabrina added, reluctantly acknowledging the fact that he hadn't given her away. "I appreciated your thoughtfulness."

"Yes, I know." Lack of sight made Sabrina's hearing more acute. She could hear the mocking inflection in

Bay's three-word answer, something her father and
Deborah were probably oblivious to. Bay knew very
well what she was thanking him for. "Maybe we'll all
see each other again some time. So long."

After their answering chorus of goodbyes, Sabrina
listened to his footsteps fading away to another area
of the parking lot. She wondered why he hadn't told
her father how they'd really met. Acting out of pity,
most likely, although he hadn't shown any earlier. In
fact, he'd been downright rude and tyrannical.

The car door was opened behind her, bringing an
end to her wandering thoughts. Her father's guiding hand helped her into the backseat.

"I thought you were going to wait in the car," Deborah said disapprovingly after they were all seated.

"It got stuffy, so I decided to get some fresh air,"
Sabrina lied.

"Well, it did put some color in your cheeks," Grant
Lane observed. "You probably should get out more."

Was that an innocent comment or a remark
prompted by a discussion with Deborah concerning
the new school for the blind, aka rehabilitation
center? It was impossible to tell. Sabrina crossed her
fingers, feeling like a little kid. It wasn't as if they
could make her go.

"So, tell me about Bay Cameron," Deborah said.
"Had you met him before?"

"No. Why?" Sabrina stiffened, feeling a little
defensive.

"It's not like you to talk to total strangers, that's
all," the redhead replied.

"You mean, not since I've been blind," Sabrina
corrected her sharply. "I've never been exactly shy.
Besides, all I did was ask about Dad."

There was a moment of uneasy silence. Her reply had held an edge, but sometimes Deborah's air of solicitude and apparent concern got on Sabrina's nerves, big time. But that was true of anybody who hovered over her.

"Do you suppose," Deborah said to break the tension, "he's one of the real-estate Camerons?"

"I can't imagine any other Cameron having a ketch in the harbor," her father replied. "After all, they're one of the founding families of San Francisco."

A native of the city, Sabrina was well aware of its colorful history. Until gold was discovered in 1849, it had been a nothing little settlement called Yerba Buena, "good herb." Kind of funny, Sabrina thought, considering how it stayed famous for other types of herbs, especially during the hippie years.

She yawned, remembering the chapter from a long-ago geography textbook. The bay was a perfect harbor for the ships racing around the tip of South America to join in the rush for California gold. The natural entrance truly became a golden gate for a lot of pioneers.

There had been a picture of bushy-bearded miners leaning on shovels and wearing the denims that had been invented for them, which were saggy and baggy and far from fashionable.

She could practically quote the caption under the photo even now. *Few actually found much of the coveted metal in the California and Nevada lodes, but fortunes were made in the goods and services the men of the new frontier required. The end result: San Francisco, a mere outpost, grew into a city.*

The Cameron family was the least well known of the original founders, she was pretty sure. It was jokingly said that they once owned all of San Francisco, and now they possessed only a quarter of the city. Hardly a step down in this day and age, Sabrina thought wryly, and it certainly accounted for the man's arrogance.

Oh well, she sighed. What was the use in thinking about him? He wasn't the kind of man you'd run into very often, not with his background.

She had liked his voice, though. Sabrina qualified the thought quickly. She had liked it when it hadn't been telling her what to do. The low baritone had been warm and vaguely caressing. She wondered how old he was.

That was one of the problems of not being able to see. She had to rely so heavily on her other senses to judge the few people she met. Still, she was becoming rather good at it. She began a quick run-through of the impressions she'd picked up in her brief meeting with Bay Cameron.

He was tall, over six foot by at least an inch. When he'd pulled her out of the oncoming car's path, she'd been against his body.

A great body and very male. Broad shoulders. Flat stomach. Lean hips. Judging by the solidness of his muscles he was in excellent physical condition. The salty tang of ocean spray that clung to him verified that he'd often sailed out in the ketch tied up in the yacht harbor and probably had that day since the scent of the sea was pleasantly strong. That told her that he was the outdoorsy type, a plus as far as she was concerned.

At the time, she had been too angry to appreciate his sense of humor, but she guessed it was there, somewhere beneath his amused mockery.

His intelligence was obvious in his educated way of speaking and quick thinking. Almost instantly he'd assessed the facts and come up with a reasonable excuse for her father as to why Sabrina had been talking to him. When it came to business, he would probably be just as shrewd.

She settled back into her seat with smug triumph. That was a great deal of information to glean from one meeting. There were only two things about him she didn't know. His age she could only narrow as being somewhere between thirty and fifty, judging by the maturity of his voice and his physical condition. The second was a detailed description of his looks— the color of his hair, his eyes, and that type of thing. Sabrina was really quite pleased with herself.

For an instant she was motionless. There was one other thing she didn't know—his marital status. That was something she couldn't be certain of even if she could see. Unless he was one of those men who faithfully wore his wedding ring. She couldn't recall the sensation of anything metal on his fingers.

Not that she cared one way or the other whether he was married or not. She had merely been conducting an exercise of her senses, a surprisingly pleasurable one at that.

Chapter 2

Sabrina licked the vanilla icing from her fingers, then painstakingly ran the knife across the top of the cake. No matter what kind of cake she made, her father invariably called it a fingerprint cake. Sabrina was never totally confident that the frosting covered the entire cake. The only way she could be sure was by feeling, hence the telltale impressions of her clean fingers all over the icing.

Placing the knife on the formica counter, she set the cake platter toward the back, refusing to give in to the sensation that there was a gaping hole somewhere exposing the dark devil's-food cake. Before the accident that had left her blinded, Sabrina had taken kitchen tasks for granted.

Now, washing dishes in the dishwasher or by hand was a study in diligence, let alone cooking a meal. She had mastered nearly everything but eggs—they turned out somewhere between a scramble and an omelet, and were never very appetizing. For the sake of their stomachs, breakfast had become the meal her father prepared.

Sunday was the day that Deborah did all the cooking, as had been the case this last weekend. Her father's fiancée was a gourmet cook. Sabrina had always been mediocre at best, which made her doubly conscious of the occasionally charred or rare meals she put on the table during the week, compared to the perfection of Deborah's. Yet her father had never complained once, and made sure to praise her efforts when the food turned out fine.

Except for a nice lady who came in twice a week to do the more thorough cleaning, Sabrina took care of the house herself, dusting and vacuuming. She actually liked what she called domestic therapy. It took her longer than the average sighted person, but she'd discovered that, with patience, there was very little she couldn't do. But patience was the key.

What with her not seeing sunlight, her natural sense of the passage of time sometimes got away from her. It seemed to escape her mind somehow, five minutes turning out to be ten, and hours dragging to interminable length. Sometimes when the loneliness of her dark world caved in about her, the opposite was true and time passed too quickly. The empty, desolate sensation invariably occurred after a surge of creative energy that she was unable to release.

Sabrina had learned to endure the myriad inconveniences that came from being sightless. She could even keep the bitterness in check until she thought about the career that had come to such an abrupt halt after the accident.

Since almost the first time a watercolor brush had been put in her hand, art, specifically painting, had been her passion. Her talent, enhanced by skills taught by some of the best teachers around, had made her a relatively successful artist at the early age of twenty-two, thanks to nearly fifteen years of training. She was just getting known for her portraits, not necessarily commissioned sittings, but more often interesting faces she had seen at Fisherman's Wharf or the Ferry Building, or while café-hopping in North Beach, and even wandering around Chinatown.

Losing that had been the cruelest thing about the car accident that had stolen her sight. To this day Sabrina didn't know exactly what had happened. She'd been driving home very late at night after a weekend spent with a girlfriend in Sacramento. She had fallen asleep at the wheel.

Looking back, her pointless hurrying home seemed so senseless, considering the month she'd spent in the hospital, recovering from broken ribs and a concussion. Not to mention the blow to her head and subsequent swelling that irreparably damaged the optic nerves.

Giving her head a firm shake, Sabrina resolutely tried to push such memories to the back of her mind. Her survival lay in the future, not in looking over her shoulder at the past. At the moment the future looked empty, but seven months ago Sabrina had not believed she would accomplish as much as she had.

Her next challenge was walking from her home to the drugstore to buy a bottle of shampoo. It was only five blocks, but it was five blocks of freewheeling San Francisco traffic and four intersections. Only in the last two months had she had enough confidence in her abilities to attempt the journey without someone going along. Her pride always kept the potential humiliation of getting lost uppermost in her mind.

The sweater jacket that Sabrina took from the closet would be warm enough and it fit well. She touched the handle of her oak cane in the umbrella stand, the smooth finish of the wood reminding her of the touch of the stranger, Bay Cameron, who she'd met at the yacht harbor last Sunday. She still didn't care what he thought and his bossy attitude rankled.

Why don't you carry a white cane?

As if it was any of his business. She would always prefer the anonymity of a wooden cane. It was bad enough blundering around in permanent darkness without drawing attention to her plight.

Entering the stairway, Sabrina walked down the steps to the front door, carefully locking it behind her. The wrought iron gates just a few feet away creaked noisily as she opened and locked them. The sidewalk sloped abruptly downward. Sabrina counted the paces slowly, accurately turning at the front door of the neighbor's Victorian house.

Pressing the intercom buzzer, she waited for her neighbor's response. As a precaution, her father insisted that she always let someone know where she was going and when she had safely returned, whether it was Peggy Collins, their neighbor for nearly fifteen years, or himself at his office.

"Yes, who is it?" a brisk female voice answered the buzz.

"It's me, Sabrina. I'm on my way to the drugstore. Do you need anything?"

"How about three more hands? Or better yet, an

all-expenses-paid trip to Cancun?" the woman replied with amused exasperation.

"It's that bad, huh?" Sabrina laughed.

"Ken called me an hour ago and said he's bringing a couple of very important clients home for drinks and dinner. Of course there's not a thing in the house to eat and the refrigerator isn't making ice and the closets just exploded, because I was looking for something I couldn't find. It looks like a cyclone hit this place. Of all days to get ambitious, I had to pick today."

"Go ahead. Rant and rave. It'll do you good." Sabrina smiled at the intercom. There always seemed to be an impending crisis at Peggy's house that she invariably got through, staying cheerful. "If we have anything you need—ice, liquor, food—you just let me know."

"What I need is a husband with better timing," Peggy sighed. "Take care, Sabrina. See you when you get back."

Humming softly, Sabrina started out again. Her neighbor's droll humor had restored her somewhat dampened spirits. The trip to the drugstore became more of an adventure than an obstacle. There was a nip in the wind racing down the hill, but there always seemed to be a nip in the winds wandering through San Francisco.

There was no warmth on her cheeks as she crossed to the usually more sunny side of the street. The sun evidently hadn't burned through the fog yet. Instantly a vision of the fog swirling around the towers and cables of the Golden Gate Bridge came to her mind.

Her concentration broke for a moment and she

had to pause to get her bearings. It was so difficult not to daydream. The tip of her cane found the drop box for the mail and she knew which block she was on.

Crossing the street, she began counting her steps. She didn't want to walk into the barbershop instead of the drugstore as she had done the last time. A funny, prickly sensation started down the back of her neck. She ran a curious finger along the back collar of her sweater jacket and frowned at the unknown cause of the peculiar feeling.

"No white cane, I see," a familiar husky voice said from behind her. "You're stubborn, Sabrina."

A disbelieving paralysis took hold of her for a fleeting second before Sabrina pivoted toward the male voice.

"Bay Cameron," she acknowledged him coolly. "I didn't expect to meet you again."

"This city isn't all that big. Here I am driving down the street and see a girl walking with a cane. I start wondering if you've been run over yet. Then, lo and behold, I realize the girl is you. Are you looking for your father again?"

His voice had an amused tone. She, however, wasn't.

"I was just going into the drugstore here." Sabrina motioned over her shoulder in the general direction of her destination. "You were driving?"

"Yes, I parked my car up the street. Do you live near here?"

"A few blocks away," she answered, wishing she could see the expression on his face. "Why did you stop?"

"To see if you would have a cup of coffee with me."

"Why?" She couldn't keep the wariness out of her voice.

Bay Cameron laughed softly. "Believe me, I don't have an ulterior motive. It's just a friendly invitation."

"I don't understand why you want to have coffee with—" Sabrina almost said *a blind girl*. But the haughtiness left her voice when she ended lamely with the single word, "me."

"Seems to me, Sabrina, if you'll indulge me in some really annoying psychoanalysis that you don't want, didn't pay for, and don't believe in—"

"You can stop now," she interrupted.

"I'm on a roll," he said. "Where was I? Oh yeah. You not only suffer from a persecution complex but feelings of inferiority as well."

"I'm also homicidal," she said sweetly, raising her cane. "How about if I do you in with this?"

He laughed and she had to smile, somewhat reluctantly. "Okay, we got that out of our systems," he said. "So where would you like to have coffee? I know a little place in the next block we could go to."

"I'm sure your wife would much prefer you spend your free time with her." She knew she was fishing for information, but she didn't care.

"I'm sure she would—if I had a wife."

"Oh." She felt a flash of elation and squelched it. "Well, I can't. I have an errand to run at the drugstore."

"Will it take long?"

Hopelessly she wished it would take an hour. She really didn't want to spend any time with him. That air of confidence he exuded did make her feel inferior.

"No," she admitted, looking downcast. "It shouldn't take very long."

"Your lack of enthusiasm isn't doing much for my ego," Bay said with a wink she swore she could hear. "Would you feel more comfortable if I waited outside for you?"

Just knowing he was in the vicinity unnerved her. Sabrina shook her head. "It doesn't make any difference."

"In that case, I'll go with you. I need some shaving gel."

She felt the brush of his arm against her shoulder as he reached around her to open the door. She entered the store more or less on her own and tapped her way to the rear counter, sighing as she heard Bay's footsteps heading toward the aisle he wanted.

"Is there something I can help you find?" a woman clerk asked her.

Before Sabrina could reply, another voice broke in, gruff but happy, male this time. "Sabrina, I was beginning to think you'd forgotten where my store was. I haven't seen you in a couple of weeks."

"Hello, Gino." She smiled widely in the direction of the reproachful voice.

"It's all right, Maria. I'll help Sabrina. You go see what that man at the prescription counter wants." In a nice way, he dismissed the clerk who'd approached Sabrina first. As the woman moved away, Gino Marchetti whispered, "Maria is new, a cousin of my wife's sister's husband. This is only her first week, so she doesn't know my regular customers."

Those who worked in Gino's old-fashioned drugstore were always related to him in some way, Sabrina had learned over the years. But she knew the information had been offered to gently apologize for the woman not knowing Sabrina was blind.

"She has a very nice voice. I'm sure she'll get the hang of it soon," she replied.

"What is it that you need today? Name it and I'll get it for you."

"Oh, shampoo." Sabrina gave him the brand name she wanted.

While he went to get it, she carefully felt through the paper money in her wallet, all of it folded in a certain way to distinguish fives from tens from twenties.

As he was ringing up the sale on a vintage cash register, Gino Marchetti said, "I still have the portrait you painted of me hanging on this wall. People come in all the time and say, 'That looks just like you,' and I say, 'Of course, it is me.' I tell them that the girl who painted it has come to my store since she was a little thing and that she painted it from memory and gave it to me on the anniversary of my twenty-fifth year in business. Everyone thinks it's a very fine gift to have."

"I'm glad you like it, Gino." Sabrina smiled wanly.

She remembered how proud he'd been the day she'd presented him with the portrait two years ago. It was that ever-present quality of pride that she'd tried to get into his likeness. He had a loving, generous face and she'd captured that too and had been relatively satisfied with the result. Now she would never know that sense of creative accomplishment again.

"Sabrina, I didn't mean—"

She heard the hint of regret and self-reproach in the elderly man's voice and guessed that some of her sadness had tugged down the corners of her mouth. She determinedly curved them upward and interrupted him.

"I'm glad you liked it so much, Gino," she said. "The painting was my way of saying thank you for all the free candy."

The sensation of being watched tingled down her neck. Sabrina wasn't surprised when Bay Cameron spoke. Her sensitive radar seemed attuned to his presence.

"You did that?" he asked quietly.

"Yes." She snipped off the end of the affirmation.

"It is very good, isn't it?" Gino prompted. "I sold Sabrina her very first crayons. Then it was colored chalk, then watercolors, then oil pastels. I carry everything, she bought it all from her allowance." He beamed at her. "In my small way, I helped her to become an artist and she gave me this portrait as a present. She always comes to my store once, sometimes twice a week. That is, until her accident." His voice became sad. "Now she doesn't come as often."

Sabrina moved uneasily and Gino's mood changed again.

"Last week I saw her walk by my store and I wonder to myself where she is going. Then I see her walk into the barbershop next door and I say to myself, 'Oh no, she is going to have that beautiful crown of hair on the top of her head cut short,' but she had only walked into the wrong store! She was coming to see me."

"Do you know the very first time I saw her and that knot of silky brown hair on top of her head, it reminded me of a crown too." There was a caressing quality in Cameron's low voice and she knew it was meant for her. Sabrina felt the rise of pink in her cheeks.

"Okay, Gino, I've taken up enough of your time," she said hastily. "I know you have work to do and other customers waiting. I'll see you next week."

"Be sure it is next week, Sabrina."

"I will. *Ciao*, Gino." She turned quickly, aware of Bay Cameron moving out of her way and following her.

"*Addio*, Sabrina," Gino responded, not showing the least surprise that the stranger was with her.

"The café is to the left," Bay instructed her as they walked out of the drugstore. "It's around the corner and down a short flight of stairs."

"I think I know which one you mean. I haven't been there in several years."

They walked side by side down to the corner. He made no attempt to guide her, letting her make her own way without any assistance.

"That really was a good portrait." Bay ended the silence. "Did you major in art?"

"I took lessons since I was a kid. And college classes." She swallowed the lump in her throat and replied calmly. "It was my career. I was relatively successful."

"I can believe it," he said. "You were good."

"*Were* being the operative word," she replied. Then she drew a shaky breath. "I'm sorry."

"Don't apologize." He seemed to shrug. "It must have been twice as hard as an artist to lose your sight. It just doesn't seem fair." He touched her arm lightly to get her attention. "The iron banister of the stairs is on your left. You can follow it to the stairwell."

When her left hand encountered the railing, his

own hand returned to his side. He had accepted the pain she felt at the loss of her career as a natural thing, not really needing an explanation. There had been no empty words like so many others had offered, nothing to the effect that some day she'd get over it.

That, Sabrina had never been able to believe.

At the base of the stairs, Bay reached past her to open the café door. A hand rested firmly on the side of her waist and stayed there as a hostess showed them to a small booth.

"Let me take your cane," he offered. "I'll hang it on the post beside your seat so it'll be out of your way."

Sabrina handed it to him and slid into the booth, her fingers resting nervously on the table top. In the past she'd avoided public eating places, too self-conscious to be at ease. She touched the edge of a menu and pushed it aside.

The waitress came to the table and Sabrina heard Bay ask for two coffees before he addressed a question to her. "They make their own pastries here," he said. "They're very good. Care to indulge?"

"No." In her nervousness she was too abrupt and she quickly added, "No, thank you."

"Okay then. We'll just have coffee."

The waitress arrived with their coffee and a little of it sloshed out when she set the first cup down. Without thinking, Sabrina reached for a napkin from the holder and mopped it up. She couldn't think of what to do with the soggy napkin for a second and then she rolled it in a dry one—and handed it to him with a smile.

"Gee, thanks," Bay said.

"Anything for you," she replied, pleased that she hadn't flubbed the simple action of cleaning up.

The waitress, who had been watching, glanced at Sabrina's cane. Surprised, she didn't say anything as she quickly walked away, looking embarrassed by her own clumsiness.

"Do you take anything in your coffee?" Bay asked.

"Nothing, thank you." Sabrina sniffed the fresh brew. It smelled wonderful and she was feeling a little more cheerful. The heat from the coffee cup made it easy to find. The fingers of one hand closed around its reassuring warmth. A silence followed, one that Sabrina was pleasantly surprised to discover was actually comfortable. Her first meeting with Bay Cameron hadn't gone well at all, considering his arrogance. Which was still in operation, proved by the very fact that he had maneuvered her into this café, but it had somehow been tempered by his understanding.

In spite of that disturbing argument about the white cane, he seemed to approve of her desire for independence. The assistance he'd given her had been unobtrusive. That, along with his matter-of-fact comment about the loss of her career, made Sabrina wonder if she shouldn't reassess him. Bay Cameron seemed to be an unusual man. She wished she'd met him before she lost her sight. He might have made an interesting subject for a portrait. Then she sighed.

"What was that for?" he asked.

"I was wishing for something."

"Do you do that a lot?"

"Only when I have nothing to distract me. You know, when I'm alone, sometimes I wonder," she ran a finger around the rim of her cup, "if I hadn't had the gift of seeing people, places, and things in minute detail early in life so I could store up a treasure of beautiful scenes to remember."

"Do you believe in fate, then?" Bay asked quietly.

"Sometimes it seems like the only explanation. Do you?" Sabrina countered.

"I believe we were given abilities and talents that are unique to each of us. What we do with them is the mark of our own character. I can't accept that I might not be the master of my own destiny." His reply was laced with humor directed at himself.

"I bet there's very little you wanted that you haven't got," she said with a faint smile.

"Maybe. Or it could be that I've just been careful about what I wanted." The smile faded from his voice. "Tell me something. How long has it been since you lost your sight?"

She was beginning to learn that Bay Cameron had a habit of coming straight to the point. Most of the people she knew or had met took special care to avoid any reference to her blindness and took pains that the conversation didn't contain words that referred to sight. Not even an ordinary "I see."

"Almost eight months." She wondered why his frankness didn't disconcert her. Maybe it was because he didn't seem embarrassed or self-conscious about her blindness.

"No days or hours?" She got the impression that he'd raised his eyebrows.

"I stopped trying to keep an exact count after the fourth specialist told me and my father that I would never see again." Sabrina tried to sound nonchalant, but there was a hopeful catch in her voice.

"What happened?"

"A car crash happened. It was late at night. I was driving home from Sacramento and fell asleep at the wheel. I don't remember anything after that." Her fingers fluttered uncertainly in the air, then returned to grip the coffee cup. "I came to in a hospital. There weren't any witnesses. Somebody driving by saw my car in the ditch—the police estimate said that was several hours after the accident."

Sabrina waited for the usual comments that followed when she related the details of the accident, the it-could-have-been-worse and the you're-lucky-you-weren't-paralyzed-or-maimed remarks. But Bay spared her that.

"What are you going to do now?"

"I don't know." She didn't have the answer to that problem. She took a sip of her coffee. "I've just been taking it one day at a time, learning all over again how to do all the things I used to take for granted. I was so positive that I was going to have a career in art that I never studied anything else outside of the core curriculum, you know, what everybody has to take. I'm going to have to make a decision about my future pretty soon, though," she sighed. "I don't want to be a burden on my dad."

"I really doubt he thinks of you that way."

"I know *he* doesn't." She didn't really mean to put qualifying emphasis on the masculine pronoun, but it was out there.

Bay Cameron was much too observant to miss it. "But someone else does, is that it?" he asked. "Do you mean your father's fiancée?"

Sabrina opened her mouth to deny it, then nodded reluctantly. "I don't blame Deborah. She wants Dad to herself—" She hesitated. "I don't want you to misunderstand me. I do like her. As a matter of fact, I'm the one who introduced her to him. She has a small antique shop here in San Francisco. It's just that we both know it would never work for the two of us to live in the same house. She wants me to go to some school she heard about where blind people are taught legitimate skills. I know the computer workshops they have are really good—they have state-of-the-art voice recognition software that was developed at Stanford just for them. And they have a job placement program, which is great, because about seventy percent of blind people are unemployed. But I don't love working on a computer, whether I can see it or not."

"What does your father think of you going to a place like that?"

"I'm not sure she's mentioned it to him. Yet." A wry smile pulled her mouth into a crooked line. "I think she wants me to feel guilty about being dependent so I'll be in favor of it when Dad brings up the subject."

"Do you feel guilty?" Bay asked.

"I suppose so. It's only natural, isn't it?" Sabrina spread out the fingers of her hands on the table top, looking at them as if she could see them. "Everyone wants to be able to take care of themselves."

"But you do."

She shook her head. "Not entirely. I mean, I help out and take care of the house and do a lot of cooking. But I couldn't keep doing that after Dad and Deborah are married. After all, it would be her house then." She continued staring sightlessly at her long fingers. "I know I could learn something new to do that was worthwhile." She blew out a sigh and folded her hands around the warm cup. "Maybe I'm too proud. Or self-important. I'm not sure which."

"Maybe you're not either one," he said in a kind voice. "Maybe you just haven't figured out what you really want to do."

"I did know. I wanted to be an artist—I was an artist," she corrected herself. "Which was so great and so meaningful to me that I'm putting off the day when I have to give up the idea of it and do something else."

"What does your boyfriend say to all this?"

"Huh? I don't have a boyfriend. Okay, I do have friends who are guys, but no boyfriends," Sabrina denied firmly.

"You're a really pretty girl. I find it hard to believe that you didn't have something going on with someone," Bay commented in a doubting voice.

"I always had my career." She shrugged. "But I dated a lot, if you really want to know. I just sort of steered clear of major involvement. True love and marriage—well, I thought that was going to happen in the future. I'm glad now that I didn't get all tangled up in a romance," she added frankly. "How many men would want a blind wife?"

"Okay, you're entitled to your opinion, but isn't that a somewhat cynical take on the male sex?"

She smiled. "Not really. It's not even a cynical view of love. It's just realistic. Being blind tends to make people who are sighted feel awkward and self-conscious. They're always trying to be so careful that they don't hurt your feelings."

"I can see how that would happen—aw, hell," he said. "Sorry."

"That's exactly what I mean. You see and I don't,

so saying some little thing like that without thinking gets people all in a tizzy. Doesn't bother me, though."

"That's funny," he mused. "Except for that dumb gaffe, I don't feel uncomfortable, awkward, or self-conscious around you. I just like being with you."

For a moment, Sabrina was flustered by his observation. Mostly because it was true. There were no undercurrents of tension flowing around her.

"Actually I wasn't thinking about you," she admitted. "I was referring to some of my other friends, male and female. They all still keep in touch, the ones that count. They call or stop by to see me or invite me out, but it's not really the same. With some of them, what we had in common was art, so I understand why they don't like to bring up the subject in front of me. The others . . . oh, I don't know. There's just a vague uneasiness on both sides. With you—" Sabrina tilted her head quizzically. "I don't really understand it. I'm talking to you about things you couldn't possibly be interested in and I don't know why." A little frown of puzzled bewilderment puckered her brows.

"Hmm," was all he said.

Sabrina sensed his smile.

"Anyway," he went on. "I wasn't at all bored. I imagine all of this has been building up inside you for some time. It can be easier to talk to people you don't know who don't have preconceived opinions. I happened to be there and ready to listen."

"In that case, what wise advice do you have to offer me?" she asked with an impertinent smile.

"My advice? Um, be careful what you say to friendly strangers." The laughter was obvious in his low tone as he dodged her question.

Hurried footsteps approached their booth. "Would you like some more coffee?" the waitress asked.

"No more for me, thanks," Sabrina said. Her fingers touched the braille face of her watch. "I have to be getting home."

"Our check, please," Bay said.

By the time Sabrina had slid out of the booth seat, Bay was at her side, handing her the oak cane. His hand again rested lightly on the back of her waist, guiding her discreetly past the row of booths and tables to the café door. She waited there while he paid the check.

Once outside and up the stairs to the sidewalk, Bay asked, "Did you say you lived only a few blocks from here?"

"Yes." Sabrina turned her head toward him, the smile coming more easily and more often to her mouth. "And it's uphill all the way."

"Well, there's one consolation. When you get tired of walking up the hills of San Francisco, you can always lean against them."

Sabrina laughed at the funny statement. "True enough."

"Hey, that's nice to hear," Bay said, brightening at her laugh. "I was beginning to think you took everything seriously. I'm glad you don't."

Her heart seemed to skip a few beats. Sabrina discovered that she wanted to believe that was a personal comment and not a casual observation. That put her on dangerous ground, so she kept silent.

"My car is right around the corner," Bay said as if he hadn't expected her to reply. "Let me give you a ride home."

It was past the hour Sabrina had told Peggy Collins

she would be gone. That was why she agreed to his offer, giving him the address of the narrow Victorian house in the Pacific Heights neighborhood. Rush hour had begun, so there was very little conversation between them in the car. Using the traffic sounds at the intersection as a guide, Sabrina was able to judge when Bay turned on the block where she lived.

"Our house is the dark gold one with the brown and white trim," she told him. "The number is kinda hard to see sometimes."

A few seconds later, he was turning the wheels into the curb, setting the emergency brake, and shutting off the motor. He had just walked around the car and opened her door when Sabrina heard her neighbor call out.

"Sabrina, are you all right?" The question was followed immediately by the sound of the redwood gate opening and Peggy Collins's footsteps hurrying toward them. "I was just coming to see if you'd come home and forgotten to let me know."

"I was out longer than I expected to be," Sabrina said, explaining the obvious.

"So I see." The curious tone of voice also said that her neighbor saw the man Sabrina was with and was waiting to be introduced.

"Peggy, this is Bay Cameron. Peggy Collins is my neighbor."

There was a polite exchange of greetings before Bay turned to Sabrina. "It's my turn to say I have to be going, Sabrina."

"Thank you for the coffee and the ride home." She offered her hand to him in goodbye.

"My pleasure." His grasp was warm and sure and all too brief. "I'll see you again sometime."

The last sounded very much like a promise. Sabrina hoped that it was. The arrogance she'd noticed in him at their first meeting was completely erased. It was really strange how readily she had confided in him, she thought as she heard the car door open and close and the motor start. Not even to her father, who was very close to her, had Sabrina been able to talk that freely.

"Where did you meet him?" Peggy asked with more than idle curiosity.

"The other day at the yacht harbor when Deborah and I went to pick up Dad," she explained, forgetting for an instant that her neighbor was standing beside her. "I just bumped into him this afternoon—well, not literally," Sabrina qualified. Her head followed the sound of the departing car until she could no longer hear it. She turned toward the older woman. "Peggy, what does he look like?"

The woman paused, collecting her thoughts. "He's tall, in his thirties, I would say. He has reddish-brown hair and brown eyes. Not dark brown but they are brown. I wouldn't call him handsome exactly. Good-looking isn't the right description either, although in a way they both fit." There was another hesitation. "He looks like a real man. Do you know what I mean?"

"Yes," Sabrina replied softly. "Yes, I think I do," guessing that his features were too strong and forceful to be classified in any other way.

"Oh, my," Peggy exclaimed suddenly. "I forgot to put the potatoes in the oven. The meatloaf will get lonely. I'll talk to you later, Sabrina."

"Okay, Peggy." Her neighbor was already retreating to her door by the time Sabrina acknowledged her words.

Chapter 3

"Are you positive you want to walk out on the docks, Sabrina?" Deborah asked sharply.

"Yes. Is that a problem?" Sabrina realized that the question probably came across as rude, which wasn't her conscious intent, but her father's fiancée exasperated her more often than not. "I mean, do you want time alone with Dad?"

"It's not that," the redhead sighed. "Grant just worries about you so much, Sabrina. There aren't any railings on the docks and he's going to be concerned about your safety."

"All parents worry, Deborah," Sabrina said quietly. "Dad feels he has more to worry about than most, of course. But I can't spend the rest of my life indoors. I'm going semi-nuts as it is."

"Believe me, if I could find a way to make him stop worrying about you, I would do it," was Deborah's response as she stepped out of the car.

Sabrina followed but more slowly, walking around the car parked in the lot of the yacht harbor to Deborah's side.

"Has Dad said anything about setting the date?"
Sabrina asked as they started toward the fence gates.

"No, and I haven't brought it up." There was a
pause before Deborah continued. "A long time ago
I accepted the fact that I am who I am."

Meaning jealous. And possessive. Sabrina said neither
phrase out loud.

"If I married your father while you were still living
at home, it would create friction among all of us.
You would be hurt, your father would be hurt, and I
would be hurt. I'm well aware that you're a very independent person, of course," she said all in a rush,
"and that you don't want to be a burden to your
father for the rest of your life."

And you're so tactful too, Sabrina added mentally.

"I respect that in you," Deborah finished up.

"Which is why you're pushing the idea of this
school." Sabrina took a deep, calming breath.

"It may not be the answer, Sabrina, but it's worth
considering," Deborah suggested earnestly.

"I need more time." Sabrina lifted her face, enjoying the ocean breeze. "I keep hoping there'll be
some other alternative. I don't know what, but there
must be something. I guess I should look it up
online. The voice recognition software reads everything aloud for me."

"Yes," Deborah murmured. "So useful—I'm glad
you have that. But do keep the school in mind."

"I am," she sighed, "whether I like the idea or not."

"Thank you." Deborah's voice trembled slightly
before it steadied with determination. "I like you,
Sabrina, but I love your father. I've waited a long
time to meet a man like him. So please understand.
It's not that I'm pushing you out of the house."

No, not at all.

The planks of the dock were beneath Sabrina's feet as the harbor gate closed behind them. "If I was in love, I would be as anxious as you, I guess. But I won't be rushed into a decision, not unless I'm sure there isn't anything else."

Deborah's manicured hand guided her on. "Turn left here."

Her father's fiancée was aware of Sabrina's stubborn streak. This would be the time to drop the subject, when she'd won a small part of the battle. A very small part. Sabrina had agreed to think about it. That was all. She changed the subject.

"Is Dad on the boat?"

"Yes, he came in a little while ago. Now he's tying himself and everything else in nice neat sailor knots," was the reply.

Score a point for Deborah, Sabrina thought. She wasn't stupid or totally without a sense of humor.

A few minutes later, Deborah called out, "Hello, Grant. Did you have a good time?"

"Of course. Maybe I shouldn't sail solo, but I love it." There was a contented happiness in her father's voice that brought a smile to Sabrina's lips. "Sabrina? I didn't expect to see you with Deborah."

She picked up on the note of worry and sighed inwardly. "It was too nice a day to wait by the car." She waved away his concern. "Don't worry, I'll be a good girl and stay in the center of the dock."

"I'll only be a few more minutes."

"Then I'll get your thermos and things from the cabin if you like, Grant," Deborah offered.

There was hesitation before the suggestion was accepted. Sabrina knew her father was reluctant to leave her alone on the dock. His agreement was probably an indication that Deborah had shot him a don't-hover look.

The creak of the boat was accompanied by the quiet lapping of the water against its hull. There was the flapping of wings near where Sabrina stood, followed by the cry of a gull. The ocean scent of salt and fish was in the breeze lifting the hair away from her forehead.

A tickling sensation teased the back of her neck. Instantly Sabrina was alert to the sound of footsteps approaching, made by more than one pair of feet. Intuition said it was Bay Cameron and she knew all along that she'd been hoping he would be there. But he was with someone, more than one, maybe three other people. The light tread of one pair of feet warned her that they belonged to someone female.

"Are you calling it a day, Grant?" Bay's voice called out in greeting.

"Bay! How are ya?" her father said with startled pleasure. "Yes, this is it for me until next week. Are you coming in or going out?"

"Out. I thought we'd take in an ocean sunset," he replied, confirming that the other footsteps she had heard were with him. He had stopped beside her. Sabrina's radar told her he was only inches from her left side. "How are you today, Sabrina?"

"Fine." Her head bobbed in a self-conscious nod. She sensed the eagerness of the others, despite their silence, to be on their way.

"I see you made it all the way onto the dock with no problems. Did you do it by yourself?" The words were spoken so low and soft that no one heard them but Sabrina.

"No," she murmured, barely moving her lips.

"Bay, are you coming?" an impatient female voice asked.

"Yes, Roni," he answered, To Sabrina, he said, "Hope to see you again." That was about it for his goodbye to her.

"Good sailing!" her father called out, but Sabrina said nothing.

A faint feeling of depression had set in, intensified when the wind carried the woman's haughty-sounding question about who "those people" were, but her acute hearing couldn't catch Bay's response.

Her fingers tightened around the handle of her oak cane. She was glad at least that her cane wasn't white and conspicuous, identifying her to Bay's pals as legally blind. She couldn't have endured sensing their looks of pointless pity. It was bad enough imagining the explanation Bay was giving them now. She wished she hadn't allowed him to talk her into having coffee with him the other day, hadn't poured out her troubles to him with a complete lack of discretion.

"Are you ready yet, Dad?" she asked, suddenly anxious to be gone, no longer enjoying the scent and sounds of the harbor.

"Be right there," he answered. "Have you got everything, Deborah?"

"Yes."

Seconds later, the two of them were at Sabrina's side, her father's arm around her shoulders, guiding her back the way she had come. For once she didn't try to shrug away his assistance. She wanted the protective comfort of his arm.

* * *

She had tried to block out the memory of that Sunday, but it remained a shadow lurking near the edges of her already dark world. The melancholy violin concerto on the sound system wasn't easing her gloomy mood. The position of the furniture in their house had long been memorized and she walked unerringly to the sound system shelves and switched off the music.

The front doorbell buzzed loudly in the ensuing silence. She reminded herself to ask her dad to install soothing chimes or anything that wouldn't make her jump at least a foot in the air every time it rang. With an impatient sigh, Sabrina continued to the intercom that linked the street level entrance next to the garage with the living area of the house.

"Yes. Who is it?" she asked briskly after her fingers found the switch.

"Bay Cameron."

A surprised stillness kept her silent for ticking seconds. There was no warmth in her voice when she asked, "What was it you wanted?"

"Well, I'm not selling anything," his amused voice answered. "The only reason I can think of for why I might be standing in front of your door is to see you."

"Why?"

"You know, I never did like talking to squawky intercoms. Come on down."

Sabrina sighed with annoyance. "I'll be there in a minute," she said and flicked off the switch.

She opened the door to the stairwell that led from the second floor to the street entrance. There were two doors at the base of the stairs, one leading to the garage that occupied the ground floor and the second to the sidewalk and the street.

Opening the second door, Sabrina walked four paces and stopped. There was a wrought iron gate less than a foot in front of her, preventing direct access to the house by people on the street. Bay was on the other side of that gate, saying hello the second he saw her.

"Here I am. What's up?" she asked.

"Can I come in?"

She couldn't say no. Her father seemed to think Bay was just peachy-keen and here he was. She unlocked the gate, swinging it open to allow him into the small foyer. Sabrina stepped back, clasping her hands in front of her in a prim pose.

"Why did you want to see me?"

He chuckled. "Because it's what a San Francisco native would call a really unusual day. There's not a cloud in the sky. The sun is shining. The breeze is light and warm. It's a perfect day for a walk," Bay concluded. "So I stopped by to see if you'd come with me."

Sabrina doubted the sincerity of his words. She couldn't believe that his motive for asking her out was a genuine interest in her company. He had to be feeling sorry for her.

"Well, sorry. I can't." She refused for a real reason.

"Why not?"

An actual no. He seemed flummoxed. Sabrina could visualize the look on his face.

"I'm fixing a pot roast for dinner. I have to put it in the oven in"—she touched the braille face of her watch—"forty-five minutes. So you see, if I went for a walk with you, we would barely be gone and we'd have to come back. An hour after that I'll have to be here to add the potatoes, carrots, and onions."

"Sounds like an awesome responsibility," he joked.

She sniffed. "I started it and I'm going to finish it."

"So that's the reason, the whole reason, and nothing but the reason?"

"That's it," Sabrina said firmly.

"Well, we can take care of that," Bay said complacently. "Your oven has a timer. While you're getting the roast ready, I'll set the timer to turn the oven on in forty-five minutes. Put the roast in now and we'll have nearly two hours for a walk before you have to be back to deal with the potatoes, carrots, and onions. My mother used to add a couple of bay leaves and five bouillon cubes at that point. You should try it."

"But—" She tried to protest but her mind went blank.

"But what? Don't you want to go for a walk? It's really much too beautiful to stay indoors."

"Oh, all right." She blew out an exasperated breath, turning toward the door.

His throaty chuckle mocked her obvious reluctance. "I'm amazed at how graciously you always accept my invitations," Bay said.

"Maybe because it's because I can't help wondering why you make them," Sabrina responded.

"I get the impression," he reached around and opened the door for her before her searching hands found the knob, "if you ever stopped being defensive over the fact that you're blind, you just might be pleasant company."

Again Sabrina bridled silently at his subtle-as-a-brick hint that she spent too much time feeling sorry for herself. When her entire life and future had been based on the ability of her eyes to see the things her hands would paint, it was only natural that she would be bitter sometimes. Even he needed to acknowledge that and cut her some slack.

Bay Cameron seemed to live on his own planet with his own laws, she decided. She led him up the stairs, through the dining room into the kitchen. By the time she had the meat seasoned and in the roasting pan, he had the oven timer set.

"Are we ready to leave now?" Bay asked.

"I have to call my father." She ran her palms nervously over her rounded hips. "When Peggy Collins, our neighbor, is gone, he likes me to let him know where I'm going and when I'll be back."

"Good plan. I'm all for it. Along with white canes and obeying the rules at intersections."

She stiffened. "You really have a thing about being protective, don't you? Have you ever considered a new career as a crossing guard?"

"Hey, crossing guards are unsung heroes, in my opinion."

She knew that he was joking—and serious at the same time. She didn't know what to say.

"Anyway, go ahead and call your father."

"Thank you, I will. I might even have remembered to do it without you reminding me," Sabrina snapped.

The receptionist at her father's law firm, well trained to keep casual callers on hold forever, put her call to him through immediately. Sabrina explained that Peggy wasn't home and she was calling to let him know she was going to be out for a while, not mentioning with whom.

"How long will you be?" Grant Lane asked.

"A couple of hours. I'll call as soon as I'm back."

"Okay. Take your cell. Not that I want to check up on you or anything, but I don't like you wandering around the streets on your own for too long, even when the weather's nice."

"I'll be fine." She wasn't eager to tell him that she was going out with Bay Cameron. "Don't start worrying, Dad."

A masculine arm reached around her and took the receiver. Sabrina tried to take it back, even pummeled him once or twice. It was no use. His chest was rock hard.

"Grant, this is Bay Cameron. Sabrina will be with me. I don't know why she didn't tell you that. I'll see that she's back in time so that your dinner won't be ruined. It's pot roast. Going to be the best you ever had."

She could hear her father laugh and make some affirmative reply, then Bay said goodbye and hung up. "He asked me to tell you to have a good time."

"Thanks," she said caustically and walked to the closet to get her lightweight coat.

Retrieving her cane from the umbrella stand, she heard Bay open the stair door.

"Got your keys?"

"Yes." She walked quickly through the opening, listening to him lock the door behind him before following her down the stairs to the street.

"I thought we'd take the Hyde Street cable car

down to Ghirardelli Square. Is that all right?" There was an underlying note of amusement in his voice, suggesting that he found her sulky display of temper pretty funny.

"Whatever you like." She shrugged her shoulders stiffly.

He didn't complain about her less-than-courteous acceptance of his plan. In fact, he said not another word. If it hadn't been for him taking her elbow at the traffic intersections, Sabrina might have been walking the blocks to the cable car stop alone. Except for a thank-you when he helped her on and off the cable car, she didn't address any remarks to him either.

"Are you finished pouting yet?" His question held barely hidden laughter as he maneuvered her, his hand at her waist, through the stream of summer tourists.

"I wasn't pouting."

"No?"

"Maybe a little," she acknowledged reluctantly, a trace of her anger remaining. "But you can be insufferably bossy at times."

"I think you just get your way too much. The people who care about you don't like to say no to you," he observed.

"I'm sure you're no day at the beach yourself," she said dryly.

"True enough." Again there was a lazy acceptance of her criticism. "But we weren't talking about me. You were the one who was pouting."

"Only because you were taking over and running things without being asked," Sabrina retorted.

"So now what? Do you maintain a state of war or

just walk with me? We could be friends." She could feel his eyes on her face. "We didn't get along too badly the other day."

Sabrina breathed in deeply, feeling herself surrendering to the potent charm of his low voice. "Friends," she agreed, against her better judgment.

Once she had succumbed it was easy to let herself be warmed by his, well, friendliness as he steered the conversation to less volatile subjects. They wandered around the fountain in the center plaza of the old Ghirardelli Chocolate factory, long since renovated into a popular area of fun little shops and upscale chain stores. They stopped at one of the outdoor cafés and sampled thin, delicious crepes, freshly made.

Their strolling pace took them by the windows of the multilevel shops in the buildings that made up the square. Bay laughingly challenged Sabrina to identify the type of store by sound and scent. She did quite well at the flower and leather shops and identifying what national cuisine was served at the various restaurants, but the jewelry, gift, and import stores she missed entirely.

When Bay stopped in front of another shop window, she gave a defeated sigh. "I'm really out of steam. Please, no more guesses."

"You got it," he agreed absently. "I'll tell you what this one is. It's a dressmaker's shop. The sign says Original Fashions by Jacobina. There's a dress in the window and I'd swear it was made for you. Come on." His hand on her back expressed his interest in it. "We'll go in so you can see it."

Instantly Sabrina moved away from him. "That's logically and literally impossible. I can't see it. Can we skip it?"

"Why?" he asked patiently. "And what's with the indignant look? Where's all that creative imagination you were bragging about the other day? I'm taking you into this shop and you're going to see this dress with your hands."

Feeling somewhat abashed—she *had* bragged— Sabrina let him escort her through the doors. A tiny bell rang above their heads as they entered. Immediately someone approached from the back of the store.

"May I help you?" a woman's voice asked.

"Yes," Bay answered. "We'd like to look at the dress in the window."

"We don't sell ready-made dresses here, sir," the woman replied politely. "That's a one-of-a-kind sample. We make another from the pattern for it using the exact measurements of each customer."

"Let me explain what I mean." His velvet charm filled his voice. "Miss Lane is blind. I admired the dress in the window and wanted her to see it. In order for her to do that, she has to touch it. Would that be possible?"

"Of course, I'm sorry. It will only take me a few minutes to remove it from the mannequin," the woman said quickly and warmly.

Her words were followed by a rustle of motion and material. Sabrina shifted uncomfortably and felt Bay touch her shoulder in reassurance. Several minutes later there was a silky swish of material presented to her.

"Here you are, Miss Lane," the clerk said.

"Would you describe it for her?"

"Of course," the woman said. "Miss Jacobina calls this dress 'Flame.' Its colors seem to change—there's red, gold, orange, and yellow in irregular panels of chiffon that curl at the end like tongues of flame." Sabrina's fingers lightly traced the edges of the many layers. "The neckline is vee-shaped but not plunging. The illusion of sleeves is created by the cutaway wings of chiffon from the neckline, draping over the shoulders and the bodice."

As she explored more of the dress Sabrina's mind began to form a picture with the help of the clerk, who had a talent for description.

"It's beautiful," Sabrina murmured.

"What size is this sample?" Bay asked. The woman told him. "Would that fit you, Sabrina?"

She nodded. "I think so."

"Can you bend the rules and allow her to try it on?" he asked the clerk, again in that incredibly persuasive tone that Sabrina was sure no woman could resist.

The clerk took a deep breath and gave a little laugh. "I don't know why not. We have a changing room in the back. Miss Lane, if you'd like to come with me—"

Sabrina hesitated and Bay gave her a little push forward. "Go on. Let's see what it looks like. It's so silky. Tell me what it feels like when you get it on."

"Oh, right. In your dreams, Bay," she said to him, but under her breath.

He chuckled.

"Why do I let you talk me into things?" she sighed.

"Because deep down you enjoy it," he teased. "Besides, I bet you haven't bought anything really nice for yourself since the accident."

"I haven't needed anything," Sabrina protested.

"When has that ever been a valid reason to a

woman?" Bay mocked. "Now go try that gorgeous dress on. That's an order."

"Yes, sir." She didn't really need to be persuaded. The vision in her mind and the feel of the expensive material already had her excited about wearing it even if she couldn't see exactly how she would look in it.

Changing swiftly out of her jeans and tops once she was in the dressing room, she only needed the assistance of the clerk with the invisible zipper, so deftly sewn in between the back panels that she almost couldn't find it. With her hand resting lightly on the woman's arm, she moved nervously to the front of the store where Bay waited.

"Well?" Sabrina asked breathlessly when the silence stretched out. Her head was tilted to one side in a listening attitude.

"You look absolutely beautiful, Sabrina," Bay said.

"That's an understatement," the clerk added. "You make that dress and not the other way around. You're stunning in it and I'm not just saying that because I work here. The sample might have been custom made for you. The style, the color—everything suits you perfectly. It's amazing, but you must have the same measurements as the figure model it was designed on."

Sabrina's fingers ran down the neckline of the dress, trailing off with a draping fold of the fiery chiffon. "Could you—would you sell this one?" she asked hopefully.

"We never do." The woman hesitated, then added with a smile in her voice, "But there's an exception to every rule, isn't there? And besides, we have the pattern safely locked up and we can always make another if we order the fabric from New York. Let me check, Miss Lane."

When the woman had left, Sabrina turned again to Bay. "Are you sure it looks that good?" she asked anxiously.

She felt the air move as he waved his hand in a dismissing gesture. "Looking for compliments?"

"No." She ran her hands over the waist and glanced sightlessly at the floating material cascading over her arms. "It's just that it's probably really expensive and I want to be sure—"

"You should be." With cat-quiet footsteps over the lush carpeting of the exclusive shop, he was at her side, lifting her chin with his finger. "I told you the truth. You look beautiful in that dress."

She wished she could see his expression. She didn't doubt the sincerity in his voice, but she had a feeling, just a shadow of one, that he was a little withdrawn. Her dark bangs hid the frown that knitted her forehead.

"Now what's bothering you?" Bay asked.

"I—" Her chin was released as he stepped away. "I was just wondering where I would ever wear this."

"Sometime there'll be an occasion and this dress will be just right for it. Then you'll be glad you bought it," he replied in an indulgent tone.

"I never asked how much it is," she murmured. Then a related thought made her shoulders droop. "I have hardly any money with me and I left my credit cards at home. Do you suppose I could give them a little to hold it and then Dad and I could come back later with the rest?"

"I could pay for it," Bay said guardedly.

Sabrina bit into her lower lip, eager to possess the

glorious dress, but unwilling to owe anything to a man who was not exactly her friend and not a stranger either.

"Hm. Well, if it wouldn't be too much trouble," her acceptance was hesitant, "you could write down your address and the amount. I'll have Dad mail you a check tonight. I'll go halfsies with him on it. He won't say no."

"You wouldn't consider accepting the dress as a gift?"

Sabrina drew back. "No way." She shook her head vigorously, ready to argue the point.

"No problem. I didn't think you would." He sounded a little disappointed. "All right, I'll loan you the money for it."

"Thank you," Sabrina breathed, relieved the interchange wasn't going to end in a quarrel.

"Instead of your father mailing me a check, why don't I stop by your house Friday afternoon?" he suggested.

"If you like," she frowned.

"I would like." The smile was back in his voice and she gave him an answering one.

The sales associate returned with the information that they would sell the sample dress to Sabrina. The price wasn't as high as she expected. While she changed back into her jeans and top, Bay took care of the purchase.

Outside the store he gave her the unwelcome news that they'd used up the two hours and it was time for him to take her back to the house. He suggested that instead of taking the cable car, then walking the several blocks to her house, that they take a taxi. At this point, Sabrina would have preferred to prolong the outing or whatever it was, but there had been a subtle change in his attitude, so she agreed to his suggestion.

"I'll see you Friday afternoon around two," Bay repeated, stopping inside the iron gate but not following her into the house.

"Would you like to come in for coffee?" she offered.

"I'll take a raincheck on that for Friday," he said.

"All right. Till Friday," Sabrina agreed with a faint smile.

Chapter 4

Sabrina touched the face of her watch. Two o'clock. She reached to be certain the check was still on the coffee table where her father had put it this morning. It was. She leaned against the couch cushions, rubbing the back of her neck to try and relax the tense muscles. It was crazy to be so on edge just because Bay was coming over, she told herself.

The front buzzer sounded and she hurried to the intercom, answering it with an eager "Yes?"

"It's me, Bay."

"I'll be right down."

Recklessly Sabrina nearly flew down the stairs. A smile wreathed her face as she opened the door and walked to the gate.

"You're right on time," she said.

"I try to be punctual." The warm huskiness of his voice swept over her as she unlocked the gate, swinging the wrought iron frame open to admit him.

"I have coffee all ready if you have time to stay," she offered.

"Great," Bay said. "Sure, sign me up."

Leading the way up the stairs to the second floor, Sabrina motioned to the living room. "Have a seat while I get the coffee tray. The check for the dress is on the table in front of the sofa."

Bay made no offer to help pour the coffee when she returned, letting her take the time to do it herself. He took the cup she held out to him, the almost silent swish of the cushions indicating that he'd leaned back against the chair next to the sofa.

"Nice house. The paintings on the wall, are they yours?" he asked.

"Yes," she said, carefully balancing a cup and saucer. "My father really likes my art, bless his heart. He chose those because he loves the sea and ships and all that. They're all ocean scenes."

"I like them too. Are they the only paintings you did?"

Sabrina sighed. "No." Her mouth tightened and she didn't say more.

"Show me the others. Later. Or whenever," Bay said softly.

"I'd really rather not." She took a sip of coffee, lifting her chin defiantly as she swallowed.

"Okay. I won't insist." He shrugged. "But I won't pretend I'm not curious why. If these are on the walls, I bet the ones that aren't are just as good."

Sabrina fidgeted nervously with the handle of her cup. Trying to act nonchalant, she set the cup and saucer on the table.

"I'll show them to you then." Not sure whether her change of mind had been prompted by the patience in his voice or by his flattery, she rose to her feet. "They're in the studio upstairs." She turned her head in his direction.

Bay got up too. "Lead the way."

Climbing the stairs to the upper floor, Sabrina trailed her hand along the wall until she came to the second door. The knob felt cold to her fingers as she swung the door open. The lingering scent of artist's paints and materials hung in the air.

"The studio isn't used anymore, so it's a bit stuffy," Sabrina explained self-consciously, stopping near the wall by the door.

Bay didn't comment. It really wasn't necessary. She listened to the quiet sounds as he wandered about the room, pausing sometimes to take a closer look at something that had caught his eye. Other times she could hear him moving canvases to see the paintings behind them. A tight sadness gripped her in its painful hold.

"They are all very good, Sabrina," he said at last. Her head turned in the direction of his voice, only a few feet from where she was standing near the door. "It's a shame to keep them hidden away up here."

"Dad and I have talked about selling them. We will some day." Sabrina swallowed to ease the constriction in her throat.

"Did you ever do any modeling?"

"Modeling? No," she replied, striving for a light tone, even though she knew neither of them would be fooled by it. "I was always the one painting the person who was posing."

"I meant modeling in clay," Bay explained. Quiet, unhurried footsteps brought him to her side. His hand touched her arm to turn her to the open door.

"Oh, that—yes. When I was studying Materials and Methods 101," Sabrina said with a slight frown. "Why?"

"Have you ever considered taking it up now that you're blind?"

"No." She shook her head.

Without thinking she had allowed him to lead her into the hallway. His question had been unexpected and it set off a chain of thoughts. The closing of the studio door brought her back to their surroundings.

The subject wasn't explored further as Bay let her descend the stairs ahead of him, maybe because he was allowing her to mull over the idea without attempting to influence her.

In spite of an understandable reluctance to do something so different from what she knew well, which was painting, the idea appealed to her.

The coffee Sabrina poured had grown cold. While she emptied the cups, there was more time to contemplate his indirect suggestion. She marveled that none of her art-scene friends had mentioned it, ever. Maybe the objectivity of someone new had been needed.

"I meant to ask," Bay said when Sabrina handed him his cup refilled with hot coffee from the insulated pot, "whether you and your dad had plans for tomorrow night."

Her own cup was half-filled, the coffee pot poised above it for a split second. "No," Sabrina answered. "Dad spends Saturday afternoon and evening with Deborah. Why?"

"I thought we could have dinner somewhere. It would give you an excuse to wear your new dress."

"No thanks." Her tone was a little curt.

"So you have other plans."

"I don't."

"Then do you mind if I ask why you don't want

to have dinner with me?" He seemed completely unfazed by her cold rejection.

"Ask away." With a proud set to her head, Sabrina replaced the coffeepot on the tray and leaned against the sofa, protectively cradling the cup in her hands. "I just don't like eating at public restaurants. You get me into the café, but it's too easy to knock over glasses and drop food on the floor. It's embarrassing," she concluded self-consciously.

"I'm willing to risk it," Bay said.

"Well, I'm not." Impatiently she took a sip of the hot coffee, scalding her tongue a little.

"Okay. If that doesn't interest you"—there was a hint of amusement in his voice—"then would you consider a less formal suggestion? For instance, we could get cooked shrimp and crabcakes to go at Fisherman's Wharf, plus sourdough bread and salad, then have a picnic somewhere along the promenade or out at Fort Point."

Sabrina hesitated. It sounded like fun, but she wasn't certain she should accept his invitation. In between the moments when she was aggravated by his arrogance, she had discovered that she liked him. But she doubted they were going to be lasting friends.

"Is it so hard to say yes?" Bay teased.

His gentle mockery made her feel foolish. She was magnifying the importance of the invitation out of all proportion. A faint flush came to her cheeks.

"It isn't difficult," she murmured, bending her head toward the cup she held to hide her embarrassment. "Okay, I accept."

"Would six o'clock be all right, or would you rather I picked you up earlier?"

"Six is fine." There was a thump from something falling to the floor. Her head came up with a start. "What was that?"

"It's a little something I bought for you as a present," Bay replied with studied casualness. "I meant to give it to you earlier, but I got sidetracked. I had it propped against my chair and I accidentally knocked it over. Here you go."

A long, narrow box was placed on her lap after Sabrina set her coffee cup on the table. Her hands rested motionless on the cardboard lid.

"Why did you buy me a present?" she asked warily.

"Because I wanted to—and please don't ask me to take it back, because I wouldn't have any use for it and neither would anyone else I know. I can't return it either," he stated.

"What is it?" Sabrina tilted her head curiously to the side.

"You'll have to open that box and find out for yourself," Bay answered noncommittally.

With a trace of nervous excitement, Sabrina eased the lid off the box and set it on the sofa. She could feel his alert gaze watching her. Her pulse accelerated slightly. Her exploring fingertips encountered tissue paper. It rustled softly as she pushed it aside to find what it protected.

The object in the box was round and hard. And several feet long, without being particularly thick. Sabrina knew what it was when her hand curled around it to lift it out of the box and she replaced it, folding her hands tightly in her lap.

"It's a cane, isn't it? White, I bet." She knew her voice sounded bitter. Well, too bad for Bay if he didn't like her response. The subject of canes was extremely touchy for her and he knew it.

"Yes," Bay admitted without any trace of remorse. "But it really isn't an ordinary white cane."

The box was removed from her lap. The action was followed almost instantly by a louder rustling of the tissue paper than she'd made, then the sound of the box being set aside.

Her lips pressed into an uncompromising line while her hands stayed folded right where they were. Bay's fingers closed over her wrist and firmly pulled her hands apart, ignoring the resistance she offered.

One hand he released. The second he held with little effort. The curving handle of the cane was pressed into her palm. Bay wasn't forcing her . . . she gave in and took hold of it.

Sabrina's first impression was of a smooth, almost glassy surface, then her sensitive touch found the carved part. Almost unwillingly her fingertips explored the design. It was several seconds before she followed the intricate serpentine lines to the handle. There—she got what it was: the head of a dragon.

"It's carved out of ivory," Bay explained. "I saw it in a shop window in Chinatown the other day. They were going out of business, so it was a final sale."

"It's very beautiful," Sabrina admitted reluctantly. The hand covering hers relaxed its grip, no longer making sure she would hold on to the cane. She held it for a few more exploring moments. "It must have cost a lot," she said, extending it to him. "I couldn't possibly accept it."

"It's artistic in design but hardly an art object." He ignored the outstretched hand with the cane. "What you really mean is it's still white."

Sabrina didn't argue with his comment. "I can't accept it."

"I can't return it," Bay replied evenly.

"Sorry." She pushed the cane into his hands and released it. He had no choice but to hold on to it or let it fall to the floor.

"I know you were trying to be thoughtful, but you knew my views on the subject before you bought it, Bay. The cane is unique and beautiful, but I won't accept it. I get along very well with the one I have."

"Hm. Is that all you have to say?"

"Pretty much." She wasn't about to feel guilty for refusing the thing.

"I suppose if I try to persuade you to change your mind, you'll go back on your agreement to go out with me tomorrow night." He sighed in a resigned way.

"Maybe." She hoped, though, that he wouldn't put her in that position.

"Then I'll save my arguments for another time." Again she heard the rustle of tissue paper and the lid being replaced on the box. "Hey, I'm not giving up," Bay warned her, "just postponing this discussion. That's all."

"I'm not going to change my mind," Sabrina replied stubbornly, but with a trace of a smile on her mouth.

"I accept the challenge." She could hear the answering smile in his voice. "While we're still on speaking terms, can I have another cup of coffee?"

"Of course." She held out her hand for his cup and saucer.

The subject of the ivory cane didn't come up again, but when Bay left a half hour later, Sabrina made sure he had the box with him and didn't "accidentally" forget it.

That evening, when Deborah came over, Sabrina discovered that Bay had tricked her. She was listening to an audiobook on her iPod, and not paying a whole lot of attention.

"Where did you get this, Sabrina?" Deborah asked in a voice that was both curious and surprised.

The tone of the question got through her headphones. The audiobook was forgotten as she set the iPod aside and took them out. "Where did I get what?"

"This ivory cane. The handle has a dragon design carved on the sides. I found it on the floor beside the chair. Were you hiding it?"

"No, I wasn't." Sabrina felt mad enough to throw something but she didn't.

"It's very elegant," Deborah said. "So where's it from?"

"Hey, let me see," her father joined in. "Is this something you found the other day when you went out with Bay Cameron?"

"Dad, you should know by now that I would never buy a white cane, much less an ivory one," she retorted. "It was a present from Bay. I refused it, of course. I thought he'd taken it with him."

"Refused it?" Deborah questioned in amazement. "Why? It's one of a kind and carved by hand, as far as I can tell."

"Because I don't want it," Sabrina answered tautly. The sofa cushion beside her sank as it took her father's weight. His hand gently covered the rigid fingers resting in her lap.

"Aren't you being a little foolish, honey?"

The question was spoken respectfully enough, but that didn't mollify her. "No, I don't think so."

"Sabrina, we both know you didn't refuse it because you thought it was too expensive or because you didn't think it was beautiful. It's because it's white. And a white cane means you're blind. You can't escape that fact simply by not using a white cane."

"I don't want to advertise it!"

"People are bound to notice, no matter what type or color cane you have. There's no shame in being blind," Grant Lane argued.

"I'm not ashamed!"

"Sometimes you act like you are," he sighed.

"I suppose you think I should use it," she challenged with a defiant toss of her head.

"I'm your father, Sabrina. Take the chip off your shoulder." The mild reproof in his voice lessened the jutting angle of her chin. "Anyway, you're too old for me to tell you what to do. You get to decide. And that's that."

"Excuse me. I'm going to my room." Sabrina set the iPod and headphones on the table and rose to her feet.

It was impossible to argue when her father wouldn't argue back. She hated it when he appealed to her logical side. It invariably overruled her emotions.

"What should I do with the cane?" Deborah asked hesitantly.

"Put it in the umbrella stand for now," her father

answered. "Sabrina can decide what she wants to do before Bay comes over tomorrow night."

As Sabrina put her foot on the first step of the stairs leading to the upper floor and her bedroom, she heard Deborah ask, "Bay Cameron is coming tomorrow night? Why?"

"He's taking Sabrina to Fisherman's Wharf," her father replied. "It's touristy but it's fun. They'll have a grand old time."

"You mean a date?" his fiancée asked with amazed disbelief.

"I suppose you could call it that. He called me yesterday at the office after he'd seen Sabrina and actually asked if I had any objections."

"Isn't that sweet," Deborah said.

"I couldn't bring myself to ask him what, ah, his intentions were, as they used to say when I was his age. God, that seems like a thousand years ago."

"You seem young to me," Deborah cooed.

Sabrina, listening, scowled.

"Anyway, I said sure, fine," her father went on. "He's really been nice to her."

"Did he mention the cane?" Deborah asked.

"No, it was a complete surprise to me," he answered.

Sabrina sighed with relief. At least her father hadn't been conspiring with Bay to keep her on a straight and narrow path. For a moment there, she'd been worried. She should have realized that her father wouldn't do anything underhanded to trick her into making a decision he thought was to her advantage. It was a shame she couldn't say that about Bay.

Still, she had to concede that Bay meant well. He

hadn't forced her to accept the cane, just left it. And its presence had produced another dilemma, thanks to her father.

A few minutes before six o'clock, Sabrina sat on the sofa, nibbling on a fingernail. She reached out for the second time to be sure the hooded blue windbreaker was lying on the arm of the sofa. Then her pensive mood was broken by the front doorbell.

Quickly she pulled on the windbreaker, stuffing a small clutch purse in an oversized pocket. She ran a smoothing hand up the back of her neck, tucking any stray strands of hair into the knot atop her head. Her question into the intercom was answered, as she'd expected, by Bay.

"I'll be right down," she said, loud and clear.

Her hand closed over the doorknob, but she hesitated. Her sightless eyes looked down at the umbrella stand next to the door. Her other hand chose the smooth oak cane. For several more seconds she remained immobile, then with a resigned sigh, she removed her hand from old faithful and tentatively searched for the carved dragon head of the ivory cane.

Slowly she went down the stairs, testing it out. It had a different heft to it, it tapped differently, but she could get used to it. She opened the outside door and locked it behind her. Squaring her shoulders, she turned toward the iron gates and Bay.

"You took your time," he commented. "I was beginning to wonder what was keeping you."

"I had to put on my jacket," Sabrina lied, waiting for him to notice the ivory cane in her hand.

"My car's right over there," Bay said as she swung open the gates and joined him on the sidewalk.

His hand guided her to it. The suspense of waiting for him to say something triumphant began to build as he helped her into the car. When Bay still hadn't said anything after he was driving the car down the street, Sabrina knew she couldn't wait for him to find the right moment.

"Well?" she challenged him finally, turning her head toward him in a slightly defiant way.

"Well what?"

"Aren't you going to say anything about the cane?"

His low, calm voice remained controlled and unruffled.

"I should think you'd be feeling pretty smug. After all, you did leave it behind on purpose."

"I gave it to you, it was a present, and I don't take back presents. It was entirely up to you what you did with it. I never insisted that you use it. If you'd wanted to donate it to charity or give it to a friend, that would have been fine with me," Bay responded.

"Well, I have decided to use it," she stated, facing straight ahead.

"Good." The car turned and went down a steep hill. She lurched forward but the seatbelt caught and held her. "Not any different than wearing that. Just common sense. Now can we talk about something else?"

Sabrina sighed. "Sure."

It seemed as if every time she thought she knew how he would react, Bay did not do the expected. He should have crowed over winning the point, or been at least a little self-righteous. Instead, he was so calm and matter-of-fact that it was impossible for Sabrina to feel resentment. She had made the decision to use the ivory cane, not Bay, and he knew it.

At the bottom of the near-vertical street, Bay turned the car again. "I thought I'd park at the yacht harbor. We can follow the seawall by Fort Mason to Aquatic Park and on to Fisherman's Wharf. Okay with you?"

"Fine," Sabrina said.

Once the car was parked and locked, they started out at a strolling pace with Bay keeping Sabrina's left arm under his right. Gulls soared above, wheeling in the air, screaming with joy over scraps and shells. As they passed Fort Mason and neared the docks, the heavier, flapping wings of pelicans accompanied the gulls. The damp, salty smell of the air held more than a hint of fish.

Although the seafood stalls were their ultimate destination, they decided to walk farther and come back. The sidewalks were filled with tourists exploring the sights and sounds of the colorful area. A few were jostling and in a hurry but most took their time, enjoying the beautiful day just like Sabrina and Bay.

The churning propellers of a tour boat indicated the start of another harbor cruise. The highlights would be a close look at the Golden Gate Bridge, the Bay Bridge to Oakland, and the former maximum security island prison of Alcatraz. Now the island was a national park, only a mile out in the bay from the wharf.

At the end of the piers, they crossed the street to the rows of shops and slowly started back to the seafood stalls.

Sabrina lifted her face to the salty, damp breeze. "Is the fog coming in?"

"Starting to," Bay said. "It's just beginning to wrap around the tops of the towers of the Golden Gate and the Marin hills north of it. It might get thick tonight."

"In that case, I'll have to lead you back to the car." She grinned impishly and Bay chuckled. "I've been meaning to ask—how did you get the name Bay, anyway?"

"My parents gave it to me—or didn't you think I had any?"

She shook her head. "Not really. I just assumed you hatched from a dragon's egg."

He laughed out loud and made a zinging noise. "Good one, Sabrina. I love your sense of humor. Even when it's directed at me."

"So tell me about your folks," she said. "Are they still living?"

"Last I heard they were. They're in Europe taking a second honeymoon." His arm tightened fractionally as a warning. "You have to step down here."

"Is Bay a family name?" Sabrina asked as she negotiated the curb at the intersection.

"I wish it were. No, I was named after the obvious, the San Francisco Bay that my mother saw from the hospital window. She was born and raised here, so it seemed like a cool name to her, I guess. I don't mind it. People don't seem to forget it," he said. "So what about Sabrina?"

"My mother liked the sound of it. And I think she saw the movie with Audrey Hepburn about a thousand times. She was very romantic."

"And you're not?" he teased.

She smiled faintly. "Maybe a little bit."

Bay blew out a breath. "Hey, we've been walking for over an hour. Are you getting hungry?"

"Very close to starving, actually."

"You should've said something."

Sabrina shrugged her unconcern and breathed in the tantalizing aroma carried by the light breeze. "There's a souvlaki pushcart just across the street, isn't there?" She laughed. "All I have to do is follow my nose."

"Are you sure you wouldn't rather eat in one of the restaurants here?" Bay checked her movement into the street and a car drove slowly by.

"Positive. But I think I would rather have seafood. As in crab."

"You do have a good nose." He took her to the long row of stalls, where she listened to Bay ask for the biggest crabcakes the proprietor had, and a round loaf of sourdough bread, a salad, and Thai-seasoned shrimp on the side.

Sabrina pressed a hand against her rumbling stomach. The delicious smells were making her even more hungry. When the order was handed over, Bay gave her the bag to hold and asked her to wait outside while he bought a split of chilled white wine to go with it.

Tingles ran down the back of her neck an instant before his hand touched her arm, signaling his return. She decided that she must have telepathic powers—or else she was highly attuned to the guy.

"Ready for a picnic?" he asked. At that moment her stomach rudely growled the answer and they both laughed.

Taking the bag of food from her, Bay added it to

the one he already had in his arms. The hand she linked in his was not for guidance but companionship as they set out for the yacht harbor and the shoreline beyond.

They were at the edge of the harbor when Sabrina noticed the fine mist on her face had intensified. "It's drizzling," she complained.

"I was afraid we were in for more than fog." Bay sighed.

"I suppose we could always take the food to the house," Sabrina suggested.

"I have a better idea. My boat's tied up here. We can go aboard her. What do you say?"

She smiled. "That sounds like fun. Sure."

"Let's go!"

Bay had Sabrina wait on the dock while he stowed the food below. He was topside again when his strong hands spanned her waist and lifted her aboard. He maintained the hold for a steadying moment, her own hands resting on the muscles of his forearms. The dampness in the air increased the spicy smell of him and heightened the heady maleness that enfolded her. The deck beneath their feet moved rhythmically with the lapping waters of the bay.

"It's been so long since I've been on the water," Sabrina said with a poignant catch in her voice. "My sea legs are a little shaky, I guess." It seemed like a reasonable explanation for the way she was feeling.

With his arm, Bay guided her below deck. Making sure she had something to hold on to, he went down the steps ahead of her. Sabrina knew it was to catch her in case she fell. Once below, he told her where the seats were and let her make her own way to them.

"Do you like sailing?" he asked. The rustling of bags indicated he was getting the food out of them.

"Love it." A rueful expression came over her face. "I used to go out every weekend with Dad."

"You haven't been out since your accident? Why?" His low voice was curious.

"Oh, a couple of times, but I had to stay below. Dad can't swim, believe it or not. He was afraid I would fall overboard and he wouldn't be able to save me. I like to be on deck when the wind stings your face and the waves break over the bow. So I don't go out anymore," she concluded.

"And you aren't afraid of falling in?"

"No, not really." Sabrina shrugged. "I mean, I know it happens, but I always wear a life jacket like everyone else. Dad even gave me a waterproof beacon to attach to it, but that was when I could see. I think it was so he could see me if I went over the side. Anyway," she took a breath, "that's over and done with."

A Thai-seasoned shrimp cocktail was set in front of her as Bay took a seat opposite her. For a time the conversation centered on sailing, then shifted smoothly to other topics as they dawdled over their impromptu meal, eventually getting around to her artwork.

"I used to really enjoy people-watching, studying different kinds of faces." She sipped at the wine. "Of course, I did it in connection with my work. Most of my better portraits were from memory, faces of people I'd seen on the streets. It's all about character— a person's attitude toward life is written on his face. The grumpy look of a cynical old man, or the open expression of a child, a young woman's eagerness for

life—there was so much to see and get onto canvas."
Sabrina exhaled slowly. "And now I have to determine
things like character and personality with just voices.
It's not easy but I'm learning. It's really hard, though,
to visualize a person's looks just from listening to
them talk."

"What have you learned about me?"

"A lot." A hint of mischief tickled the corners of
her mouth. "Do you really want to know?"

"I think so."

"You're self-confident," she began, sensing him
relax at what he probably assumed was a compliment. "And arrogant," she added. "Hmm. What
else—you're well-educated, accustomed to having
authority over others. You obviously enjoy the outdoors and especially the sea. You have a quick
temper, but you can be thoughtful when it suits you."

He groaned. "Fair enough. Have you put a face
with my voice yet?"

Sabrina quickly ducked her head, avoiding his
gaze. "Only an impression of strength. But it's just
an impression." She pushed her plate away. "That
was good."

"Why haven't you asked to look at me?" Bay ignored her attempt to change the subject to food.

"W-what?" she stammered.

"I mean the way you did with the dress," he explained.

Humor hovered on the edge of his voice after she
shifted uncomfortably. The thought of exploring his
face with her hands was a little strange.

"I could fill in the blanks for you," he said cheerfully. "I have green hair and purple eyes, and a long,

ugly scar down the side of my face. I keep it hidden with a bushy silver beard."

"So far, so good, and so ZZ Top," she laughed.

"That's not all. I have a tattoo of a skull and cross-bones on my forehead—and I'm not going to tell you what's on my chest."

Sabrina grinned.

"Don't you believe me?"

"Hardly. Besides, my neighbor's already told me what you looked like." Sabrina's tension had dissolved.

"So you were curious."

"Well, yes. She said you had reddish-brown hair and eyes."

"Cinnamon, according to my mother."

Sabrina nodded. "Do you get it from her?"

"I guess so. She's been coloring her hair for years, though. C'mon, what else did your neighbor say about me?" he coaxed.

"Oh, Peggy isn't all that good at descriptions," Sabrina hedged, unwilling to pass along the "real man" comment.

"All the more reason for you to see for yourself," he challenged her.

There was the clatter of plates being stacked, then movement as the dishes were carried away. Bay's actions gave her time to think of an excuse to avoid the exploration he'd invited her to make. Try as she might, Sabrina was unable to come up with one that didn't reveal her nervousness about that level of intimacy.

When Bay returned, he didn't take his seat across from her but one that placed him beside her. Before she could voice her half-formed protest, he had taken her wrists in a light but firm grip and carried her hands to his face.

"You don't have to feel shy or self-conscious," he scolded gently as she tried to pull away. "It doesn't embarrass me."

The hard outline of his powerful jaw was beneath her hands, pressed by his on either side of his face. As her resistance faded, he released his hold. The initial contact had been made and the warmth of his skin eased the cold stiffness of her fingers. Tentatively Sabrina began to explore his face.

From the jawline, her fingertips stroked his cheeks, stopping on the hard angles of his cheekbones. Fluttering over the curling lashes of his eyes, she reached thick brows and the wide forehead. Then up. His thick, somewhat wavy hair had a hint of dampness from the fog and the drizzle. Then down. There was an arrogance, to be expected, in his Roman nose and a gentle firmness to his male lips. After inspecting the almost forceful set of his chin, her hands fell away.

It was a very masculine face, Sabrina thought with satisfaction. There was no doubt about that. No one would ever refer to him as conventionally handsome, but his looks were certainly striking. Heads would turn when he walked into a room.

"What's the verdict?" Bay asked, in a deep voice that was also soft as velvet.

She guessed her approval showed in her expression and slight blush. She averted her face slightly from his gaze, sensing it.

"The verdict is," she answered with false lightness, "that I like your looks. You have a strong face."

His finger tucked itself under her chin and

turned her head back toward him. "Thanks," he said. "And just in case you don't know it, you're gorgeous when you blush. And when you don't blush."

She turned redder, she could feel it. He'd noticed.

The warm moistness of his breath caressed her cheek for a warning instant before his lips touched hers. Initial surprise held Sabrina rigid under his kiss, but the gently firm pressure of his mouth transmitted a sensual heat that got to her. Her heart seemed to start skipping beats. With expert persuasiveness, his mouth moved over hers until he got the pliant response he wanted. Then slowly, almost regretfully, he drew away from her.

Sabrina could still feel the imprint of his mouth throbbing on hers. She had to resist the impulse to carry a hand to her lips. A wonderfully satisfying feeling filled her. Oh my, oh my, was all she could think.

"Why the thoughtful look, Sabrina?" Bay's husky voice asked gently.

"I—I've never been kissed like that before," she murmured.

"Liar," he mocked softly. "That was no inexperienced maiden who kissed me back just now."

"I meant"—the words did not come easily—"since I lost my sight."

"That I will believe." Bay took hold of her hand in a casual, not intimate grip. "Tell you what. Let's go get ourselves a cup of coffee at a restaurant somewhere."

Sabrina was willing enough to leave the ketch. For some reason the decking beneath her feet didn't feel very steady. She wanted the security of solid ground beneath her again.

It was a few minutes past ten o'clock when Bay parked the car in front of her house and walked her to the wrought iron gate. He didn't follow her inside the small enclosure and Sabrina turned to him hesitantly.

"I had a wonderful time. Thank you," she said.

"So did I. Therefore, no thanks are necessary," Bay said with a smile in his voice. "I'll be in L.A. all of next week. I'll give you a call when I get back."

"Okay," Sabrina said easily. She didn't want him to think that he was under any obligation to see her again.

"Talk to you soon," he said gently. "Goodnight, Sabrina. I'll wait in the car until I see a light go on inside, so don't forget."

She nodded. "I won't. Goodnight, Bay."

He swung the iron gate closed and Sabrina locked it. She felt his gaze follow her to the door. Cinnamon brown eyes he had. Nice. To go with his cinnamon hair. She wished she could see him and realized that in her way, she could.

Chapter 5

The switch on the sound system was clicked off by the remote in her hand. There was nothing soothing about the music as far as Sabrina was concerned.

What was there to do, she wondered tiredly. She didn't feel like domestic therapy, getting into cooking or cleaning even if it was needed, which it wasn't. She was tired of reading. Besides, her fingers were still slow to read the raised braille letters, so the task required her total concentration. In this restless mood, she knew her thoughts would wander.

An inner voice blamed—unfairly—her state of mind on Bay Cameron. Although why his business trip to Los Angeles should affect her this way, Sabrina didn't know. These restless moods had been with her before anyway, even prior to the accident. Then she had channeled the surging energy into her paintings. Now there was no outlet.

Have you ever done any modeling—in clay, I mean?

Bay's voice spoke clearly in her mind as he was standing beside her. The idea that had been planted several days ago began to germinate.

Walking to the telephone, Sabrina felt for the receiver, picked it up, then hesitated. Before she changed her mind, she pressed a fingertip quickly to each number. Excitement pulsated through her at the sound of the first ring.

"Art Supply Depot," a voice answered on the second ring.

"Sam Carlyle, please." Sabrina twirled the corkscrew curl of the phone cord. A few minutes later, a familiar male voice came on the line. "Hey, Sam. This is Sabrina."

"Sabrina, how are you?" he exclaimed in happy surprise. Then his tone changed immediately to apologetic. "Listen, I'm sorry I haven't called or stopped by for so long, but what with one thing and another—"

"That's all right," she interrupted quickly. "Actually I was calling to see if you could do me a favor."

"Name it and it's yours, Sabrina."

"I wondered if you could send over about twenty-five pounds of modeling clay—"

"Sure, sure. Harry's heading for the van right now."

"And an inexpensive set of sculpting tools for soft media."

"You got it. You taking up sculpting?"

"I'm going to give it a try," Sabrina said. "That's why I only want the bare necessities to see if I'm going to like it or be any good at it." She added several more items to the list anyway.

"I think it's a tremendous idea!" Sam enthused. "A stroke of genius!"

"So tell Harry where I live."

"Right, right. I'd come myself if I could, you know. There's Harry, drinking coffee—" Sabrina held the phone away from her as the man bellowed for him, then came back to her. "Sabrina, you still there?"

"Yes. With what's left of my hearing."

Sam guffawed. "He'll be there in about ten minutes and I'll make sure your place is his first stop."

"Thanks, Sam." A contented glow spread over her face.

"Hey, listen, I'm just sorry I didn't suggest something like this to you before," he replied, ignoring her thanks. "I'll get this stuff out to you right away. We'll get together soon, okay?"

"Yes, Sam, soon," Sabrina agreed.

Barely half an hour had elapsed when the delivery was made. She had already cleared a small area in the studio where she could work, realizing that her father would have to give her a hand this evening getting the heavier items onto her storage shelves. The delivery man had thoughtfully offered to carry the packages wherever Sabrina wanted them so she hadn't had to carry them to the studio.

After he'd left and she had returned to the studio, a thrill of excitement coursed through her. Her old smock was behind the door, smelling of oil paints and brush-cleaning fluid. Soon, the earthy odor of clay would wipe out that smell, she told herself happily as she donned the smock and made her way to the work table.

All sense of time vanished. She started out with simple shapes, using fruit she'd taken from the kitchen for her hands to use as a guideline. Her name was called for the third time before it finally penetrated her consciousness. It was another full second before she recognized her father's voice.

"I'm upstairs in the studio!"

She stepped back, wiping her hands on a rag as she listened to his hurrying steps on the stairs. Apprehension and joy mingled in the face Sabrina turned to the open doorway.

"I was getting frantic," Grant Lane declared with an exasperated sigh. "Why didn't you answer me? What are you doing up here anyway?"

"Working," Sabrina replied softly, but she could tell by the tense silence that her explanation wasn't necessary. Her father had already looked beyond her and seen for himself. She waited interminable seconds for his comment. "What do you think?" she asked breathlessly.

"I . . . I'm speechless," he told her. "How—when?"

Then he laughed at his inability to get his questions out and came the rest of the way into the room, throwing an arm around her shoulders and giving her a fierce hug. "You are one fantastic daughter. I'm proud of you." His voice was choked with emotion.

"Yes, but what do you think?" she repeated anxiously.

"If you're asking whether I can tell the apple from the pear, the answer is a definite yes. I can see that's a cluster of grapes you're working on now," her father smiled. "And I don't need that assortment of real fruit spotted with clay to make the identification either."

"Do you really mean it?"

"There's something else. You somehow got the soul of that apple, if you know what I mean. Not just the likeness." Sabrina beamed. "Now how about an explanation? When did you decide to do all this?

You never mentioned a word about it to me. Where did you get the art supplies?"

"From Sam. Had them delivered. But it was because last week Bay asked me if I'd ever worked in clay. I guess that's when I started thinking about it, subconsciously at least. This morning I decided to try it and called the Art Supply Depot."

"This morning? And you've been working ever since? You must be exhausted."

"Huh?" She turned to him, her wide mouth smiling broadly. "No, Daddy, I'm alive. For the first time in a very long while."

There was a moment of silence. Then her father took a deep breath. "Just the same, you'd better call it a day. No sense in overdoing it. You clean up here and I'll see about the dinner you forgot," he teased.

"All right."

For the rest of the week, Sabrina spent every waking minute she possibly could in the studio room. The end results were more often failures than successes. It didn't do any good for her father to insist that she couldn't be perfect as a beginner. But Sabrina demanded perfection of herself. Nothing less would satisfy her.

On Sunday morning Grant Lane ordered her out of the studio. "For heaven's sake, Sabrina," he declared, "even God rested on the seventh day!"

The mutinous set of her chin softened as she sighed her reluctant surrender to his logic. Her fingers ached to feel the molding clay beneath her hands, but she knew her father was right.

"I've got some work to do on the boat. Why don't

you come with me this morning?" he suggested. "Deborah is going to be busy in the kitchen. If you have nothing to do, I know you're going to sneak back up here the minute I leave."

"I wouldn't do that," Sabrina laughed softly.

"Oh, wouldn't you?" he mocked. "You're coming with me."

"I think it's awful that you don't trust your own daughter!" She clicked her tongue in reproof. "But if that's the way you're going to be, I guess I'll have to go with you."

"There's a pretty stiff breeze blowing in from the Pacific, so dress warmly. But make sure it's something you wouldn't mind getting dirty," her father added. "I thought I'd put you to work cleaning below deck."

Sabrina nodded sagely. "That's why you want me to come along. It has nothing to do with my health."

"You didn't think it was your company I wanted, did you?" he teased as he walked to the stairs.

The wind was chilly, Sabrina discovered. It had not yet blown away the morning fog, so the sun hadn't warmed the air. Below deck, she didn't feel the cool breeze. Wiping the sweat from her forehead that had separated her dark silky bangs into damp strands, she wished she could feel it.

She shoved up the sleeves on her navy blue pullover and set to work scrubbing the galley sink. The sweat was making the wool blend of the turtleneck's collar tickle the sensitive skin of her neck, but she couldn't very well scratch it with her soapy hands. As soon as she finished, Sabrina decided she would call her father down for a cup of coffee. From the sound of voices overhead, he was doing more chatting with fellow sailing enthusiasts than work.

Maybe she should take the pot of coffee and offer it around. There was a waterproof container of cookies in the cupboard with a patented anti-soggy lid to keep them nice and crisp. She smiled to herself. That would ensure nothing was accomplished today.

The quiet tread of rubber-soled shoes approached the steps leading below. Sabrina was rinsing the soap from the sink when they began their descent. She stopped, turning slightly in the direction of the footsteps.

"I thought I would bring some coffee up as soon as I finish here, Dad. I'll bring extra cups if you think the others would like to join you."

"That sounds fine."

"Bay! You're back!" The exclamation of delight sprang unchecked from her lips.

"I got in late yesterday afternoon," he acknowledged. "I thought I might see you here today with your dad. I never guessed he would make you a galley slave."

Sabrina smiled at the teasing voice. "Did you have a good trip?"

"Yes, I had some investment property to check on and inspected some other land I've been interested in acquiring. I even ran into an old friend I went to college with. He's topside talking to your father. Why don't you come and meet him?"

She had half expected it to be a woman, and she wondered if her relief was reflected in her expression. She hoped not. She didn't want Bay to think she was jealous. They were only friends.

"I'll be through here in a minute," she said. "If you'd like, you can take the coffeepot on up. There are some mugs in the cupboard. I can bring the sugar and mini-creams."

"All right," Bay agreed.

A few minutes later, Sabrina joined the others on deck. The wind lifted her bangs and she turned her face into the caressing flow of air.

"Here, Sabrina, let me take those." Her father took the packets of sugar and the mini-creams from her hands and helped her on deck.

"This is Grant's daughter, Sabrina Lane," Bay said. "This is my old fraternity brother, Doctor Joe Browning."

"You'd better watch who you call old," said a gruff male voice in a fake-serious tone. Then Sabrina's hand was taken in greeting. "I'm more commonly known as Joe or Doctor Joe to my patients."

Cold fingers raced icily down her spine. "How do you do." Her greeting was stiff. Since her accident and the string of doctors and specialists she'd been to, Sabrina had developed an aversion to anyone with the letters MD after his or her name.

"So call me Joe if you like," he said. "Your father tells me you've been blind for only a year. You seem to be getting along rather well."

"I really don't have a choice, do I?" she retorted.

"Of course you do. You could always get along badly."

His nonsensical reply brought an unwilling smile to her face. She'd always expected that even outside the office doctors were professional and unemotional, spouting platitudes and sending bills. This one seemed to be different.

"I ran into my share of furniture and buildings in the beginning," she admitted.

"Do you use a cane or do you have a seeing-eye dog?" He didn't give her a chance to reply. "I hear they're using standard poodles as well as shepherds and other breeds as seeing-eye dogs."

"Poodles? Hope they skip the silly haircut," she said.

The doctor laughed. "Can you imagine a poodle prancing down the street with its pompadour and that ball of fluff on his tail leading a blind person? Please, no. Not that I have anything against the intelligence of poodles."

Sabrina laughed too. She liked his irreverent attitude and her wariness disappeared. The relaxed sound of her laughter began a natural flow of conversation among all of them. Doctor Joe Browning dominated most of the topics with his dry wit.

Some time, Sabrina wasn't sure when, the subject became centered on her blindness, the accident, and the damage to her optic nerves that had resulted from the head injury. She was suddenly aware that the inquiries weren't all that casual but had a professional undertone.

"Wait a minute," she interrupted the doctor in mid-sentence. "Exactly what kind of doctor are you?"

"The best," he quipped. "A surgeon, to be specific."

"What kind?" Then she raised her hand in a halting gesture and said almost angrily, "No. let me guess. You're an eye surgeon."

"Right. You got it on the first guess. Now that's the mark of someone who pays attention," Joe Browning replied without the least embarrassment.

"What were all those questions for? Was that a subtle examination?"

"Yes," he admitted simply.

Seething with indignation, Sabrina turned in Bay's direction. "You put him up to this, didn't you, Bay? And you must have been in on it too, Dad."

Her father blew out a huge sigh. "You seemed so ambivalent about getting examined again. I just didn't want to lose time, if it came to that."

"I contacted him initially," Bay offered.

She wasn't sure which one of them she wanted to beat up more. It wasn't right to play games like that, not on her. She was the one who got to make decisions about her medical care and no one else.

"But the rest was my idea." Her father's voice was contrite. "I hoped you wouldn't have to go through the whole rigmarole again, maybe unnecessarily."

"That's why you pretended," Sabrina said tautly, "that he was your old school chum. How very chummy of both of you. And how very manipulative. Who do you think you are, Bay?"

"I am, though. That happens to be the truth," the doctor replied. "And it's also the truth that we bumped into each other in Los Angeles. He had no idea I was there since I've been on the East Coast for the last few years. He mentioned you to me and professional curiosity took over."

"I'm sorry, Sabrina," Bay offered quietly. "I knew you'd be upset when you found out."

"*Upset*? That's much too tame a word. Why did you try to trick me?"

"I felt I should respect your father's wishes. And there was the likelihood that you wouldn't find out, not if Joe didn't think there was any hope that your vision could be restored."

Sabrina could feel the steam building up, but she wasn't going to howl at them in public, much as she wanted to. "Really. I may be in the dark, but you two are in the freakin' Dark Ages. Do not ever do that again." She enunciated the last sentence with furious clarity. "And as for you, Doctor Joe, tell me what you think. Now that you've completely shattered my trust." Her chin tipped proudly toward him. Despite this ridiculous ruse, she was here, he was here, and she might as well listen to what the eye surgeon had to say.

"I'd like to run some more tests before I give you a definite answer, Sabrina," he said honestly. "I would guess that there is no more than a ten percent chance, if that, for a surgical cure."

"Four specialists told my father and me that I would never see again. What makes you think that you can help me?"

"I don't know that I can," Doctor Joe answered. "But I don't know that I can't either. On occasions, the body's natural healing processes repair some damage, making a condition that was inoperable shortly after the injury operable months later. It has happened."

"I see," she snapped. "And that's what you think has happened to me."

"I don't know, but I think we should explore the possibility," he replied. "To be absolutely sure, I'd have to admit you to a hospital and run some advanced tests. I have friends in the San Francisco medical community and I can wangle admitting privileges up here. But I don't want to raise false hope, Sabrina. You have a very slim chance of having your vision restored, right next to none at all. The decision is yours."

Not even the scent of roses that her father had brought could overcome the strong medicinal and antiseptic odor of the hospital. In the corridor, there were the hushed voices of a pair of nurses walking swiftly by her door. Sabrina listened to the even breathing of the female patient who shared her room.

Visiting hours were over. The lights were out. She knew that because she'd heard the flick of a switch when the nurse left the room a few minutes ago.

Her dark world seemed blacker this night. She felt very much alone and completely vulnerable. She was afraid to hope that the tests tomorrow would be encouraging. Yet it was impossible to be indifferent to the reasons she was here.

Her hand doubled into a fist at her side. Damn Bay for running into his doctor friend, Sabrina thought dejectedly. She'd accepted her blindness, stopped fighting the injustice of it and had started living with it.

Since Bay was partially responsible for her presence in the hospital, the least he could have done was come to visit her. But no, he'd sent a message of good luck with Doctor Joe, passed on when Sabrina had been admitted.

She trembled all over, a trembling that wouldn't stop. She hadn't realized she was so scared. Her chin quivered.

She wanted to break down and cry. The brave front she'd put up was crumbling and she didn't care.

A swirl of air blew over her face. She had come to recognize that as the silent opening of the door to her hospital room. Someone was approaching her bed and she had the sensation that it wasn't the nurse. A spicy scent of aftershave lotion drifting to her nose confirmed it.

"Are you awake?" Bay asked softly.

"Yes," Sabrina whispered, struggling to sit upright and keep the flimsy hospital gown around her. "Visiting hours are over. You're not supposed to be here."

"If they catch me, they can ask me to leave, right?" His smile was in his voice. "How are you doing?"

"Fine," she lied. The edge of the bed took his weight. "I thought Doctor Joe said you had to go to a party or something."

"I did go," Bay acknowledged, "but I slipped out to see you. Is that okay?"

"Fine with me. So long as it's fine with the lady you were with," she added unhappily.

"What makes you think I was with anyone?"

"I sure hope you were, because otherwise you're wearing some very expensive French perfume." Her fingers clutched the bedcovers tightly. It was important that she maintain this air of lighthearted teasing so Bay wouldn't guess her inner fear.

"Aha. The blind detective," he said gently.

"Elementary, Mr. Cameron." She shrugged. "After all, you were at a party. That makes it only logical to assume that you would turn on the charm for the prettiest woman there."

"Now that's where you're wrong."

"Why?" Sabrina tilted her head to the side in mock challenge.

"Because I've been turning on the charm only for a certain blind lady I know. She's prettier than anyone," Bay responded lightly.

Her throat constricted. "I find that difficult to believe."

His big hand covered hers for a moment, then pried them away from the sheets. "Your hands are like ice, Sabrina. What's the matter?"

His question set an uncontrollable shiver quaking over her shoulders. Giving a shaky sigh, Sabrina admitted, "I'm frightened, Bay—of tomorrow."

He said nothing for a minute. She felt his weight shift a little on the bed. Then his arm circled her shoulders and he drew her against his chest, the back of his hand cradling her head near his chin.

"Let's think about this," he murmured calmly. "It's not the thought of the tests the doctor is going to do that frightens you. That only leaves two alternatives. One is that you're afraid to have your sight restored and the other is that you won't, right?"

Sabrina nodded, feeling numb. The steady beat of his heart beneath her head and the protective circle of his strong arms was blissfully comforting.

"I know you can't be afraid of seeing again," he continued. "That result would have everyone rejoicing. That only leaves the second."

"I—" she began hesitantly. "I had accepted the fact that I was blind, did I tell you that? I'm a total coward. I wish I'd never agreed to these tests. I wish I'd never met Doctor Joe. I don't want to go through the agony of accepting all over again that I'm permanently blind."

"Where is that gutsy gal who was always trying to thumb her nose at the world?" Bay asked softly. "You aren't a coward, Sabrina. A coward wouldn't be here in the hospital taking the slim chance that Joe offered. If the tests are negative, you aren't going to wail and tear your hair out. The Sabrina I know is going to shrug her shoulders and say, 'Well, I gave it a go.'" She felt him smile against her hair. "You have everything to gain and nothing really to lose."

She sighed. "That's what I keep trying to tell myself."

"The secret is to stop saying it and start admitting that it's true." He didn't seem to require a reply as he held her for more long minutes. The strength seemed to flow from his arms into her, chasing away her unreasonable fears. "Are you all right now?" he asked finally.

"Yes." She smiled faintly, staying where she was.

"Then I'd better be going before the nurse comes in and gets the wrong idea about what we're doing," Bay teased softly.

Very gently he shifted her onto the pillow, tucking the sheet around her chest. As he started to straighten, Sabrina reached out for his arm.

"Thank you for coming, Bay," she whispered.

"Don't thank me for something I wanted to do." Then he bent over her and there was a tantalizing brush of his mouth on hers. "Goodnight, Sabrina. I'll be seeing you."

"Okay. Goodnight, Bay."

There were soft footsteps, then the swish of air as the door opened and closed.

The hospital bed felt like a pincushion. Sabrina knew it was the waiting. She'd had two days of different tests, and enhanced CAT scans and super-digitized MRIs and everything else ophthalmology had dreamed up to look inside the human eye and the bones around it. Doctor Joe would be explaining the results any minute. The unemotional tone of his voice the last few days had convinced Sabrina that the results had no new hope to offer.

Her father walked again to the window in her room. She knew he had no interest in the parking lot below, his patience giving way to restless pacing. She wished she could join him. In mid-stride, he stopped and turned abruptly. A second later air from the corridor fanned her cheek and she turned toward the door.

"Good morning, Sabrina, Grant." Doctor Joe Browning greeted them with his usual informality. At least that went both ways, she thought idly. He didn't seem to expect anyone to bow down to him, not that she was in awe of any doctor or surgeon by this point. She heard him walk to the window.

"Good morning, Doctor Joe," Sabrina said, feeling like she was about six years old.

"Dreary out, though, isn't it?" he said. "I never have gotten used to the fog."

But her father skipped the small talk. "Are all the results in?"

"Yes."

Sabrina felt a little sick. She called out hesitantly. "Bay?"

"Hello, Sabrina," he answered quietly.

"Don't tell me my patient is psychic," the doctor laughed.

Sabrina was beginning to be hugely annoyed by his jokes, even though he meant well.

"She has a keen sense of smell," Bay corrected in an amiable voice. It occurred to her that he was picking up on her miserable mood and trying to keep things light. "She probably recognized my aftershave."

Sabrina didn't correct him. She wasn't certain herself how she'd known he was there and she couldn't be positive that she hadn't unconsciously caught a whiff of the spicy fragrance.

"Well, to get back to the business at hand," Doctor Joe said. "I've analyzed the test results twice and consulted with a team of specialists."

He paused and Grant Lane prompted. "And?"

"We knew at the outset that Sabrina regaining her sight would be a long shot." The flat tone of his voice was all the warning Sabrina needed to brace herself for the rest of his answer. "There isn't anything more that can be done. I'm sorry."

The silence from her father told Sabrina that he had been hoping for a miracle. So had she, for that matter. But she wasn't as crushed as she'd been the other times that the verdict was pronounced.

She summoned a wan smile. "We had to take the chance, Doctor Joe." Her smile deepened as she remembered Bay's words that first night in the hospital. "We had to give it a go."

The doctor walked to the bed and clasped one of her hands warmly between his. "Thank you, Sabrina."

As Doctor Joe said goodbye to her father, apologizing again, she heard Bay approach the bed. He stopped somewhere near the side. She felt his penetrating gaze run over her face.

"Are you all right?" he asked quietly.

"Yes," she whispered and she knew suddenly that it was the truth and not brave words.

"I knew that gutsy gal would come back," he told her.

"With your help, she did," Sabrina answered.

"I can't take the credit for strength you already had," Bay said, "but we'll argue the point another time. How about Saturday night?"

"Saturday night?" she repeated.

"Yes, we can have dinner together. I'll pick you up around seven."

There was a breathless catch in her voice. "Is that an order or an invitation?" she asked unevenly.

"Both, depending on your answer."

"I'd be happy to have dinner with you, Bay." Sabrina accepted with a demure inclination of her head.

More than happy, she added silently to herself. She found she was eagerly looking forward to Saturday night.

Chapter 6

Sabrina slowly descended the steps to the second floor, fingering the soft knit of her top uncertainly. A tiny frown of indecision pulled her brows together. In the living room she could hear her father's and Deborah's voices. She walked to the open doorway and paused.

"Deborah, can I talk to you for a minute?" Sabrina asked, a hint of anxiety in her voice.

"Of course." Footsteps muffled by the carpet quickly approached the open doorway where she waited. "What is it?"

"Is what I'm wearing too dressy?"

"No, I don't think so." Deborah sounded confused. "Bay's taking you out to dinner, isn't he?"

"Not to dinner exactly," Sabrina explained. "We'll pick up something to eat at Fishermen's Wharf like we did the last time and have a makeshift picnic somewhere. He's not taking me out to a public restaurant." Her hand touched the necklace at her throat. "But maybe I should wear something simpler."

"I don't think so," Deborah decided after several

seconds of consideration. "If that's the plan, you really can't go wrong with nice jeans and a good sweater."

"Good," Sabrina sighed with relief. It was so difficult sometimes trying to judge how outfits looked. The front doorbell rang. "That must be him."

"Your purse is on the table," Deborah said. "I'll tell Bay you're on your way down."

Retrieving her purse, Sabrina slipped the ivory cane from the umbrella stand, hooked it over her arm and opened the stairwell door, calling a good-bye to her father before closing it. She darted eagerly down the stairs and through the street door to the gate.

"I'm ready," she declared, unlocking it and walking through.

Bay's hand touched her arm in light possession as he guided her to his car. "I was hoping you'd wear that new dress tonight and set the world on fire."

"That dress?" Sabrina laughed softly. "I'd look pretty silly wearing that to a picnic."

"Huh? We aren't going on a picnic. We did that. It was fun, but I'm taking you out to a real dinner."

"But—" she stopped short.

"What is it?" He paused patiently beside her.

"You know that I don't eat in public places," she stated, punctuating the sentence with a tap of her cane.

"Yes, I remember what you said." His arm crossed her back and he moved her nearer to the car. The door was opened and he helped Sabrina inside, even though she wasn't sure she wanted to be helped.

"You're not paying attention to what I'm saying now," Sabrina accused him.

"I can't give you all my attention and drive too," Bay said logically, starting the car and turning it away from the curb with one hand. "We're going to a nice little Italian restaurant. It doesn't look like much on the outside, but the food is excellent."

"I'm not going. You can't make me."

"Sabrina, you can't keep avoiding things on the off chance that you'll do something embarrassing." The firm tone of his voice said his patience was thinning.

"You're going to look pretty silly dragging me into that restaurant," she commented smugly.

"I hope you aren't counting on the fact that I won't, because if that's the only way to get you in the door, I'll do it," Bay said.

In that flashing second, Sabrina realized that he meant it. No stubbornness or anger on her part would change his mind. He was actually going to get her into the restaurant one way or another.

"Forget it!" she hissed. "I don't know why I ever agreed to come with you tonight. I should've guessed you'd do something like this."

"You'd better be careful," he warned jokingly. "I could change my mind and take you to a Chinese restaurant and put a pair of chopsticks in your hand. Now that would be a challenge."

The pouting line of her mouth twitched as her sense of humor resurfaced. She had to suppress a snort of amusement but she did smile, hoping he was looking at the traffic and not her. After all, she'd never mastered the use of chopsticks when she could see. Any attempt now that she was blind would be absurd.

"I see that smile," Bay laughed softly. "That's

much better. You just keep that positive attitude going, okay? And don't be embarrassed if you spill something. Sighted people do it all the time."

"Why can't I ever win an argument with you?" Sabrina sighed but with humor.

"The answer is obvious," he announced. "It's because I'm always right."

Surprisingly, as far as Sabrina was concerned, the dinner went well. Bay laughingly threatened to order spaghetti for her, but she'd beat him to the punch by asking for lasagna, which was excellent.

She leaned back in her chair, a hand touching the coffee cup so she wouldn't forget where it was. A tiny sigh of contentment came from her.

"What was that for?" Bay inquired softly.

"For a very enjoyable meal," she responded. "Thank you for making me come."

"I prefer the word 'persuaded.'" Amusement danced in his voice.

"Persuaded me to come, then." She gave him a dimpling smile.

"So—no depression because of the negative test results?" Despite the teasing tone, there was an underlying hint of seriousness.

"You had to change the subject," she said wryly. "No, not really. I wish it had been otherwise, but I don't mind as much as I might have. Partly because of your brilliant idea to work in clay and partly because I'd already started working again, in a creative sense. My life as a blind woman wasn't without purpose when I went into the hospital this time. Before, when the specialists gave me their verdict, I had nothing to look forward to and I was scared half to death. Now I have a goal."

"I'm really glad to hear that. When are you going to show me what you've done so far?"

"When I can stand some criticism." Sabrina smiled ruefully.

"And you think my judgment would be critical?"

"I don't think you'd let me slide or do mediocre art simply because I'm blind," she said.

"I actually don't think you would lower your standards for that reason or any other reason."

"I couldn't," admitted Sabrina with a nod of her head. A fervent note crept into her voice. "I want to be more than just so-so or even just good. I want to be great. It's the only way I'll be able to support myself with art as my career."

"And that's very important to you, isn't it?"

"Yes. Not just for pride's sake or to be independent," she went on earnestly, "but because I don't want to keep being a burden to my father. I know he doesn't think of me that way, but I know that because of me he hasn't married Deborah. Earning money by myself is the only way to prove to him that I'm capable of living on my own again."

"You could always get married. That's the old-fashioned way to leave home, but I understand it still works."

"There happens to be two obstacles to that solution." Sabrina laughed, not taking his comment at all seriously.

"What are they?"

"First, there isn't anyone I happen to be in love with, and it would be a huge, huge mistake to marry just to get out of the house."

"And the second?"

"The second is even more crucial. There would

have to be someone around who was willing to marry me." She shook her head as if that would never, ever happen.

"Is that so unlikely?"

"If they're sane, it would be." She laughed quietly again.

"I've always considered myself to be sane. I guess that puts me out of the running, doesn't it?"

Sabrina felt his gaze searching her face, alert to her reaction. She was suddenly self-conscious about the subject they were discussing.

"It certainly would," she answered firmly.

"I guess that settles that," Bay stated. The nonchalance in his voice didn't match the sensation Sabrina had that he had been interested in her answer. Maybe he thought she wanted to take advantage of his apparent wealth. "Would you like some more coffee, Sabrina, or should we go?"

"No more, thanks. I'm ready if you are." Her hand found the ivory cane hooked over the arm of her chair.

After that first successful dinner, Bay took Sabrina out several times during the following weeks. The restaurants he chose were seldom crowded but served excellent food.

The only twinges of self-consciousness she experienced came when friends of Bay's stopped at their table to say hello. She sensed their surprise upon learning she was blind and guessed that they wondered why Bay was with her.

Now and then, she wondered why herself, but the answer had ceased to be important. It was enough to enjoy his company without constantly questioning his motives for being with her. In a way she didn't want to find out. She was still afraid his reason might be charitable. Although she'd come a long way out of her shell, she still didn't want pity, most especially not from Bay.

Carefully she smoothed the arm of the clay figure, letting her fingers transfer the image to her mind's eye. A shiver of subdued elation trembled over her at the completed sculpture of a ballet dancer captured in the middle of a pirouette that her mind saw. With each passing week, her hands had become more sure and adept. The successes had begun to outnumber the failures.

Someone came up to the studio from the stairs. Quelling her excitement, Sabrina stepped back from the work stand, a smile of triumph tickling the corners of her mouth. Wiping her hands on the towel, she turned slightly toward the door as the somewhat heavy-sounding footsteps came nearer. An eagerness she couldn't conceal was in her stance.

"Come in, Dad," she called when he paused. "I've finished the third version of this. I want you to see it."

The instant the door opened, her head tipped sideways in a listening attitude. The person entering the room was not her father but Bay. She knew it instinctively.

"What are you doing here?" she said with surprise. "You said you wouldn't come until seven. It can't be that late." She had removed her watch to work with the messy clay, so she couldn't check the time.

"It isn't. It's the middle of the afternoon," Bay said cheerfully. "Since you haven't invited me to see your work, I persuaded your father to let me come up here rather than have you come down."

In an instinctive, protective movement, Sabrina moved a few steps to block his view of her work-in-progress. Only her father and Deborah had seen the result of her many hours of labor in the studio. She wasn't ready yet for someone outside her immediate family to see what she had done.

"That doesn't explain what you're doing here in the middle of the afternoon," she said defensively.

"Doesn't it? I thought it did." She could hear the smile in his tone. "Actually, you're right," Bay conceded. "I had another purpose for coming other than to sneak into your studio. I'm afraid I have to cancel our dinner date tonight, Sabrina."

"That's all right," she fibbed.

It wasn't all right, but she didn't want him to realize how much she looked forward to an evening with him. She didn't even like to admit it to herself. There was no future in it. No, the future was here in this studio with her work.

"I don't know whether I should be pleased or insulted that you take it so calmly."

Sabrina sensed that he wasn't really angry, just curious as to her reasons.

"You could show a little regret," he went on.

"Look, I would've enjoyed the evening, I always do." Her pride kept her from going on and on about it, though. "I mean, whatever it is must be important or you wouldn't have canceled." Striving for lightness, Sabrina added, "I certainly hope you've warned your jealous girlfriend that she doesn't need to start a catfight or anything."

"Huh? What makes you think a jealous girlfriend changed our plans?"

"I don't know for sure," she answered with a teasing smile. "But I hope you don't expect me to believe that you're a monk or something."

"Okay," he deadpanned. "Let's be really clear about that. I am not now, nor do I ever plan to become, a monk. I don't think I could take all the gloomy chanting and I don't see myself in a scratchy brown robe tied with a rope. And the no-girls thing? No deal."

She had to laugh. "Sorry. I guess that was silly of me."

"Not entirely," he said dryly. "What's on your mind?"

"Oh, Bay," she said. "We're friends, right? Nothing more."

"Strictly platonic?" he asked.

"Of course." She frowned, trying to puzzle out his mood at the moment and failing.

"In that case, when are you going to step aside to let a 'friend' see your work? My view is limited with you in the way."

Sabrina decided that she had imagined the sharpness in his "strictly platonic" question. She'd only been stating the obvious and he had agreed in an indirect way.

For a hesitant moment, she stayed where she was, wanting and not wanting his opinion of her sculpture.

"Some of my first attempts are on the side table," she said hesitantly. "And they're not very good, but I've been improving. Right now I'm working on a series of ballet figures. I thought I'd do a small *corps de ballet* with the central figures being a dancing couple. I'm nowhere near done with the secondary figures, though."

The silence that followed stretched on endlessly.

Sabrina thought she would burst with the suspense of waiting. Her hands were unconsciously clasped in a praying position.

"Have any of your friends seen your work?" Bay asked absently. "Your art-world friends, I mean."

She shook her head quickly, not really wanting to answer. "Only Dad and Deborah."

"I'm no critic, Sabrina," he murmured. "I only know what I like and I'm impressed by what I see here. You've really never done any work in clay before?"

"Never," she said. "Do you really think it's good? You're not just saying that because I'm blind, are you?" She needed to hear his approval again.

"I wouldn't do that," he said seriously, "and you know that what you've done is more than good. I can see that it is. A professional is the only person who can tell you how good you are and have you believe it, though. If you want my suggestion, I think you should talk to someone who can give you that answer."

"No—not yet," Sabrina said. Her confidence in her work was far from the point where she could endure the scrutiny of her work by an art expert. "I'm not ready for that. I need more time."

"Just don't postpone it forever."

"I won't." She ran her palms nervously over the sides of her clay-stained smock, wishing there was some way she could distract him at the moment. "Hey, there's coffee and homemade cake downstairs," she said brightly. "Want some?"

"Bet it's good, but no. I have to go," Bay said in a warm way. "And my schedule is kinda full otherwise for a while. I do have a couple of tickets to the San Francisco Light Opera next Saturday if you're willing to accept that as a raincheck for tonight."

"I'd love to go." Sabrina smiled.

"Great. Then that's a date. Oh, by the way, there's something I meant to give you as an apology for tonight."

"What? Not that you have to give me anything," she added.

She listened to him reach into his pocket and heard the faint rustle of paper. He placed a small, wrapped box in her hand, long and thin, similar in shape to a jeweler's box.

"Open it," he ordered, laughing at her hesitation. "It's nothing expensive, if that's what's bothering you. In fact, you might decide to throw it at me when you find out what it is."

"I'm beginning to think I would enjoy that," she said softly. She began unwrapping the package. Removing the top of the box, her exploring fingers touched a pair of tapering, extremely narrow pieces of wood. She turned her bewildered face to Bay.

"Sticks?" she questioned in disbelief.

Bay clicked his tongue in mock reproof. "Not just sticks," he chuckled. "They're chopsticks. I'm giving you a couple of weeks to practice before I take you to a Cantonese restaurant in Chinatown."

Laughter bubbled in her throat and she bit her lower lip to hold it back. "I suppose I should be grateful that you gave me some warning."

"Yes, you should. Either that or you can give me a swift kick."

"Gee, what if I miss? I'll have to practice that too." Sabrina couldn't hold back her laughter. "Okay. All I'm going to eat is egg rolls, soup and fortune cookies. All the rest will end up on the floor or the tablecloth."

"I'll take the chance." Bay smiled. "As for next

Saturday, I think a formal occasion calls for that sophisticated flame-colored dress."

"Is that an order?"

"If it is, will you obey it?" he countered.

She nodded, giving him a big smile. "Yes."

After Bay's approval of her work, Sabrina strove even harder for the perfection she demanded. The renewed effort made the week pass swiftly. The performance of the Light Opera Company the following Saturday seemed like a reward.

The initial nervousness she'd felt at the prospect of going to such a very public place, a see-and-be-seen venue, vanished under Bay's genuine praise of her appearance. She'd taken extra pains, enlisting Deborah's help with her hair and makeup. The two of them had gotten along much better since Sabrina had started working in the studio again. Deborah hadn't mentioned the special school for the blind since then, either. It was as if they were both counting on what was happening in the studio for the future happiness of each.

Sabrina hadn't intended to take her ivory cane, mostly from—she had to admit it—vanity. She didn't want to be easily identified as blind by the crowd attending the opera. However, Bay handed her the cane from the umbrella stand as they walked out of the door of the house. She'd known he would chide her for not wanting to carry it, so she'd said nothing.

Now the cane was hooked over her arm as they stood in the foyer of the theater. It was intermission. Had Sabrina been with anyone else she would probably have remained in her seat, but Bay had ushered her into the outer lobby.

Bay just wasn't a man to be overlooked by anyone around him. His stature drew attention to him even if his male magnetism didn't. That was how Sabrina knew she was the object of interest and curiosity, especially once people saw the cane on her arm, because she was in his company.

Several people acquainted with Bay stopped, politely including her in their greeting. Bay didn't encourage conversation with anyone and they gradually drifted away after the initial exchange. Sabrina wasn't sure whether it was because he was aware of her uneasiness with strangers or because he was self-conscious that she was blind. The last didn't seem to fit with his personality and she dismissed it.

"Bay Cameron!" an older woman greeted him effusively. Unconsciously Sabrina edged closer to be nearer his protection. "I haven't seen you in ages!" the woman exclaimed. "Where have you been hiding, hmm? Is this young lady the reason for your disappearance from the social whirl?"

His hand moved to rest on the back of Sabrina's shoulders, moving her slightly forward as he introduced her. "Sabrina, this is a very dear friend of mine, Pamela Thyssen. Pamela, I'd like you to meet Sabrina Lane."

"It's a pleasure!" Pamela said.

Bay leaned down and spoke in a loud stage whisper, "Um, she tends to be a little overpowering and maybe even nosy, but Pamela is all heart."

"Don't you believe one word he says," Pamela chirped in a cultured voice. "My bite is every bit as bad as my bark, so beware, Sabrina Lane." After a pause, she added, "Miss, Mrs., or Ms.?"

"Do you see what I mean, Sabrina?" Bay chuckled. "She's a terrible busybody."

"Oh. I'm not married, Pamela," she said with a smile. "Miss or Ms. Either is fine."

She would agree that Bay's description of Pamela Thyssen was correct. Although inquisitive and forthright, the woman seemed to be kind.

"We single women must stick together," Pamela Thyssen averred. "Not that I intend to remain single. I've outlived two husbands and they always say the third time's the charm. As for you, my dear—are you and Bay an item?"

Sabrina flushed deeply. "No."

"I guess you know where you stand, Bay!" the woman laughed loudly.

"She's too independent," he said with faint amusement, yet Sabrina sensed a hint of unhappiness with her answer in his tone.

"I must get to know Sabrina better. Bring her to my party after the performance." It was a command, not a request, and the older woman said goodbye before Sabrina could prompt Bay to refuse.

"You aren't actually intending to go, are you?" she asked him when they were alone.

"Why not?" he countered smoothly. "Pamela's parties are always a hoot. Lots of interesting people. Consider yourself honored that she asked."

"Maybe so," Sabrina replied uneasily. "But I'm just not comfortable with a room full of strangers."

"It's about time you got over that," Bay responded, the hand on her back prodding her into movement. "Now we only have a few minutes to find our seats before the curtain goes up."

Chapter 7

Sabrina curled her fingers into the soft fake fur of her black evening jacket, pushing the collar up around her neck. The corners of her mouth drooped downward in frustration as she nibbled at her lower lip. The closed window of the car didn't completely block the sound of other cars exiting the theater lot.

"Why can't you take me home and go to the party by yourself?" Her suggestion had a faintly desperate ring.

"The invitation was for both of us," Bay reminded her.

"Mrs. Thyssen doesn't know me. She wouldn't even miss me if I wasn't there," Sabrina reasoned.

"Yes, she will." A smile lightened the firmness of his tone. "Especially since you were the one who got her to do the inviting."

"I did no such thing!"

"Let me rephrase it," he said patiently. "It was after meeting you and getting curious that she invited us to her party."

"She never gave us a chance to say whether we

could come or not. We could've made other plans for all she knows," Sabrina argued.

"But we don't have other plans, do we? There isn't any actual reason why we can't go to her party for a little while."

"I don't want to go. That's a good enough reason for me." Her chin jutted out defiantly.

"No, it isn't," Bay replied in a voice that said he wouldn't be swayed by any more arguments.

"You're a bully, Bay Cameron!" Sabrina accused him in a low voice, slumping in her seat.

"A gentle one, I hope," he chuckled softly.

"A bully," she repeated with no qualifying adjectives.

Bridling at the way Bay had maneuvered her again into a situation she didn't want to be in, Sabrina couldn't concentrate on the direction they were taking. She lost track of the turns and eventually stopped guessing at the streets. The lack of traffic indicated they were in a residential area, but she had no idea what part of the city they were in.

The car slowed down and eased to the curb. "Here we are," Bay announced, switching off the motor and reaching for the driver's side door handle.

Sabrina said nothing, sitting in mutinous silence as the door opened and closed on his side. In her mind, she watched him walk around the car to her door, judging almost to the second when he would open it. Stubbornly she didn't move.

"Are you coming in with me or are you going to sit in the car and sulk like a little kid?" Bay asked.

"If I have a choice, I'll stay in the car," she declared coldly.

"Sabrina." His sighing voice held indulgent patience in its gentle tone. "Are you really that afraid of meeting new people? C'mon, tell me."

"You know that's not the reason."

"Actually, I don't."

"I'm not afraid," Sabrina said forcefully.

"Of course not," Bay said in a deliberately disbelieving voice.

"I'm not!"

"Whatever you say." He agreed with her again in the same annoying tone. "Okay. If you're going to stay in the car, I suggest you lock all the doors. I'll be gone about an hour."

"Wait a sec. You're not really leaving me here." Sabrina frowned, not sure any more if he was teasing or serious.

"You said you'd rather stay," Bay reminded her complacently. "I'll put in an appearance and explain why you couldn't come."

"As if you would have the nerve to tell Mrs. Thyssen that I'm sitting out here in the car," she breathed. But that comeback was met with silence—a silence that held an affirmative answer. "You have no shame," she grumbled, turning to slide her feet out of the car.

He didn't reply, but his hand reached out for her arm to guide her safely to the sidewalk.

A maid admitted them into the house. The sound of warm, friendly voices filled the foyer entrance. It seemed to come from several directions, indicating that the party was larger than the small gathering Sabrina had imagined.

With her evening jacket whisked off to a closet somewhere by the maid, she let Bay take her arm and lead her in the direction where the majority of the voices seemed to be coming from. Her lips pressed together as she mentally prepared herself.

"Smile." Bay whispered the single word near her ear.

"No." But the tight nervousness in her expression lessened.

Sabrina was unaware of the faintly regal tilt of her head, or the way it accented the swanlike column of her neck as they entered the room. Her queenly posture and the softly draped flame-colored gown got her as much attention as Bay. Since he was acquainted with most of the people there, most of the greetings were offered to him.

Not that she was left out. But, stubbornly, Sabrina didn't acknowledge any of them. Only the white knuckles of the hand clutching the ivory cane revealed her inner apprehension at being in a room full of strangers.

From their right, the instantly recognizable voice of Pamela Thyssen called out to them. "Bay—Sabrina! I'm so glad you could come."

Sabrina's greeting when the woman was beside them was no more than a polite hello. She wasn't going to lie by saying how happy she was to be there.

Bracelets jangled on the older woman's wrists. The hand that clasped Sabrina's free hand was heavy with rings, small and large. Her perfume was a comfortable, old-fashioned scent of violets.

"Bay, be a dear," Pamela Thyssen commanded. "Go and fetch drinks for Sabrina and me. I'll have my usual—Sabrina, what do you want?"

"Um, nothing, thanks." Sabrina started to say more but Bay had already moved from her side. She was stuck with her ebullient hostess.

"Actually, my usual is iced tea," the woman confided. "So I don't think that really qualifies as a drink."

"No, it doesn't." Sabrina braced herself for a barrage of small talk.

"That's a little secret between you and me," Pamela murmured. "A hostess is expected to drink at her own parties or the guests don't feel free to imbibe. Iced tea looks just like scotch on the rocks and no one thinks twice. So relax, my dear. We won't ply you with intoxicating beverages."

"I doubt if you could," Sabrina answered almost under her breath.

"You have spunk, do you know that? I like it," Pamela pronounced. "You just fit right in with us— and did you know I'm Bay's godmother, by the way? Did he tell you?"

"No." Was that the reason for the woman's obvious curiosity about her, Sabrina wondered to herself.

"His parents are in Europe on a second honeymoon. Louise—that's Bay's mother—and I grew up together. We've always been very close friends."

"He mentioned they were in Europe," she said, since there seemed to be no other comment she could offer.

"I've been admiring your cane. It's ivory, isn't it?" She didn't wait for an answer. "It's a beautiful old piece, and such fine workmanship. Quite elegant, I would say. Where did you find it?"

"It was a gift—from a friend," Sabrina added after a second's hesitation. Bay could tell the woman himself if he wanted her to know it was from him.

"Oh. A friend." Pamela put an annoying emphasis on the last word.

"That's right," was all Sabrina said.

"How long have you been blind, Sabrina?"

Oh please, she thought to herself. Bay's bluntness must run in his family, extended and otherwise. But she might as well answer. It wasn't classified information.

"Almost a year." Her chin lifted fractionally as if to ward off probing questions about her past. Enough already.

"And how long have you known Bay?"

"About two months. Mrs. Thyssen—" Sabrina began, taking a deep breath in the hopes of changing the subject of conversation to some other, less personal topic without offending the other woman.

"Speak of the devil," Pamela murmured, cutting her off in midsentence. "That didn't take you very long, Bay. Thank you."

The clink of expensive rings against a glass accompanied the words. In the next instant, Bay's voice said, "Here you are, Sabrina." He placed a cold glass in her hand. "How have you two been getting along while I was gone?"

"Just fine. Not like you were away for a week." Sabrina smiled at him sweetly.

He didn't speak to that. "I can see by the tilt of her nose that you must have been asking too many questions, Pamela."

"I wasn't prying, Bay," Pamela corrected with a laugh. "I was just trying to find out more about her. You never brought an actual goddess to a party of mine before. Can you blame me for being curious?"

"Um, thanks, but—" Sabrina didn't get a chance to finish.

"I bet you don't like to be talked about as if

you weren't here." Pamela Thyssen finished the sentence for her. "I actually do know what you mean and don't like it myself. I'm sorry. It was meant as a compliment. Anyway, Bay, Sabrina and I don't need a referee, so why don't you go and circulate or something? Let me monopolize her for an hour. I'll take care of her."

Sabrina turned in Bay's direction, her lips parting in a silent plea for him not to desert her. For a fleeting second she thought he was going to argue with his godmother's request.

He didn't.

"You're in good hands, Sabrina," he said quietly. "Pamela is one hell of a talker and she'll keep you entertained. See you later."

"I like that," Pamela said indignantly as he moved away.

Sabrina's mouth thinned with annoyance. First he maneuvered her into coming to a party packed with people she didn't know and probably would never meet again, then he handed her off to their much-too-chatty hostess. Her irritation seethed beneath her polite demeanor. She couldn't escape from here on her own. Independence could only be sustained to a certain point, and after that she had to rely on whoever was around her.

"Come, my dear." Pamela hooked her arm in Sabrina's. "I want to introduce you properly. My friends are wonderful and there isn't a snob among them."

Sabrina took that in. All well and good, but she wasn't going to kick off her shoes and dance on the piano. She really couldn't relax at all. Gritting her teeth, she forced herself to accompany her hostess. The following flurry of introductions and new voices were difficult to assimilate and put the correct name to the right voice.

But at least there wasn't one awkward remark concerning her blindness. The main topic of conversation was the performance that evening. Several of the people she'd met had seen her at the theater before and asked her opinion. Everyone's interest in her seemed friendly, without prying overtones. Gradually Sabrina's defensiveness ebbed away.

"Tommy, why don't you let Sabrina sit in that loveseat with Mrs. Phillips?" Pamela suggested in a tone that was actually an order. "The armrest is just to your left, dear."

The glass of iced tea, empty now, was taken from her hand as the searching tip of her cane found the front edge of the small sofa. Willingly Sabrina sat down. The flood of strange names and voices was beginning to overwhelm her and she guessed that her hostess had sensed it. She conceded, but only to herself, that Bay had been right when he'd said she was in good hands.

"That's an absolutely stunning dress you're wearing, Sabrina," the woman at her side said, obviously the Mrs. Phillips that Pamela had mentioned. "I noticed it in the theater."

The compliment was followed by a lengthy discussion of the difficulty the woman had finding clothes that fit her well and how unflattering the trendy styles were to her figure. Sabrina just listened, inserting a monosyllabic answer when she thought one was required but letting the other woman carry the conversation.

The sensitive area on the back of her neck began to tingle. Sabrina instantly guessed the cause. Bay

Cameron had to be somewhere near. Her radar was seldom wrong where he was concerned. Pretending to concentrate on the woman speaking to her, she strained her hearing to catch any sound that might pinpoint his location.

Then came the husky, caressing sound of a feminine voice, vaguely familiar although Sabrina couldn't place it.

"Bay—hey, honey. I didn't expect to see you here."

"Uh, what a surprise," she heard Bay answer calmly. "I thought you didn't like Pamela's parties. Too tame for you, right?"

"A girl can change her mind, can't she?" the voice purred.

"And a guy can always wonder why," Bay countered.

"Actually, a little bird spotted you at the theater tonight."

Whoever Bay was flirting with was disgustingly coy, Sabrina thought.

"I took a guess that you might bring her here tonight," the voice said.

"Did you," was his noncommittal reply.

"Uh-huh," she cooed. "I don't think I'll ever understand your charitable streak, Bay," the woman said silkily. "I mean, why do you have to take an interest in that poor thing? You don't have to squire her around. Just give her money or something and be done with it. You certainly can afford it."

Sabrina stiffened, sure she'd turned as red as her gown. She couldn't help it. The only saving grace in the whole situation was that no one here but her possessed the acute hearing that blindness had

given her. Bay's flirty conversation with the unknown woman wasn't being overheard by anyone
but Sabrina.

"That would be your solution, Roni," he murmured in a low voice. "Sometimes I think that when
they were handing out compassion, you got shorted."

Roni. That was the name of the girl who'd been
with him that day at the yacht harbor. Sabrina also
remembered that Bay had said they were going to
take in an ocean sunset, a romantic offer if she'd
ever heard one.

"I'm not that bad, Bay," Roni answered. "Or maybe
I'm just bad in a good way." Her voice was a passionate whisper that Sabrina could barely understand
but it still irked her tremendously.

"Not in certain situations." He sounded amused,
as if he was remembering times when he'd enjoyed
her so-called badness. Sabrina's blood started to
boil, temper bubbling hotly to her nerve ends.

"Tell me, honey . . ." Sabrina got the impression
that the woman had moved closer to Bay in an inti-
mately confiding way. "You aren't trying to use that
blind girl to make me jealous, are you? Isn't that a
little ridiculous?"

"She's gorgeous and she's a great person," Bay
said, without denying the charge.

"But she's blind," Roni reminded him. "I know
you must feel sorry for her. All of us feel pity for
those less fortunate."

All of us minus one. You, Sabrina thought with fury.
Not that she wanted pity from anyone, ever.

"But it will be so hard for her when she eventually
discovers that all the attention you've been giving her

is because of pity," Roni said in a persuasive but unpleasant tone. "I don't think she'll thank you."

"You're right about that. Knowing Sabrina, she'd probably slap my face," Bay said, cheerfully enough.

Sabrina didn't listen to the rest as he went on. She'd heard enough. Her stomach was twisting in knots. Nausea attacked, swirling in sickening circles as she rose to her feet, not listening to Mrs. Phillips's chatter either.

"Excuse me," she interrupted the flow. "Mrs. Thyssen?" Her questioning voice searched for the location of her hostess somewhere nearby.

"Yes, Sabrina?" Pamela was instantly at her side, a curious note in the voice that answered her summons.

Sabrina swallowed, trying to calm her frazzled nerves and make her tone as natural as possible.

"Where is the bathroom?"

"Right this way. Come with me." A ringed hand guided her from the small group. "Are you all right, Sabrina?" Pamela asked in a concerned tone. "You look pale."

"I'm fine." Sabrina forced a smile of reassurance.

Winding through the guests, they turned into what Sabrina guessed was a hallway. Her nerves were raw. The voices in the other room seemed to take on a higher pitch. Although she tried desperately, she couldn't block her hearing.

"Here we are," Pamela said. "The door is directly to your left."

Sabrina stopped, letting her cane determine the distance to the door before she turned to her hostess. "Thanks very much."

"It's a standard layout," Pamela said understandingly.

"And uncluttered—that's my pet peeve. So you aren't likely to stumble."

"Great. Thanks again."

Pamela turned to go. "Do you want me to wait for you out here? I don't mind at all."

"No. That's not necessary." She drew a breath and calmed herself. "I can make it back on my own. I can't keep you from your guests. Just give me an idea of where I am and I'll find my way back. I'm really quite good at following directions."

The older woman hesitated, then gave Sabrina simple directions to follow back to the main party area.

After thanking her and assuring her again that she was all right, Sabrina walked unerringly to the door, aware that Pamela watched. She went in, grateful for the closed door that reduced the voices to a low hum.

The exploring tip of her cane touched a chair leg. Sighing heavily, Sabrina sank onto the velvet cushions. So much for simple, clutter-free decorating. A vanity counter was in front of her and she rested her arms on its smooth surface. But the silence didn't stop her mind from racing.

She had always wondered—she had always questioned Bay's motive for seeing her. Secretly she'd stopped believing it was out of pity. Bay had used the word compassion, but not even that less offensive word eased the stabbing hurt of the conversation she'd overheard. And he was letting pity for her serve a twofold purpose. While he was oh-so-nobly spending an evening or two with Sabrina, he was trying to make this Roni jealous.

Her fingers balled into tight fists. She moaned silently. No, another voice inside remonstrated, she

should be glad she'd discovered his real motive. She
was lucky she'd regarded him as nothing more than
a friend and found out the truth before she'd begun
to misinterpret his attention. How awful it would
have been if she'd started to care for him as a man.

The problem was—what was the next step?
Should she confront him with what she'd figured
out? That was what she wanted to do. She wanted
to throw his pseudo-charitable, pitying words in his
face. But what good would that do? He would just
deny it the way he had all the other times before.

Bay Cameron was just too smooth—that was
something Sabrina couldn't overlook any more.
First he'd maneuvered her into accepting the ivory
cane and using it, then into going to a public restaurant with him, and finally coming here tonight to a
party packed with strangers. Well, the last had back-
fired. Now Sabrina knew his true colors.

The door opened and a woman walked in. Her
voice as she greeted Sabrina was familiar, but she
couldn't recall the woman's name. Self-consciously
Sabrina smoothed the back of her hair, pretending
that she was in front of the vanity mirror to check
her appearance. She hoped the woman wouldn't
dawdle. Unfortunately she did and each passing
second ticked loudly in Sabrina's head.

At last Sabrina knew she couldn't stay any longer
without arousing suspicion. She'd already been in
here a while. She didn't want Mrs. Thyssen sending
in a search posse for her. If only she could slip away
from the house, she wished, as she rose to her feet.
She didn't want to go back to the party. It was taking
on the overtones of a nightmare.

But where would she go, she asked herself, pushing

open the door to the hall. Even if she could sneak away unseen, there was little likelihood there would be a taxi cab cruising in this residential neighborhood. Pamela Thyssen would make a huge fuss if she asked her to call one for her. And on this night of all nights, she'd left her cell phone at home. She doubted very much if she could hold her tongue during the long ride home with Bay.

Not concentrating on where she was going, she bumped into a small table sitting against the hallway wall.

Instinctively her hand reached out to prevent whatever was on the table from falling to the floor. A vase started to tip but she set it upright again. As she started to withdraw her hand, her fingers encountered a smooth, familiar object—the receiver of a telephone.

Saved. Not caring who might be glancing her way, Sabrina picked up the receiver, her fingers quickly dialing 411 and getting the number of a taxi company. Thank God you could now request an automatic connection to the number you'd asked for, she thought. She did just that, too upset to memorize it at the moment.

When the dispatcher answered, Sabrina said quietly, "Would you please send a cab to—" She stopped. She realized she didn't know where she was. Footsteps were approaching.

Don't let it be Bay, she prayed. "Just a minute," she said sotto voce to the dispatcher. Taking a deep breath, she turned to the person coming nearer. She had to take a chance. "Excuse me, but could you tell me what the address is here?"

"Yes, ma'am," a courteous female voice replied and gave her the address.

Something about the way she spoke prompted Sabrina to ask, "Are—are you the maid?"

"Yes, I am." Sabrina knew she'd noticed the white cane in Sabrina's hand.

"Would you bring me my jacket? It's black fake fur."

"I remember it," the maid said. "Of course. Right away."

At the departing footsteps, Sabrina removed her hand from the mouthpiece and gave the address to the dispatcher patiently waiting for it. Maybe not so patiently. He was cussing a blue streak over the radio at a lost cabbie, but he stopped abruptly when she said "Hello?"

"Right here. Sorry you heard—"

"Not a problem," she said but she hoped he wouldn't send that cabbie. She gave him the address and he promised only a few minutes' wait. With the receiver safely replaced, Sabrina turned away from the table.

Footsteps approached again from the direction the maid had taken. Sabrina couldn't tell if it was the maid and she held her breath, fearful she might be stopped on her way out by Bay or Pamela.

"Here you are, ma'am," the maid said. "Shall I help you on with it?"

"Please," Sabrina agreed nervously.

The maid deftly assisted her into the jacket. "Should I let Mrs. Thyssen know you're leaving?"

"No, that won't be necessary. I've already spoken to her," she lied, feeling bad about it. She hoped Mrs. Thyssen wouldn't worry and made a solemn promise to call her the second she got safely home. "The cab will be here any minute. I'll wait outside. The front door—is it straight ahead, down this hall?"

"Yes," the maid replied. "But the fog is awfully thick tonight. It would be best to wait inside."

"I'd prefer to be in the fresh air. It just got so stuffy in there." She didn't want to risk being discovered when she was so near her goal.

"Very well." The maid went about her business as Sabrina said an almost inaudible thanks to her.

As quickly as her searching cane would permit, Sabrina traveled the length of the hallway to the front door. Her hands were trembling with excitement as she opened the front door and stepped into the night.

The cool air was a soothing balm to her taut nerve ends. She moved away from the door, seeking the shadows she knew would be at the side of the entrance. The cocooning fog dampened everything, including her face. The thick walls of the house shut out the noise of the party within. The night was profoundly still. She relaxed a little.

A smile turned up the corners of her mouth as she imagined Bay's confusion when he discovered she was nowhere to be found. He might be genuinely concerned for her safety, if nothing else. But she knew it wouldn't be long before the maid would be asked about her. She would tell him that Sabrina had taken a taxi. He would be angry, but that was just tough. She really didn't care. Whatever debt she might have thought she owed him for his assistance and supposed friendship had been paid in full tonight.

Time went by slowly, but it always seemed to do

that when she was waiting anxiously for something. Sabrina remained in the shadows, hoping she was concealed from anyone who might decide to leave the party early or nicotine fiends stepping outside for a smoke. Finally the steady growl of a car engine sounded down the street. She waited to see if it stopped at this house or continued past. It halted at the curb and a car door slammed.

As she stepped from the shadows, a man's husky voice spoke to her. "You call for a cab, lady?"

"Yes, I did." She walked as swiftly as she could toward him, a spring in her step. A car door opened. She used the sound to judge the distance. The man's hand took her elbow to help her into the rear of the cab. "I want you to take me to—"

Sabrina never got her home address out. The front door of the house opened and she just stood there, feeling frozen. She had nearly made it.

Maybe she still could. There wasn't much time. Bay's long strides were already eating up the distance from the front door to the taxi.

As she tried to slip into the rear seat, an arm circled her waist and drew her back to the sidewalk.

"Let me go!" She struggled against that familiar arm.

"Sure thing, Sabrina. As soon as we get a few things straightened out." He tightened his hold and then she heard the crisp sound of money being removed from his pocket with his other hand. "Hey, pal," he said to the cabdriver. "Sorry you had to come out for nothing. But I'll see her home."

She sagged in his embrace, not wanting to cause a public scene and get him in serious trouble. He maneuvered her so he could hand over a few bills to the cabbie and shut the door.

He wasn't going to force her to walk back with him. She had decided to go of her own accord. But Bay didn't lead her to the house. They went to his car, parked at the curb some distance down the street.

"Would you like to explain what's going on?" he requested in an I-mean-business voice.

"Isn't it obvious? I was going home," Sabrina retorted.

"If you wanted to leave, why didn't you look for me? I never said we had to stay at the party until the last minute." His fingers held her wrist, which he absently stroked on the inside. His gentle touch effectively kept her in place. She wished she wasn't so easily led.

"I didn't want you to take me home, that's why!" she snapped.

"Then you should've left your cane behind. Maybe no one would've noticed you leaving if it hadn't been for that little white stick." He was really annoyed. It vibrated through his controlled voice.

"I didn't think of that." She refused to be intimidated by him in any way, no matter how minor.

"So, why after all this time would you suddenly not want me to take you home?" Bay demanded.

"I don't have to give you a reason," Sabrina said haughtily.

"Yes, you do. And I really want to hear it," he informed her.

Sabrina stopped short and Bay did likewise. "Maybe I'm tired of your pity and your patronizing attitude," she began. "And that's just for starters."

She tilted her head so he could see the dislike in her expression. "I don't need you or anyone else to feel sorry for me!"

"What?"

She sensed his alertness, knew she had his complete attention. "Go and join the Boy Scouts!" Her voice grew shrill. "I'm tired of your good deeds!" Her chin gave a traitorous quiver.

"Pity? Is that what you think I feel?" The accusation exploded around her.

Sabrina opened her mouth to retaliate, and in the next instant she was pulled against him. The strength of his action sent her cane clattering to the sidewalk. An arm curved around her and a gentle hand cupped the back of her head. Without knowing exactly why, she stood on tiptoes and—

He kissed her. Her low sound of protest was muffled by his sensual mouth. He hardly allowed her to breathe but she secretly didn't mind. If he was that into it, so would she be. She kissed him right back.

An elemental tension crackled in the air when he raised his head. His hands moved, closing over her slender shoulders, keeping Sabrina in front of him.

"I—you—we shouldn't have done that," she managed to say. It wasn't as if she'd been unwilling. But the kiss was unexpected and he'd caught her off guard.

"Oh no? You didn't seem to mind." His voice was low and a little ragged, something she found incredibly sexy.

Again he gathered her to his chest, pressing her against the rock wall while the muscles in his arms rippled around her. Sabrina had not yet recovered from the sensation of his first kiss when she gave in to the second. She strained against him, not surrendering entirely, not sure what she was doing.

As her token resistance faded, she became more aware of the passion within him, transmitted to her by his demanding lips. A feverish warmth enveloped her and she began to respond even more to the hard, commanding mouth that possessed hers.

Her hands stopped pushing against him and her fingers curled into the lapels of his jacket. Through the rainbow explosion of her senses, Sabrina realized she was falling for the virile skill she'd warned herself against.

As suddenly as it all began, it ended, with Bay holding her an arm's length away. Her equilibrium was completely gone. Up was down and down was up. And it was because of Bay and his irresistible embrace.

"Get in the car." The blunt command snapped her out of it.

But even that abrupt return to reality couldn't make Sabrina move. Bay had to do that, guiding her to the passenger seat and getting in himself, then firmly clicking the buckle of her seatbelt when she just sat there with the strap pulled across her without fastening it. Her voice didn't return until he drove the car away from the curb.

"Bay—" Her voice was barely above a whisper.

"Shut up, Sabrina."

His tone was tense and she guessed his mouth was too. She knew his jaw was clenched without having to touch it.

"Maybe when I can think," he went on, "I can say I'm sorry. Maybe."

Chapter 8

Obeying his command, Sabrina hadn't spoken during the tense ride to her home. She had been too frightened to speak. Not because she thought he would subject her again to his much too intriguing kisses. Sabrina had been frightened by herself. For a few fleeting moments in his arms, she had not been a blind woman, only a woman. Fully alive.

Her tender mouth retained the burning fire of his hard, demanding kiss. The racing of her heart kept right on pounding in her ears as if she were on a runaway locomotive and couldn't jump off. The sensation of the strong arms that had locked her in his embrace didn't feel like it would ever go away.

Her body remembered the solid rock pressure of his chest and thighs, implanting the hard masculinity of him so firmly in her mind Sabrina thought she would never be able to uproot it. The scent of his maleness and spicy cologne clung to her skin. She really didn't want to wash it away.

What was worse, she didn't want to erase anything else. That was why she was still frightened two days after the fact. Over and over again she'd asked herself why he had kissed her that way.

Had his passionate strength been heightened by anger that she had found out his true motive? Could he have used her as an outlet for his frustration? His plan to make Roni jealous had failed. Considering what Sabrina had overheard, that was the most likely explanation. Probably it was a combination of several things, though.

Sabrina would not consider the possibility that Bay had been prompted by any physical desire for her. Not that she believed there would never be a time when she would meet a man who truly loved and wanted her. But visualizing Bay Cameron as that man was something she couldn't do. He had social standing, lots of money, charm, and good looks. There were too many other women he could have at his side in an intimate sense.

Her blindness had touched him. It didn't matter which noun was used to identify the emotion he felt—pity, compassion, sympathy. They were all one and the same thing.

Pain gnawed at her heart. Pride said she couldn't regard Bay as a friend any longer. A true friend might commiserate but he would never seek her company because he felt sorry for her. But Sabrina's heart honestly acknowledged the main reason why she had to reject him. *She* was the one who'd stopped regarding him as a friend and started thinking of him as a lover. For her, that was dangerous and foolish.

A sob rasped her throat, choking her with its futility. Sabrina buried her face in her hands, letting the misery wash over her. For a little while in the solitude of the afternoon, she would feel sorry for herself and not regret it. She'd earned the right.

Before the first tears slipped from her brown eyes, the phone rang. *No.* Sabrina silently denied that she'd heard it. The ringing persisted.

The urge was there to ignore it, to let it ring until the person on the other end gave up. Grimacing at the possibility that it was her father, she knew it was wrong to make him unnecessarily concerned. Reluctantly she rose to her feet and walked to the phone.

"Lane residence," she answered in a pseudo-calm voice.

"Sabrina."

The sound of Bay's husky baritone nearly made her drop the phone. It was as if a bolt of lightning had struck her. Weakness made her knees quake and she quickly sought the support of a chair.

"Are you there, Sabrina?" he asked when she failed to reply right away.

"Yes—hello, Bay." Her tone was strained and unnatural but it didn't matter any more.

"How are you?" It was not a casual question. There was too much guarded alertness in his tone.

"Fine. And you?" She was distant and polite, just to be safe.

Bay ignored her routine question. "You know why I'm calling, don't you?"

"How could I possibly?" Sabrina asked without interest.

"Would you have dinner with me Saturday night?" A certain grimness in the way he spoke turned the invitation into a challenge.

But Sabrina had guessed that if Bay did make any conciliatory gesture as he'd indicated he might, it would be wrapped in a suggestion for a Saturday night date. She realized now that he always chose Saturday night because that was the evening her father devoted exclusively to Deborah and Sabrina spent it alone—at least, she had before she met Bay. Yesterday she'd invited an old friend, Sally Goodwin, over on Saturday night.

"Sorry, can't. I have other plans," she answered truthfully and a shade triumphantly.

"You do?" The mocking inflection held obvious doubt.

"Yup. I do know other people besides you, Bay."

A tired and annoyed sigh came over the wire. "Let me guess. You *arranged* to be busy on Saturday night."

"You can guess whatever you want." She wasn't going to affirm or deny it.

"I get it. Because of my—indiscretion the other night, you've decided not to see me again." He didn't let her reply. "You didn't make any allowances for the possibility that I might have had the right to lose my temper because you walked out without leaving a message or telling where you were going. Listen, Sabrina, you need to grow up some."

He had a valid point, but Sabrina wasn't going to give him credit for it. "It's done. There isn't any point in discussing it."

"Then that's your decision. You aren't going to see me again," Bay stated. "Was it that big a deal? Hasn't anyone ever gotten angry at you before? We were just getting to know each other, sharing some good times—I guess that didn't mean much to you."

Oh, poor guy. But his challenge had to be answered. "It was fun, until you had to go and tell me that you felt sorry for me. I told you once I don't need anyone's pity."

"Whoa. Sorry I was nice," he snapped. She heard him draw a deep, calming breath. It was just too bad if he didn't like what she'd said.

"I don't think that counts as an apology."

He was quiet. "You really don't listen when other people are talking. And you like to test my patience, don't you? How many times do I have to tell you that I don't feel sorry for you before you'll believe me?"

"Then explain to me why you see me," she demanded defiantly.

"There has to be an ulterior motive, huh?" Bay answered. "It can't be because I might"—he paused for an instant, choosing his words— "admire you, especially your courage when you aren't being unreasonably stubborn. Hey, let me put the question to you. Why do you go out with me? Am I a convenient way to get out of the house? Do you simply tolerate me because I take you places you want to go? What's your ulterior motive, Sabrina?"

"I . . , I don't have one," she answered, taken aback by his bluntness.

"Come on. You must," he said. "You had to have a reason for going out with me."

"No, I don't," Sabrina insisted, feeling more than a little confused. "I just enjoyed it. I had—"

Bay interrupted. "Yet it's inconceivable that I just enjoy your company too?"

"How could you?" she protested, looking to regain the offensive. "I don't listen and I test your patience. You said so yourself."

"And I'm arrogant and full of it."

"Six of one and half a dozen of the other," she said. "Both true, though."

He deflected her argumentativeness with mocking humor. "That makes us equal with two flaws apiece."

The corners of her mouth twitched with reluctant amusement. Her stand against him was weakening. She could feel her resolve crumbling under his cocky charm and—not her favorite word in the world—logic.

"You're smiling, aren't you, Sabrina?" he said with a soft chuckle. "Okay, don't bother to answer. I know you'll deny it. I won't ask you to cancel your plans for Saturday evening but how about going sailing with me Sunday?"

"Sailing?" Of all the invitations Bay could have extended, her own love of the sport made this the one she wanted to accept.

"Yes, sailing," he repeated. "You know, boats, water, yo ho ho and a bottle of rum, and all that."

"I—" Sabrina couldn't get the words *no, thanks* out.

"I'll pick you up bright and early around 7 A.M. We'll make a day of it."

"Oh. Um, then I'll be ready. At seven." Her awkward acceptance came from her in a breathless rush, before better judgment made her change her mind.

"All right. See you!" Bay hung up fast, as if he'd had the same thought.

Sabrina didn't change her mind. She had a multitude of second thoughts, but none of them had lasted long enough to bring her to the point of canceling. Any thought that her father might take the decision out of her hands had ended the same day Bay had called.

When she told her father about Bay's invitation that evening, his reply had been, "Yes, Bay called me this afternoon to make sure I had no objections. I don't, and I promise you I won't worry. You'll be in good hands. You can swim and he's a champ. On the swim relay team in college or so he said."

My, my. Bragging to her dad. Bay was really determined.

Sunday morning found Sabrina aboard his trim ketch *Dame Fortune.* Fog and not a whisper of wind delayed their departure for nearly an hour, and Bay was too much of a traditionalist to use the motor.

Now they were under sail, the stiff breeze ruffling the scarf tied around Sabrina's hair, the salty taste of blowing spray on her lips. Passing under the echoing span of the Golden Gate Bridge and negotiating its strong currents, Bay had veered south into the open sea, past Cliff House and Seal Rocks. He continued beyond the ocean beaches, explaining in off-and-on shouts that the treacherous undertows and riptides restricted people there to sunbathing and strolling.

Sabrina patted the bulky life vest he'd put on her, donning one himself, joking that he looked like Mae West on a bad day. She had no idea how she looked, but it was nice that he didn't care about anything besides keeping her safe. The deck was slanted sharply beneath her, heaving with each swell, as Bay expertly took advantage of the prevailing wind and stayed on course.

The billowing nylon of the sails, the waves slapping the sleek hull, and the groans of a ketch at sea were the only sounds now. He really had to concentrate. She'd hardly said five words herself since they'd left the yacht harbor. Conversation wasn't necessary and wouldn't have added anything to the exhilarating experience. Each seemed to sense the other's deep pleasure and nothing needed to be said.

It was some time, even hours, before Sabrina noticed there had been a change in their course. The sun wasn't in the place it normally would've been in their initial heading. Blocking out the song of sea and sail, she listened intently, trying to determine their location and failing.

She turned to Bay. "Where are we?"

"In the waters of Monterey Bay near Santa Cruz. Were you daydreaming?" She heard the smile in his voice.

Instantly she visualized his ruggedly handsome features, tanned by the sun and the wind, cinnamon brown hair dampened by the salt spray and tousled by the breeze. The sun was directly overhead. His light brown eyes would be narrowed against its brilliance, crinkled at the corners because of that flashing smile she had detected in his voice. It was disturbing how vividly clear her picture of him was, so vitally alive and masculine.

Her heart beat a rapid tattoo against her ribs. "Daydreaming or sea-dreaming, I don't know which," she murmured.

Again there was a change in the motion of the ketch. The wind was catching less sail and their speed had decreased. The deck beneath her had begun to right itself.

"What are you doing now?" Sabrina asked.

"Taking her in close to shore. We just passed the

natural bridges north of Santa Cruz. I thought we'd anchor southward for lunch. There's a small cove there that I hope no one else has discovered."

"Sail on, Columbus," she teased him.

He did and came about, eventually dropping the anchor with a little help from Sabrina. This close to shore, wavelets lapped gently against the hull. She turned her head inquiringly toward Bay and felt his gaze moving over her face. A sensual warmth suffused her body and she was pretty sure she was blushing. She was suddenly and intensely aware that they were alone, the two of them, a man and a woman. She put the brakes on that line of thought.

"I'll go below and fix lunch." She pivoted sharply away. "What are we having?"

"Sandwiches, a salad. It's all fixed," Bay answered. "What about a swim before we eat, though? The water is warmer here than up the coast and there aren't any riptides."

"Um, no." Sabrina waved away his suggestion. "You didn't tell me to bring a swimsuit and I didn't."

"No problem." Bay dismissed her excuse. "I always keep extra suits on board in case someone wants to take a dip. I'm sure one of them will fit you."

"But—" She hadn't been in any water but her bathtub since before the accident.

"But what? You can swim, right?"

"Yes, I can swim," she said tightly.

"I'll point you in the right direction so you won't head out to sea if you're worrying about losing your reference points. And I'll be right there with you. Go and change."

He told her which locker he kept the suits in and

Sabrina went below. It was probably better to go for a swim than stay on the small deck alone with him.

She needed to cool off.

Most of the swimsuits were two-piece, some mere triangles of cloth. Sabrina chose a close-fitting maillot with diamond cutouts at the waist crisscrossed with ties. At least in it she felt less naked when she walked up on deck. Her long hair was tumbling down over her shoulders. The water would've pulled it free of its knot eventually, so she had done it first.

"I'm ready," she said nervously.

Bay didn't comment on her appearance. "I've put a rope ladder over the side." He took her hand and led her to the rail. "I'll go in the water first."

When he released her hand after her silent nod of agreement, Sabrina tightened the hand into a fist to retain the warmth of his touch a little longer. It was kind of silly of her, because this wasn't a romantic outing, more a just-friends thing. Which was why the sensations she was feeling were bothering her.

The deck rocked slightly, followed by the sound of a body slicing into the water, and Sabrina knew that Bay had simply dived in. A second later she heard him surface and turned her head his way. A few clean strokes brought him to the bottom of the ladder.

"Come on in. The water's great!" he called to her.

While Bay held the ladder steady, Sabrina started down, her toes feeling for the rope rungs. In the water, which was neither warm nor cold, Sabrina clung to the security of the ladder for a few minutes, adjusting to the eerie sensation of having nothing solid beneath her feet.

Of course she knew how to swim, but this was the

first time she'd tried since becoming blind. The chattering of her teeth was from nerves and not the cool water.

"Are you ready?" Bay was still beside the ladder.

"I think so," Sabrina answered, clenching her jaw so he wouldn't hear the chattering of her teeth.

He moved a few strokes from the ladder. "Swim toward my voice."

Forcing her hand to release the rope, Sabrina took a deep breath and struck out toward him. At first she was hampered by nervousness and lack of coordination, but both soon faded as she became accustomed to the watery environment. She could hear Bay's strong, cleaving strokes keeping pace beside her and drew strength and reassurance from his presence.

It seemed as if they had been swimming a long time. Sabrina began to get tired. Her reaching arms were feeling heavy and hard to move. She stopped to tread water and catch her breath, and Bay did the same.

"How much farther?" she asked as she swallowed down gulps of air.

"About another fifteen feet before we touch bottom." He wasn't at all out of breath. "Can you make it?"

She didn't answer but started out again, maintaining a steady rhythm that wouldn't wear her out too quickly. Surprisingly, it didn't seem that she'd gone far at all before a kicking foot scraped the sandy bottom. Sabrina righted herself quickly, wiping the salt water from her face and tucking her long wet hair behind her ears.

"You made it." Bay spoke from somewhere near her left side. "How do you feel?"

She managed a smile. "Exhausted, but good otherwise."

"Let's go ashore and take a breather."

Her hands were resting lightly on top of the almost chest-high water. She let the gentle swells roll over them instead of splashing. The waves would have told her which way the shore was if she'd been in doubt, but Bay took her hand anyway and led her to the beach.

"You're going to like this. The beach comes equipped with its own sunning rock," he said as they waded onto the sand, packed smooth and firm beneath her feet. "It's a little hard but better than the sand when you don't have a towel." The pressure of his hand stopped her after they'd gone a few yards. "Here."

Before Sabrina could protest, his hands were around her waist and he was lifting her onto the hard, sun-warmed surface of the stone. Her fingers automatically gripped the sinewy wetness of his arms for balance. Her flesh was heated where his hands had covered the open diamond areas of the swimsuit waistline. It was several seconds before her heart stopped thumping so much. By then he was on the rock too.

"Did you have a good time last night?" he asked after he moved into a more comfortable position. He was sitting, Sabrina could tell by the direction of his voice.

"Last night?" She frowned and shifted more fully onto the rock. Had the seawater dissolved her short-term memory? Maybe not. Then she remembered. "Yes, I did." Actually it had been a quiet evening.

She and Sally had sat around and talked and listened to music.

"Where did you go?"

"Nowhere. Sally and I stayed at the house." She shrugged, turning her face to the warmth of the sun, letting it chase away the shivers on her damp skin.

"An evening of gossipy girl talk, is that it?" He didn't sound thrilled.

Sabrina wasn't sure whether he was dismissing her uneventful plans or that she'd chosen not to spend time with him. From what she knew of Bay, the first seemed more likely.

"Men gossip just as much as women do," she replied. "Plus they do a lot more bragging."

He didn't argue the point.

An awkward silence followed. At least it was awkward for Sabrina. She was too aware of Bay, physically aware of him. She leaned back on her hands,

"The sun feels good," she said.

"I think I'll stretch out and enjoy it," Bay replied.

At the same time that he spoke, his movements matched his words. And the silence that Sabrina hadn't wanted took over, broken only by the slow, repeated rush of the ocean to the shore. There was little for her to do except to follow suit.

Her searching hands found a small, smooth hollow in the rock behind her, a natural headrest. Sabrina lay down on her back. For a long time she listened to the sound of Bay's even breathing. Her own was shallow, her chest muscles constricted with tension. Finally the heat of the sun and the rock it warmed coaxed her into relaxing.

Sabrina didn't fall asleep, but she did drift into a

strange state of drowsiness. She was aware of her surroundings and the man beside her, yet deaf to them at the same time. Then something brought all of her senses to full alert. Her eyes blinked uselessly as she tried to determine what had disturbed her. She turned her head slightly in Bay's direction and accidentally brushed his hand with her cheek. She felt a tug—he was holding a lock of her silky brown hair.

"Do you know this is the first time I've ever seen you with your hair down?"

"I—I don't like to wear it down. It gets in the way." There was an odd tremor in her voice as she sensed how close he was to her. She could almost feel the heat of his body stretched beside hers. His voice had come from a position slightly above her, indicating that he was most likely lying on his side, propped up on his elbow.

Bay didn't seem to pay any attention to her explanation.

"When you wear your hair up in that little topknot, you look regal."

"Regal? That sounds old," she blurted out, realizing that she sounded vain.

He laughed. "Then, you look like a young queen."

"Hah."

He hummed a little. "But with your hair down like this," he twined the strand around his finger, "you look even prettier. Windblown. A little wild."

Her pulse was picking up speed. It was impossible to roll away from him. The edge of the rock was too near.

"Do you think we should be heading back?" Her throat was tight and so was her voice.

"What's the matter? Am I not supposed to admire your hair? Sorry."

"No big deal." Sabrina shook her head, freeing the lock of hair from his fingers and feeling it fall against her bare shoulder. "I'm going to wear it up because it's the easiest to take care of, no matter what." He could probably finish the rest of what she was thinking himself. *No matter what you want, pal.* Sabrina really wasn't interested in his opinions on the subject.

Bay reached back and gave her hair another annoying tug. "Then you'll probably be sorry to hear that I prefer that silky knot. The way it is now is just right for a bedroom."

The sensual implication of his statement made Sabrina draw in a fast breath. Her heightened awareness of him in all his half-bare glory made this type of conversation impossible. She wasn't capable of idle flirtation, this suggestive playing with words. She started to push herself back into a sitting position to escape his nearness, but Bay was already straightening, and getting up.

"We should be heading back," he said as he towered above her.

Thankful for the reprieve, Sabrina swung her legs to the edge of the rock. Bay was on the sand, his hands gripping her waist to lift her down before she could slide the short distance to the sand. Straining away from his unwanted assistance, her effort to keep from landing too close to him brought a heel down on a partially buried outcropping of the rock.

The unexpected, jarring pain sent her against his chest. He tightened his hold to steady her.

"Are you all right?"

Her unspoken answer was negative. It couldn't be otherwise when the nakedness of his muscular torso and thighs pressed against her was playing havoc with her heart. Soft, curling chest hairs tickled sensually on her skin. His head was inclined toward her, his warm breath stirring her dark bangs.

The desire was strong to slide her arms around his broad shoulders and nestle her head against his neck. To resist the nearly overpowering impulse, she moistened her lips nervously and tipped her head back.

"I'm all right," she assured him in a shaky voice. "I stepped on a sharp rock or something."

A sudden breath of wind tossed a thin lock of hair across her face. It clung to the gleaming wetness of her lips. Sabrina started to push it away, but her hand was only partway there when Bay's fingers drew it gently away, pushing it back with the rest of her long hair.

His hand remained along the side of her face, his thumb absently caressing her cheekbone. She held her breath, motion suspended under the magical spell of his touch.

The intoxicating sweetness of his mouth barely touched hers before Sabrina sharply twisted her head away. Her defenses couldn't withstand a kiss. Not even a casual kiss.

"Don't, Bay, please!"

"I wasn't going to hurt you." Her words brought a rigid stillness to his touch as he misinterpreted the reason for her trembling.

"I just don't want you to kiss me." Sabrina pulled free of his unresisting arms and took several quick steps away until common sense kicked in and she realized that she didn't know where she was going.

She wrapped her arms tightly around her, trying to fight off the chill that shivered over her where his strong body had warmed her.

Bay walked over to stand beside her. She could feel his gaze move over her. Her lashes fluttered downward in case her sightless eyes mirrored the heady sensations swimming in her mind. For an electric moment, she hardly dared to breathe.

"We'd better head back to the boat." The edge in his voice betrayed tightly leashed emotion. Sabrina couldn't tell if he was angry and whether whatever he was feeling was directed at himself or her.

The hand that gripped hers and led her toward the water was cold and impersonal. Sabrina was glad when the water became deep enough to swim and he had to release her. She hadn't thought it was possible that his touch, which usually started a fire, could chill her to the bone.

It was not a leisurely swim back. Sabrina set herself a pace that took every ounce of her strength to maintain. It was a form of self-punishment for being stupid enough to let Bay persuade her to come along on this outing when it would have been a lot smarter to stop seeing him.

She was just about done in when Bay reached out and pulled her to the rope ladder, but she climbed aboard without his assistance. She paused on deck to catch her breath.

"If we'd been anchored another ten feet away, you never would've made it. What were you trying to prove?" Bay snapped.

"Nothing." Sabrina averted her head and self-consciously felt her way to the steps leading below deck.

"When you're dressed, you can get the lunch ready. I think you can find everything. In the meantime, I'll get the boat under way," he said tersely.

"Don't you . . . don't you want to eat first?" she faltered.

"I think we're both in a hurry to get back, aren't we?"

There was a challenge in his voice that dared her to deny it. When she didn't reply, he added grimly, "I'll enjoy the food as much as you once we're under sail."

Actually Sabrina found the food tasteless. Most of it wanted to stick in her throat but she forced down several more mouthfuls. There was no atmosphere of friendliness when they sailed back to the yacht harbor. Although he was preoccupied with handling the boat, their mutual silence when they looked at each other was rife with tension.

Bay's acceptance of her polite thanks at the conclusion of the day was as cool and aloof as her offer had been. When the iron gate closed behind him, Sabrina knew why she was so totally miserable. She had plenty of time to ponder the reason on the way back. She had fallen in love with Bay Cameron. She was literally a blind fool.

Chapter 9

Bay's last parting remark to her had been "I'll call you." In Sabrina's experience, those particular words had always signaled the end of a relationship. It was Friday night and he hadn't.

Another tear slipped down her cheek. She wiped it away with her fingertips, leaving a streak of dark clay to smudge her face. At least she could still cry—somehow that was better than nothing.

There was a knock on the studio door. She'd kept it closed this last week, not wanting anyone to pop in without the warning click of the doorknob. She had told her father it was because she wanted to block out any distractions. The truth was she could work in the middle of rush hour traffic. Lately, however, she'd found herself simply standing and crying. It was this she didn't want her father or anyone else to see.

Sabrina took the hem of her smock and wiped her face carefully just in case there was a betraying tear she'd missed. "Come in," she called in answer to the knock.

A cloud of perfume swirled into the room, a scent her mind labeled as Deborah's. The light sound of shoes that were undoubtedly expensive confirmed that.

"I came to remind you that we would be leaving in an hour so you would have plenty of time to clean up here and change clothes," her future stepmother said brightly.

"I don't think I'll go," Sabrina murmured, centering her attention on the partially completed clay bust on the work pedestal.

"Grant has been looking forward to the three of us dining out tonight," Deborah reminded her.

"I know, but I'd rather keep working a while longer. I'm right in the middle of this piece. I want to keep going while the concept is still fresh in my mind," she lied.

"Are you sure?" came the slightly troubled question.

"I've just really grasped the form and I don't want to lose it," Sabrina assured her.

"I didn't mean about the work," Deborah said hesitantly.

"What did you mean then?" Her hand was poised along the half-formed ear of the bust. Was Deborah's womanly intuition at work?

"I . . . I wanted to be sure you weren't refusing because of me. I don't want you to think you would be a third wheel tonight," the attractive redhead explained self-consciously.

"No, Deborah, it wasn't because of you." Sabrina gave a silent sigh of relief. "We'll go out another night. I probably shouldn't have started this so late, but now that I have, I want to work a little longer."

"I understand. I know how important this is to you. And don't worry, Sabrina." There was the warmth of a smile in her voice. "I'll explain to Grant."

"What were you going to explain to me?"

"Grant!" Deborah explained in a startled voice. "You shouldn't sneak up on a person like that."

"I didn't sneak. You just didn't hear me." There was the faint sound of a kiss exchanged. "Now, I repeat, what are you going to explain to me?"

Sabrina answered for Deborah. "I've decided to stay in and work tonight instead of going out to dinner with you two."

"The two of us were going out to dinner with you, not the other way around." Her father frowned.

"Then we'll go out another night." She was determined not to let him change her mind.

"Nope. No deal. Tonight."

"Grant!" Deborah interjected a silent plea into his name.

"Damn it, Deborah, she's working too hard," he declared forcefully. "Look at the dark circles under her eyes and the hollows in her cheeks. She doesn't sleep. She doesn't eat. All she does is work, work, work from dawn to dusk—no, midnight."

"Dad, you're exaggerating," Sabrina sighed. "Besides, doing art is really important to me." It was the only thing that kept her sane but she didn't want to say that. Without it, the emptiness of a life without Bay would be more than she could stand. "I promise as soon as I can leave this piece I'm doing I'll fix myself something to eat and go straight to bed. How's that?"

"I think that's a fair bargain, don't you, Grant?" Deborah murmured.

"I—" He took a deep breath, exasperated, but arguing with the two women he loved was not something he enjoyed. He sighed heavily. "All right. I surrender. You can stay home this time. But next week we're all going together and no excuses. Now, why don't you let me have a peep at this work of art that is too important to leave?"

Sabrina stepped to the side as he walked closer. "I only have it roughed in right now. I'm doing the head and shoulders of Gino Marchetti as he was in his youth. Over a year ago, he showed me a picture taken at his wedding. I had intended to do a painting, but—" She left that unfinished for obvious reasons. "He looked very Roman, very proud and very strong."

"Gino, the pharmacist?" Grant Lane repeated with a hint of disbelief.

"It's only a rough version," Sabrina said.

There was a moment of silence as he studied the partially completed head of the sculpture. Then he turned to Deborah suddenly. "Deborah, who does it look like to you?"

"Well—" Her hesitation was pronounced. "I don't know Gino very well."

"I've known him for years. I'm sorry to be the one to tell you, Sabrina, but that doesn't look like him at all, not even when he was younger," he said emphatically.

"When it's finished—" Sabrina began.

"It will look exactly like Bay Cameron," her father finished the sentence for her.

"You must be mistaken," she responded evenly,

but she clenched her hands tightly together until they hurt, punishing them for having betrayed her. "It doesn't look at all like Bay, does it, Deborah?"

"Um, it does bear a slight resemblance to him," the other woman admitted reluctantly, "but as you said, it isn't finished."

"The man has an interesting face. If you could see it, Sabrina, I know you would want to put it on canvas. But nevertheless, I'm not going to argue with you. You're the artist, not me. If you say it's Gino, it's Gino. I suppose there's Roman characteristics in both of them." He put his arms around her shoulders and gave her a reassuring hug. "Now if you two ladies will excuse me, I came up here to shower and change."

After bestowing a paternal kiss on Sabrina's cheek, he left the room. Sabrina stared sightlessly at the mound of clay on the work pedestal, her heart crying with pain. For a moment, she had forgotten Deborah was still in the room, until the faint click of a heel reminded her.

"Sabrina, about Bay—" The gentle voice paused.

"What about Bay?" Sabrina's tone was cold and aloof.

"You aren't becoming—too involved with him, are you?" Deborah hesitated as if sensing she was trespassing on private territory. "I mean, I admire him very much, but I don't think you should—"

"Take his attentions too seriously," Sabrina finished for her. "I'm well aware that he only sees me to be kind." She couldn't bring herself to use the word pity.

"I'm glad." There was a note of relief in the redhead's statement. "I'm sure he likes you, Sabrina. I just don't think it would be wise if you became too fond of him. After all you've been through, it wouldn't be fair."

"I am fond of him," she asserted. "He helped me a lot. Bay was the one who suggested that I try sculpture and start with clay." She had to admit, if only silently to herself, that it wasn't a fair trade to give away her heart for a career, but when was anything having to do with love fair? "But don't worry, Deborah, I haven't misinterpreted his motives."

"You always seem to have your feet on the ground," was the faintly envious response.

Only this time my head was in the clouds, Sabrina thought to herself. She mumbled an absent reply when Deborah said she would leave Sabrina to her work.

As the studio door closed behind her father's fiancée, Sabrina's hands reached tentatively toward the sculpture, lightly exploring the roughed-in features, confirming for herself that it was indeed Bay. A cold fury pervaded her.

Destroy it! Smash it! her mind ordered. *Turn it back into an ordinary lump of clay!*

Her hands rested on either side of the face, but they couldn't carry out the order. One tear fell, then another. Finally heart-wrenching sobs racked her slender form, her shoulders hunching forward at the excruciating pain in her chest.

But her hands didn't remain immobile. Shakily they began working, painstakingly defining each detail of his face in the yielding clay. It was a labor of love and what pieces of her heart she hadn't given to Bay went into his likeness.

Later, Sabrina wasn't conscious of how much time

had passed. Her father knocked once on the door and opened it. She didn't have time to wipe the tears from her face, so she kept her back to the door.

"We're leaving now," he told her. "Don't forget your promise. Eat and go straight to bed."

"Yes, Dad," she answered tightly. "Have a good time."

The interruption checked the onslaught of tears. She suddenly realized how drained she was, emotionally and physically. When the front door leading to the stairwell to the street closed, signaling the departure of her father and Deborah, Sabrina sank onto the work stool. She buried her face in her hands, not wanting to move or expend the energy to breathe.

A pounding began. For an instant she thought it was coming from inside her head. Then she realized it was coming from the door downstairs. She made a wry face as she rubbed her cheeks, trying to freshen up a little so she wouldn't scare whoever it was.

Her father must have forgotten his key. She slipped off the stool, but her legs refused to be hurried as she made her way out of the studio and down the stairs to the second floor. The knocking continued, more demanding than before.

"I'm coming!" Irritation raised her voice and the sound stopped.

Her neck was stiff and tense, and she rubbed the muscles at the back of it wearily as she turned the deadbolt and opened the door.

"What's the matter? Did you forget your key?" She tried to make her voice airy and teasing, but it was a hollow attempt. Her greeting was met with silence.

Sabrina tilted her head in a listening attitude. "Dad?"

"Did you know there's a smudge of clay on your cheek?"

Sabrina recoiled instinctively from the sound of Bay's voice. Her hand moved to shut the door, but he blocked it effectively and stepped into the room.

"How did you get up here? What do you want?" she demanded angrily.

"I met your father and Deborah on their way out. He let me in," he explained calmly.

"Why?" She pivoted away, unable to face him, a hand nervously wiping the clay from her cheek.

"Why did he let me in?" Bay questioned. "He said something about you working too hard."

"Well, I'm not!" she said emphatically. "And I meant why did you come?"

"To ask you to have dinner with me."

"No." Sabrina tipped her head back, her lashes fluttering down as she prayed silently that he would leave her alone.

"I won't accept that," he stated. "You have to eat and it might as well be with me as alone."

"You'll have to accept it, because I'm busy. It doesn't bother me in the least to eat by myself." A solitary meal was something she had better get used to, she told herself.

"Sabrina, stop being stubborn," Bay told her. "There's no need to change clothes. Just take off your smock and go as you are. We'll eat and I'll bring you back here to finish your work, if it's so essential that it get done tonight."

"I'm not going to be talked into going," she warned.

With a fluid step, Bay reached out and untied the sash of her smock. Quickly she tried to tie the bow again, but his fingers closed over her wrist to prevent it.

"You are not going to bully me this time, Bay Cameron," Sabrina muttered, straining to free her wrist from his grasp.

He held it easily. "It's going to be a long night then, because I'm not leaving here until you agree."

He was just arrogant enough to do it, too. And she had a feeling that she might not be able to hide her feelings or hold her tongue if she tried to outwit him.

Sabrina closed her mouth tightly for a moment. "If I agree just this once, do you promise that from now on you will accept my decisions about going with you as final?"

Her request was met by guarded silence. "Sure," he finally said. "I'll promise anything if you'll explain the reason why you can't stand me all of a sudden."

"I don't know what you're talking about," she said coolly. Her heart started pounding in a frantic fight-or-flight reaction. She couldn't really do either.

Bay ignored her denial. "I promise, you promise."

She gave a sigh. "All right, you have it. Now let go of me." Her wrist was freed. "But I still don't know what you're talking about," she lied.

Her attitude toward him had changed, but not for anything did she want him to find out why. Pity because she was blind was one thing, but pity because she loved him was something she refused to tolerate.

"We'll see," Bay murmured.

She hated his air of confidence. Sabrina flung her

smock in the general direction of a chair and stalked to the umbrella stand to get her cane, the ivory cane that Bay had given her.

"Let's go, so we can get this over with," she declared.

"Aren't you forgetting your bag?" he said. "You might need your key to get back in unless you plan to spend the night with me."

"Perish the thought," Sabrina said.

But the thought stayed with her as she hurried up the stairs to her room. It did hurt, though, that Bay could joke about making love to her, especially when it was something that she wanted so very much.

Downstairs with her purse in hand, she brushed past him through the door.

"Are you ready?" he asked.

Obviously.

Her continued silence in the car was for her own protection, not to be rude. She couldn't begin to guess Bay's reasons for not speaking. He was an enigma. She didn't understand why he did anything he did. For instance, why did he want her company when she'd made it so clear that she didn't want his?

Poignantly Sabrina realized that this was probably the last time she would be with Bay, if he kept his word. It was really impossible and impractical to keep going out with him when she knew the truth of her feelings. It would only bring more pain.

She knew he hoped to change her mind and persuade her to continue their relationship. He had succeeded the last time when she hadn't been aware of her love.

Naturally he was sure he could do it again—why, she didn't know. She had to guard against his charm. She couldn't let him linger when they separated.

Her thoughts were centered on the man behind the wheel. Nothing else around her penetrated her consciousness. She couldn't hear the traffic. Up or down a San Francisco street, it didn't matter. She couldn't care less where he was taking her, although at some future time she would probably do her damnedest to avoid the restaurant.

"Sabrina."

The faint command for her attention drew her out of the sheltering cocoon of her misery. She sat up straighter, realizing that they had stopped. The engine had been turned off. Pink heightened her cheekbones but she knew the dimness of the car concealed it.

"Are we here?" She tipped her head to a haughty angle.

"Yes," Bay answered.

Her fingers closed tightly around her cane while she waited for Bay to walk around the car to open her door. The dragon head carved into the ivory handle left an imprint in her fingers. Since she didn't know where she was going, she had to accept the guidance of his hand on her elbow. Several paces farther, he opened a door and ushered her into a building.

Footsteps immediately approached them and a woman's voice greeted them in pleased surprise. "You're here so soon. Let me take your coat."

Bay shrugged out of his overcoat. "Yup, it didn't take me as long as I thought. Mrs. Gibbs, I'd like you to meet Sabrina Lane. Sabrina, this is Mrs. Gibbs."

"Hello." Sabrina greeted the woman warily, her

ears straining to hear the typical sounds of a restaurant. Nothing.

"I'm pleased to meet you, Miss Lane." Then the footsteps retreated.

"What kind of a restaurant is this?" Sabrina whispered, not sure if anyone could overhear.

"It's not a restaurant." His hand was at her elbow again, leading her forward.

Sabrina frowned. "But—"

"This is my home, Sabrina," Bay said quietly.

She stopped right where she was. "You said you were taking me out to eat."

"But I never said to a restaurant." He released her elbow and curved his arm around the back of her waist, propelling her forward. "And you never asked."

Sabrina twisted away from his arm. "You've tricked me for the last time, Bay Cameron." Her voice trembled with emotion. "You can just take me home right now."

"I gave Mrs. Gibbs a list of your favorite things. She's gone to a great deal of trouble to cook a meal you'll like. She'll be very disappointed if you don't stay."

"Don't guilt me into it. Besides, you were never concerned about my feelings," she reminded him sharply. "Why should I worry about hurting hers?"

"Because essentially you're a gentle and sensitive woman and because"—his low voice got even lower—"you gave me your word."

"And I'm supposed to honor it even when you don't keep yours." Sabrina swallowed back a sob of frustration.

"I've never lied to you."

"No, you've only tricked, maneuvered, and bullied me into doing what you want, but after all, you are Bay Cameron. You can make up your own code of ethics, can't you?" she snapped.

"Let's go into the living room." A fine thread of cold steel ran through his voice and Sabrina knew her barbs had pricked.

Paradoxically she felt remorse and satisfaction at hurting him. She loved him desperately, but she hated him too, for seeing her only as a pathetic blind person and not as a woman with physical and emotional needs. She didn't oppose the arm that firmly guided her forward. They turned to the right and his steps slowed.

"Why did you bring me here, Bay?" Sabrina asked.

"We couldn't spend the evening in the hallway." He deliberately misunderstood her question.

"You know very well I was referring to your home," she said.

"We need privacy for the talk we're going to have."

"We could get that in your car or at my house," Sabrina reminded him.

"No way. In a car you could lose your cute little temper and jump out the door and get run over," Bay explained. "Your house wouldn't work either. You know it better than the back of your hand. As stubborn as you can be sometimes, I would probably end up talking through the door of some room you'd locked yourself into. Here, in my home, you don't know which way to move without running the risk of falling over furniture or banging into a wall."

"Aren't you nice," she said. "I can't believe you just said any of that. And you wonder why I've suddenly begun to dislike you." Sabrina edged away but she was unable to move swiftly.

He had essentially set a trap. The tip of her cane raced out to search for any obstacles in front of her and contacted a solid object.

"The sofa is directly in front of you. There's a chair to your right," he said. "Take one step backward and turn to your right and you'll avoid the chair."

"What's in the way after that?" she asked caustically.

"Why don't you see for yourself?"

Slowly Sabrina followed his instructions, putting distance between them as she crossed an empty space with the aid of her cane. Finally the ivory-white tip touched what appeared to be a table leg. She carefully sidestepped around it only to find the table had been situated against a wall. Or at least it was something solid, maybe a door. But that didn't make sense. Sabrina reached out to investigate and sheer, filmy curtains met her fingers.

"The window overlooks San Francisco Bay." His voice came from the center of the room. "There's an unobstructed view of the Golden Gate Bridge and the harbor."

Sabrina didn't know what she had hoped to discover—a way out, maybe. Frustrated, she turned away from the window and partially retraced her steps, stopping before she came too close to where she guessed he was.

"Bay, take me home, please," she asked softly.

"Not yet."

The carpet was soft and thick beneath her feet. She wondered at its color and the furnishings that surrounded her. She really wanted to explore this place where he lived and slept. She shook her head firmly. She couldn't think about that.

"If you don't take me home, I'll just call a cab." She raised her chin defiantly.

He made a sound that was somewhere between a growl and a sigh. "Oh, I give up. This is an exercise in futility. You have a cell phone, go ahead. But I will take you home and you don't have to spend money on a cab—"

"I'm not going to ask you for it! I'm not going to ask you for anything!"

"Just make the call. You're not a prisoner. I shouldn't have brought you here."

"No. You shouldn't have. And don't add insult to injury by asking me why I'm upset!" she cried angrily.

"Is that all? I think there's more to it than that."

His voice was moving closer, the plushness of the carpet muffling his steps. Sabrina turned to face him, trying to use her five-senses radar to pinpoint his location.

"Maybe I'm tired of being treated like a child," she suggested icily.

"Then stop acting like one!" Bay snapped.

With a start, she discovered that he was closer than she'd realized. His hands touched her shoulders, but she quickly shied away.

"For God's sake, Sabrina, why are you afraid of me?" he demanded. "Every time I come near you now you tremble like a scared rabbit. You've been like this ever since Pamela's party. Is that what upset you? Why you're afraid to let me near you?"

Her breathing was shallow and uneven. "It didn't

inspire me to trust you," Sabrina lashed back, unable to explain that it had precipitated the discovery that she was in love with him.

"I was angry. I never meant to frighten you," Bay said forcefully. This time his hands closed over her shoulders before she could elude them. His touch was firm but he was giving her wiggle room.

"Isn't it a little late to be regretting it now?" She lowered her chin so he couldn't study her face as she made the sarcastic retort. "We can't be friends, Bay, not any more."

"Then I'll undo the damage," came his low, clipped response.

He pulled her toward him. Her hands automatically pushed against the solidness of his chest. It was the last resistance Sabrina offered as his mouth closed over hers. It took all of her strength and will to keep from responding to the persuasive mastery of his kiss. At all costs she had to prevent him from finding out the effect he had on her. He could never know the fiery desire in her that nearly made her limp in his arms.

The kiss seemed to go on forever. Sabrina didn't know how much longer she could hold back the raging passion that Bay had ignited. Before the shuddering sigh of surrender escaped, he dragged his mouth from her throbbing lips.

"Sabrina." The husky, whispering tautness of his caressing voice was very nearly the final blow.

Her heart was in her throat, but she forced the words of rejection through. "Now will you let me go?" she demanded in a strained voice.

"What is it, Sabrina?" he asked guardedly. "My kiss doesn't frighten you, or my touch. I don't think you're frightened of anything, but there's something wrong, some explanation why you don't want to continue to see me."

She stood silently for a minute, realizing he wasn't going to free her immediately. Sabrina took a deep breath and tossed back her head. She was about to make the biggest bluff in her life and the most important.

"Do you want the truth, Bay?" she said boldly. "Well, the truth is that when you first met me I was lost and lonely. I was nothing and my destination was nowhere. You got me out of my shell and gave me companionship. More important, you gave me back a chance for a career in a field I love more than anything else in the world. I'll always be eternally grateful to you for that."

She paused for an instant, sensing his stillness. "I wish you hadn't forced me to say this, Bay. I don't mean to be unkind, but I'm not lost or lonely anymore. I have my career and a goal, and that's all I've ever wanted in life. I've enjoyed the times we spent together. But you tend to dominate and the only thing I want to dominate my life is my work. To sum it all up in one sentence, I simply don't need you anymore."

"I see." His hands fell away from her shoulders as he stepped back. His voice was deeply sad. "I don't think you could have put it more clearly."

"It was never my intention, consciously or unconsciously, to use you. I hope you'll believe that," Sabrina explained. "About two weeks ago I realized that I wanted to devote all of my time to my work, but I didn't know how to tell you that without sounding ungrateful for all you'd done. All you were asking in return was a casual friendship, and I was too selfish to even want to give you that. So I tried to pick a fight with you, thinking that if you got angry, you might be the one to break it off. I'm sorry, Bay."

A tear slipped from her lashes at the magnitude of her lie. Mostly it was untrue, but his silence told her that he believed it all.

"Would you mind taking me home, Bay?" Her voice was choked with pain.

"I don't think either one of us has much of an appetite," he agreed bitterly. "Not a surprise, is it?"

An impersonal hand took her elbow. Not another word was spoken. Bay made no comment on the tears that ran freely down her cheeks. He didn't even tell her goodbye when he saw her to the door, but his sardonic "good luck" echoed in Sabrina's ears all the way to her room where she sprawled on her bed and cried.

Chapter 10

"Sabrina! Would you come down for a minute?" Grant Lane called from the base of the stairs.

She sighed heavily. "Can't it wait?"

"No, it's important," was the answer.

Reluctantly Sabrina covered the lump of clay just beginning to take shape. If she had her druthers, she probably could have persuaded her father to postpone whatever it was, but she was simply too tired to argue. In the last two weeks, she'd worked hard and barely slept.

"I'll be right down," she said as she scrubbed at her hands with a wet washcloth and forced her legs to carry out her statement. "What did you want, Dad?" Halfway down the stairs she felt a prickling down the back of her neck. For a few steps, she blamed the sensation on strain and tired nerves. She stopped abruptly on the last step, her head turning toward the stairwell door.

"Hello, Sabrina. I apologize for interrupting your work." The sardonic tone in Bay's voice cut her to the quick.

Blanching slightly, Sabrina tipped her head down and managed the last step, shoving her trembling hands in her pockets. "What a surprise, Bay." Her own voice sounded anything but delighted. "What brings you here?"

"Bay stopped to—" her father began to explain.

"You might call it my last good deed," Bay interrupted blandly. "I want you to meet Howell Fletcher, Sabrina."

"Is this the new artist you've been telling me about?" a cultured, masculine voice asked. Its owner stepped forward to greet her. "Ms. Lane, it's a pleasure."

Bewildered, Sabrina offered her hand. It was gripped lightly by smooth fingers and released. "I'm sorry—I don't think I understand."

"Howell is here to see your work and give his considered opinion on your talent and potential," Bay explained. The total lack of warmth in his voice almost made him seem like a stranger. There was none of the gentle mockery or friendliness she was accustomed to hearing.

"I don't think—" Sabrina started to protest stiffly that she didn't believe she was ready to have her work critiqued by a professional.

"You might as well find out now whether or not your work will sell. I'd like to see it," Howell Fletcher said.

Good deed. That was what Bay had said his motive was. Sabrina couldn't help wondering if he wasn't wishing she'd blow this unexpected interview somehow.

"I keep all my work in the studio upstairs." Her chin lifted proudly. "Are you coming, Bay?"

"No, I won't be staying." The outcome apparently

didn't matter to him. He said goodbye to her father and his friend, or whatever Fletcher was to him. Sabrina he ignored.

On autopilot, Sabrina led Howell Fletcher to the studio. The man didn't say a word as he slowly studied each piece but she didn't mind. Oddly, she didn't really care what his opinion was. There was only one man in her life who mattered and Bay had walked in and out before her broken heart could start beating again.

Her work was a way of filling the empty, lonely hours, providing a challenge and a reason to get up each morning. Some day, she hoped her labors would allow her to be independent of her father. She wanted him to marry Deborah and be happy. It was only right that one of them should have the person they loved. She would never have Bay.

"How much of this work have you done since you became blind, Ms. Lane?" the man asked thoughtfully.

"In clay? All of it," she answered. "The paintings were done before my accident."

"I understood that you've only known Mr. Cameron for a few months."

"Yes, that's right." Sabrina wearily rubbed the back of her neck.

"How did you manage to sculpt this bust?"

A wry smile curved her mouth. "Blind people see with their hands, don't you know that?"

He paused before speaking again. "You haven't asked what I think yet. Aren't you curious?"

"It's been my experience that criticism comes without asking for it. Compliments, too."

"You're wise for your years," he commented.

"Not so much." If she ever figured out how to love wisely, that would be a miracle.

Then Howell Fletcher launched into an impromptu critique. He didn't temper his words, just talked tough, uncaring or unaware that it was her future he was judging. He analyzed the merits and potential value of each piece of artwork. Every flaw, no matter how minute, was called to her attention. Each object was pushed into her hands so she could examine it for herself.

On and on he droned until Sabrina wanted to yell at him to stop. The weight of potential failure was making her hunch her shoulders and draw into herself. Her expression changed into a bleak look, but pride kept her chin up as the last piece was disposed of with the same analytical surgery as the others. A heavy silence followed his final assessment.

"Well, well." Sabrina took a deep breath. "I never realized I was such an incompetent amateur."

"Oh, no, not at all," Howell laughed. "You're neither. Yes, some of the pieces are clumsy and need work on the flow of their line. But the others are fantastic. The pride and the power you've stamped in Bay's portrait are unbelievably accurate. And the virginal figure is very touching—that poignant quality in the tilt of her head, for one thing." He rattled on. "Like your paintings, your sculptural talent is in portraiture. You bring some of these to life, heighten the qualities that attract people."

She couldn't believe she was hearing him correctly. "Then you think I should keep working?"

"If you can keep up this pace and this standard, I can promise you a showing within six months," Howell declared.

"You must be joking."

"My dear, I never joke about money. And if you'll pardon my saying so, your blindness is going to attract a great deal of beautiful publicity. What we will do is combine a display of your very best paintings with the very best clay models and start out with an invitation-only showing for all the right people—" The plans kept on coming long after the shock of his announcement wore off.

"You aren't saying this because of Bay, are you?" Sabrina interrupted, suddenly afraid that Bay had used his influence to arrange this.

"Are you asking me if I was bribed or something?" He sounded affronted.

Hesitantly, Sabrina nodded.

"Bay Cameron did ask me to come here, but I would never risk my reputation for anyone. If you had no talent or potential, I would have told you so."

Sabrina believed him. Success was within her grasp. She let Fletcher talk on, knowing that success wasn't sweet at all without being able to share it with the man she loved. The triumph was as hollow as she felt.

A private show within six months, Howell Fletcher had declared. After careful consideration, he pushed the date ahead to the first week of December, timing it for the holiday season and open wallets. Sabrina had silently realized that his appreciation of art went hand in hand with his appreciation of money.

"I think you've done it, Sabrina," her father murmured so he couldn't be overheard by the people milling about. "All I've heard is positive comments."

Sabrina smiled faintly, not at his words but at the

deep pride in his voice. She could imagine the beaming smile on his face.

"Yes, praise is great, Grant." Howell had moved to Sabrina's other side. There was triumph in his voice. "You're a hot property, Sabrina, because our guests are putting their money where their mouth is."

"Thanks to you, Howell," she said softly.

"Always the diplomat," he kidded. "It took both of our talents, as you very well know. Excuse me, I have to circulate. You stay here and look beautiful."

"Sabrina." A warm, female voice called her name, followed by the pleasing scent of violets. "It's me, Pamela Thyssen. You were at my home several months ago."

"Of course, Mrs. Thyssen, I remember you very well." Sabrina extended her hand and had it clasped by beringed fingers. "How are you?"

"A little upset, if you must know," the woman said jokingly. "How come you didn't volunteer any information about your remarkable talent, hmm? And wait until I get my hands on Bay. I'll teach that godson of mine a thing or two about keeping me in the dark."

"At the time, there wasn't anything to tell." She swallowed nervously. Every time his name was mentioned, her heart started skipping beats and an icy cold hand would close around her throat.

"I should think Bay would be here tonight, helping you to celebrate. Surely he could've cut his Baja sailing trip short for an occasion like this," Pamela said.

"Oh, is that where he is?" Sabrina tried to sound unconcerned. "I haven't seen him lately. I've been so busy getting ready for this show and all."

Pamela Thyssen obviously wasn't aware that she

and Bay had parted company several months ago. Sabrina didn't intend to enlighten her either.

"The bust you did of him is positively stealing the show. Everyone is talking about how you captured his character and not just his features, although it is a wonderful likeness of him," Pamela said, sounding a little curious. "Howell must have realized how successful it would be, judging by the price he put on it."

Sabrina shrugged to indicate that she had nothing to do with that aspect of the show. "I'm only the artist."

She hadn't wanted to exhibit the sculpture at all, but Howell had been adamant, insisting that she shouldn't allow her emotions to get in her way. When she'd finally given it, it was with the proviso that the bust would not be for sale.

That was when she'd learned that Howell Fletcher's shrewdness wasn't limited to money and art. He had asked if she wanted to raise speculation as to why it wasn't for sale. It would be better, he suggested, to put an exorbitant price tag on it, too high for anyone to purchase it. Sabrina had finally agreed.

"What was Bay's reaction when he saw the model you did of him?" Pamela asked.

One of the other guests chose that moment to offer his congratulations and comments, and Sabrina was infinitely grateful that he did. A few others stopped after that. Eventually Pamela was sidetracked by someone she knew and Sabrina was able to dodge the question completely.

"What a fabulous show," a woman gushed. "Absolutely stunning. The paintings, the statues—they're all so breathtakingly real."

Sabrina nodded politely, not knowing how to deal with the woman's effusive praise, other than saying a simple, "Thank you."

"Excuse me, Mrs. Hamilton, but I have to steal Sabrina away from you for a moment," Howell Fletcher broke in, his smooth hand tucking itself under Sabrina's elbow.

Sabrina made some excuse to the woman and was happy that Howell guided her away. The ivory cane tapped its way in front of her. She had learned that Howell seemed to forget she was blind and he sometimes let her run into things.

"Who are you spiriting me off to see this time?" she asked, wiping a damp palm on the skirt of her black dress.

"I don't know exactly how to tell you this, Sabrina." There was an uncharacteristic note of apprehension in his statement. "We seem to have a buyer for the bust and he wants to see you."

"A buyer?" She stiffened. "You know it's not for sale."

"I tried to explain that you were very reluctant to part with it, that its real worth was something less than the price. I couldn't very well tell him how much less—the information could get around and the other prices could be questioned," he replied defensively.

"You shouldn't have talked me into displaying it in the first place. You guessed how I felt about it," she accused him.

"Well, I did," he agreed quietly. "Maybe you can appeal to his better nature and persuade him to choose something else. He's waiting in my office, so you'll have privacy for the discussion."

"I'm not going to sell it," Sabrina said emphatically as they left most of the guests behind to enter a back hall. "I don't care what the consequences are."

Howell didn't comment, slowing her down and turning her slightly as he reached around to open the door. She walked into the room with a determined lift of her chin. There was a murmured wish for good luck from Howell and he closed the door. She turned back, startled, expecting to have his support.

Then she heard someone else rise to his feet. She'd been in the office many times and knew the potential buyer had been sitting on the Victorian sofa against the left wall. Fixing a bright smile on her face, she stepped toward the sound.

"Hello." Sabrina extended a hand in greeting. "I'm Sabrina Lane. Howell told me you were interested in purchasing a piece of mine that you really liked."

"That's right, Sabrina."

The voice went through her like a bolt of lightning. Her hand fell to her side as she fought to remain composed. The floor seemed to roll beneath her feet but it was only her shaking knees.

"Bay—Bay Cameron," she identified him with an audible catch in the forced friendliness of her voice. "What a coincidence. Pamela Thyssen was just telling me a few minutes ago that you'd gone sailing somewhere around Baja. It must be difficult to be in two places at once."

Howell, that traitor! Why hadn't he warned her that it was Bay who was waiting for her? No wonder he'd sneaked away and left her alone.

"Oh, that was an understandable mistake. Pamela

just assumed—anyway, I hadn't planned to return for some time," he replied in that impersonal tone that made her feel cold. "So, tonight you're a big success. How does it make you feel?"

Miserable, her heart answered. "Great," she lied.

"You're looking very sophisticated in that black dress. And the single strand of pearls is just right. Not to mention the expression," he said. "Pale. Hauntingly beautiful. As if you've experienced a great tragedy and risen above it. The media must be having a field day," Bay commented cynically.

She longed to tell him that her tragedy had been losing him and not her sight, but she kept silent, trying to ignore the sarcasm underlining his words.

"I would've thought that by now you would've ditched that cane and gotten another." The reference to the carved ivory handle she held made her grasp it more tightly as if she was afraid he would try to take it back.

"Why should I? It serves its purpose," she stated, shrugging.

"I wasn't going to accuse you of attaching any sentimental importance to it," Bay responded dryly. "Although when I saw the sculpture you did of me, I was curious. Did our, um, association leave you with any good feelings toward me?"

"Of course." Her voice vibrated with the depth of her own emotions. "Besides, I told you once before that I liked your face. Your features are strong and proud."

"Howell did tell you that I'm going to buy it, didn't he?"

"Yes, but I never realized you were an egotist, Bay."

Her laughter was brittle. "Imagine buying an image of yourself."

"It'll remind me of times I probably should forget."

"Bay, I—" Sabrina pivoted slightly to the side, feeling the play of his eyes over her profile, cold and chilling. "Th-there's been a mistake. Howell came to get me because . . . well, because it isn't for sale."

"Why not?" He didn't sound upset by her stammering announcement. "I thought the purpose of this show was to sell what was on display."

"It is, but not this piece," she protested. "That's why we set the price so high, so no one would buy it."

"I'm buying it," Bay said evenly.

"No! I'm not letting you have it!" she lashed out sharply in desperation. "You've taken everything else from me. Please let me keep this!"

"Taken everything from you?" His hand unexpectedly clasped her wrist. "What have I ever taken from you? Aren't you forgetting that I'm the one who got used? Why not take my money? You got everything else of value I had to give!"

"Pity? Sympathy? Charity?" The end of her cane tapped the floor in punctuation to her angry words. "When were those humiliating things ever worth anything? And to whom? Certainly not to me! You never cared about me, not really! I was only a charity case to you!"

"You don't still believe I felt sorry for you?" He heaved a weary sigh.

"You really don't love me," Sabrina sniffed.

"And if I had," his hand moved to the back of her neck, turning her face toward him, "would it have made any difference?"

If only he hadn't touched her, Sabrina thought, a fiery sensation racing down her spine, maybe she could have withstood the agony tearing at her heart. Now she felt herself go limp inside, her pride unable to support her, and she swayed against his chest.

"If you'd loved me just a little, Bay," she sighed wistfully, inhaling the spicy fragrance clinging to his jacket, "I might not have minded loving you so desperately. But I don't want to be with a man who just pities me because I can't see."

"Granted, you're blind, Sabrina," he said. A great weight seemed to leave his voice. His hand slipped from her neck to the back of her waist while the other hand gently stroked her cheek. "But I never pitied you. I was too busy falling in love with you to waste time with that emotion."

"Oh, Bay, don't tease me," she cried in anguish, twisting free from his tender embrace. "Haven't I made enough of a fool of myself without having you make fun of me?"

"I'm not teasing. Believe me, the hell I've been going through these last months hasn't been funny at all," Bay said.

"I'm blind, Bay. How could you possibly love me?" she pleaded with him.

"My brave and beautiful blind queen, how could I possibly not love you?" His tone was incredibly warm and caressing. The sincerity of it almost frightened Sabrina.

"You aren't trying to trick me again, are you, Bay? Don't do this to me if all you want is the sculpture I did of you. You can have it. Just don't lie."

A pair of hands closed over her shoulders and she was drawn against his chest. He placed her hands on his heart, rapidly thudding against her palms. Her own heart raced wildly. Cupping her face, Bay bestowed soft kisses on her closed eyes.

"Being blind doesn't make you feel less of a woman when I hold you in my arms, honey," he whispered tightly.

"You never let me guess what you really felt, not once," Sabrina murmured, leaning her head weakly against his chest.

"I wanted to—a hundred times in a hundred ways." Strong arms held her close as if he was afraid she would try to escape again. "I loved you almost from the beginning. Maybe it started that night we got out of the rain. I don't know. But I told myself to take it slow. You were proud, stubborn, defensive, and very insecure. I didn't try to convince you in the beginning that I was in love with you, because you wouldn't have believed me. That's why I set about trying to help you build confidence in yourself. I wanted you to learn that there was nothing you couldn't do if you set your mind to it. And believe it or not, I thought after that was accomplished, I'd just make you fall in love with me. You can imagine what a blow it was to my self-esteem when you told me you didn't need me anymore."

He smiled against her temple and Sabrina snuggled closer. "I needed you. I wanted you desperately," she said fervently. "I was terrified you would guess and feel even sorrier for me."

"I never felt pity. Pride, but never pity."

"Pride?" She turned her face toward him, questioning and bewildered.

"I was always proud of you. No matter what challenge I made, you always accepted it." Lightly he kissed her lips.

"Accepted with protest," she reminded him with an impish smile.

"No one could ever accuse you of being patient. Stubborn and independent, yes, but never patient. You made that plain the first time we met and you slapped my face," Bay laughed softly.

"And you didn't slap me back." Sabrina let her fingertips caress his cheek. "It made me angry. Eventually I realized that you get what you give."

He quickly gripped her hand and stopped the soothing movement, pressing a hard kiss in her palm. "Will you tell me now why you ran away from me at Pamela's?" he demanded huskily. "The truth this time."

Her heart skipped a beat. At the moment she didn't want to talk, not after the sensually arousing kiss on her palm.

"I heard you talking to a girl named Roni," she said a little hesitantly. "She said you'd brought me with you because you felt sorry for me and because you were hoping to make her jealous. You didn't deny it, Bay. I kept hoping you would at least say I was your friend, but you just let her keep rattling on about me being a charity case and a poor unfortunate. I thought she was telling the truth. That's why I ran away," she admitted.

She heard and felt the rolling chuckle that vibrated from deep within his chest. It was throaty and warm and strangely reassuring.

"One of the first things I'm going to have to remember when we're married is how acute your hearing is," Bay declared with a wide smile of satisfaction against her hair. "If you'd eavesdropped a little longer, you would have heard me tell Roni to take a flying leap to the moon and that I didn't appreciate her comments about the woman I was going to marry."

"Bay!" Her voice caught for a moment, full of the love that welled in her heart. "Are you going to marry me?"

"If that's a proposal, I accept."

"D-don't tease," she whispered with a painful gasp.

His mouth closed over hers in a tender promise. Instantly Sabrina responded, molding herself tightly against every hard male curve. Hungry desire blazed in his deepening kiss as he parted her lips to savor the softness of her mouth. His love lit a glowing lamp that chased away all the shadows of her dark world.

Long, heady moments later, Bay moved her gently out of his arms. She swayed toward his chest, feeling its uneven rise and fall with sensitive fingers. He did his best to hold her at a distance.

"Bay, I love you so," Sabrina whispered achingly. "Just hold me a little longer."

"I'm not made of iron, my love." The teasing note in his voice somehow made the deeper emotions beneath seem stronger.

Her mouth curved in a small smile of pleasure and anticipation. "The door has a lock, Bay."

"And there's a horde of people who must be wondering what happened to the star of the show," he reminded her.

"I don't want to be a star," she said.

"Your work—" Bay began.

"Oh, right. My work. That's what I'll be doing

when you're not around," Sabrina declared in a husky murmur. "And you know how much I want you around me."

"You're not making it easy to maintain my self-control," he growled, letting her come back into his arms.

"I know," she whispered in the second before his mouth closed passionately over hers.

More by Bestselling Author

Janet Dailey

Bring the Ring	0-8217-8016-6	$4.99US/$6.99CAN
Calder Promise	0-8217-7541-3	$7.99US/$10.99CAN
Calder Storm	0-8217-7543-X	$7.99US/$10.99CAN
A Capital Holiday	0-8217-7224-4	$6.99US/$8.99CAN
Crazy in Love	1-4201-0303-2	$4.99US/$5.99CAN
Eve's Christmas	0-8217-8017-4	$6.99US/$9.99CAN
Green Calder Grass	0-8217-7222-8	$7.99US/$10.99CAN
Happy Holidays	0-8217-7749-1	$6.99US/$9.99CAN
Let's Be Jolly	0-8217-7919-2	$6.99US/$9.99CAN
Lone Calder Star	0-8217-7542-1	$7.99US/$10.99CAN
Man of Mine	1-4201-0009-2	$4.99US/$6.99CAN
Mistletoe and Molly	1-4201-0041-6	$6.99US/$9.99CAN
Ranch Dressing	0-8217-8014-X	$4.99US/$6.99CAN
Scrooge Wore Spurs	0-8217-7225-2	$6.99US/$9.99CAN
Searching for Santa	1-4201-0306-7	$6.99US/$9.99CAN
Shifting Calder Wind	0-8217-7223-6	$7.99US/$10.99CAN
Something More	0-8217-7544-8	$7.99US/$9.99CAN
Stealing Kisses	1-4201-0304-0	$4.99US/$5.99CAN
Try to Resist Me	0-8217-8015-8	$4.99US/$6.99CAN
Wearing White	1-4201-0011-4	$4.99US/$6.99CAN
With This Kiss	1-4201-0010-6	$4.99US/$6.99CAN
Yes, I Do	1-4201-0305-9	$4.99US/$5.99CAN

Available Wherever Books Are Sold!

Check out our website at **www.kensingtonbooks.com**

Thrilling Suspense from
Beverly Barton

__Every Move She Makes	0-8217-6838-7	$6.50US/$8.99CAN
__What She Doesn't Know	0-8217-7214-7	$6.50US/$8.99CAN
__After Dark	0-8217-7666-5	$6.50US/$8.99CAN
__The Fifth Victim	0-8217-7215-5	$6.50US/$8.99CAN
__The Last to Die	0-8217-7216-3	$6.50US/$8.99CAN
__As Good As Dead	0-8217-7219-8	$6.99US/$9.99CAN
__Killing Her Softly	0-8217-7687-8	$6.99US/$9.99CAN
__Close Enough to Kill	0-8217-7688-6	$6.99US/$9.99CAN
__The Dying Game	0-8217-7689-4	$6.99US/$9.99CAN

Available Wherever Books Are Sold!

Visit our website at **www.kensingtonbooks.com**